THE BROTHERHOOD
WOLF

PENELOPE BLACK

Wolf
The Brotherhood

For Veronica Mars and Buffy Summers.
MacKayla Lane and Katniss Everdeen.
Daria Followhill and Hermione Granger.
Arya Stark and Daenerys Targaryen.

For all the fictional women who inspire us,
and for all their wonderful creators.

And for Tarryn Fisher for being an absolute inspiration.

Playlist

Florence + The Machine—"Dog Days Are Over"
Madilyn Bailey—"Titanium"
Joseph—"California Dreamin'"
BØRNS—"Electric Love"
Arcade Fire—"Keep the Car Running"
Fleetwood Mac—"The Chain"
Fleetwood Mac—"Go Your Own Way"
David Bowie—"Modern Love"
Marvin Gaye—"Ain't No Mountain High Enough"
Queen—"Bohemian Rhapsody"
The Clash—"Train in Vain"
Yeah Yeah Yeahs—"Maps"
Joe Cocker—"With A Little Help From My Friends"
Radiohead—"Creep"
Lady Gaga + Bradley Cooper—"Shallow"
Mark Ronson ft. Amy Winehouse—"Valerie"

prologue

"CONGRATULATIONS, CLASS OF 2020! It's been my absolute pleasure to watch you ladies achieve your goals these last four years."

I tune out the words from the principal of St. Rita's All-Girls Academy as my gaze zeroes in on the reason I'm here: the redhead with doe eyes in the fifth row. Judging by the way she's searched the stands every sixty seconds for the last twenty minutes, she's waiting for someone to show up.

Lucky for her, I did.

The air conditioner closest to me hums to life, adding to the low murmur of the crowd around me. A makeshift stage sits in the middle of the gym, red and silver balloons framing all four corners. A bead of sweat rolls down my back as the New York City heatwave bakes everyone inside this glorified tin can.

I tug my ball cap lower to shield my face and tuck my hands back in my pockets as I lean against the wooden accordion bleachers. The last thing I need for someone to recognize me, and with a face—and hands—like mine, it's inevitable. Technically, I'm in neutral territory, but I don't put it past those weaselly fucks to jump on an opportunity while I'm alone. And I don't want to spill blood here today.

My gaze tracks her every movement, and when they call her name, she glides across the stage, her smile wide and bright. She waves to a group of familiar faces cheering for her in the stands, but her shoulders never lose their tension.

Ah, so my little bird wasn't waiting on any of them, I muse.

She tips her chin higher as she poses for a photograph at the end of the stage, and my black heart squeezes at the sight.

She's the most stunning creature I've ever seen.

And she will be my queen.

chapter one

Alaina

"KISS A STRANGER."

An involuntary cough wracks my body as my straw-berry wine cooler gets caught in my throat. "Sorry," I say as I put a hand to the base of my throat and set my drink on my desk. "It went down the wrong pipe when I thought I heard you say I have to kiss a stranger." I pin my cousin, Maddie, with a glare.

"That's because I did." She quirks an eyebrow at me and flips her long, straight red hair over her shoulder. "Although I'm not sure why you're surprised, because this isn't my dare."

"Well, it's not my dare, so . . ." I turn to look at Maddie's twin sister, Mary, with a new appreciation. "Color me impressed," I murmur.

"What?" Mary huffs and crosses her arms over her chest. "We're eighteen now—"

"Ahem." I point at myself with a wry smile. "Some of us are almost nineteen."

"Well, *we're* eighteen"—Mary gestures to herself and Maddie—"and your birthday isn't for another week. I thought we could step up the game a little." Mary's cheeks are pink by the time she's done talking. "Plus, we just graduated!"

Mary and Maddie are fraternal twins, and while their physical differences are minor, their styles couldn't be more different. Mary wears her red hair in a lob—a longer bob—that she straightens every day, and Maddie wears her long and curled. With matching ice-blue eyes, they're total knockouts. And they're my best friends.

"I think it's a great idea, but you guys are going to be disappointed because I definitely added 'binge-watch *Vampire Diaries*' in there last week," I tell them with a laugh.

Mary's stiff as she sits on the end of my twin bed in our shared dorm suite at St. Rita's All-Girls Academy. Technically, we're no longer high school students here, but since we're enrolled in the sister school—St. Rita's College, we're opting to keep the same living arrangements.

Mary's arms are still crossed tightly across her chest, and she stares at the cream-colored carpet as if it's holding all her secrets.

I glance at Maddie and nod toward her sister. With a sigh, she sets the colored popsicle stick with the dare on it on my dresser and crosses the room to her sister.

"Babe. It's totally fine. And you know I'm all for you kissing whoever you want—whenever you want."

"Yeah, you can have this dare if you want, Mary," I offer.

"No take-backs, Lainey. You know the rules," Maddie interjects.

Mary lifts her head, a wry smirk on her face. "No worries, all five of my dares last week were 'kiss a stranger.'"

A giggle escapes my lips before I can catch it, and Maddie joins in. After a few seconds, Mary loosens up a little, and before long, she's giggling right along with us.

"Who knew we'd still be playing the silly game we made up with an extra mason jar and colored popsicle sticks when we were twelve?" I muse as I take a drink of my wine cooler.

"Me. I did," Maddie sasses, lifting her chin and leaning back.

"That's because you came up with the idea." Mary rolls her eyes with a smirk.

"And what a good idea it was! Besides, what else were we going to do? We couldn't leave the dorm, and we needed something fun to look forward to since they dumped us in the city and left without a backward glance." Maddie's smile is hard and forced, her eyes narrow.

"Ah-ha! I knew you cared that Mom left us here and went to Europe that summer!" Mary exclaims, her earlier tension long forgotten.

Maddie tilts her chin up. "Don't be ridiculous, Mary. I did not. I was only making a point. And Mom brings us with her to Europe every summer now."

Watching my cousins trade quick retorts is like watching a tennis match. I sip my drink and settle back into my chair.

"Exactly! Because you pitched a fit that one summer, so now Mom's afraid to leave us here. Honestly, I don't even know why you want to go over there anymore. Being a *wingwoman* to your middle-aged mother while she picks up guys fifteen years younger lost its appeal years ago." Mary practically sneers the word wingwoman, and I do a double-take. The expression is more Maddie than her. I feel like I'm missing something here.

11

"That *one* summer? You mean the one where we were attending summer courses, and you got your period in the middle of ceramics, but I pretended it was me, and Becky Parsons made fun of *me*"—Maddie jabs a finger into her chest—"for months. That summer?" Her lips flatten, and a flush of anger creeps down her neck.

This is a familiar discussion they've had many, many times over the years. The thing is, Mary always apologizes—again—and Maddie always accepts. They hug, and then they move on. I'm not sure what it is about that one instance that has Maddie still hung up, but it's time for me to step in, like usual.

I stand up and face them, hands on my hips. "Alright, girls, are we going to kiss some strangers tonight or what?"

Both girls stop and turn to face me, their cheeks pink, arms crossed, and eyes guarded. I swear, they're so alike sometimes, it's like they're the same person.

This time, it's Mary who deflates first. She turns to face Maddie. "I'm sorry, Maddie."

Maddie turns toward her. "I'm sorry too. Don't worry about it. I'm just getting hangry, I guess." Maddie leans into Mary and wraps an arm around her shoulders. "Okay, let's pick our dares for tonight."

Maddie leaves her twin on the end of my bed and walks to the mason jar on my dresser. Somewhere along the years, we started keeping the dare jar in my room. The colorful popsicle sticks nearly fill the jar. We pick from the jar once a week, sometimes more, but always when we're together. Now that I'm working at the coffee shop a few blocks away, tutoring a couple of middle school kids in the afternoons, and singing for fun with the girls nearly every Friday, we have to be a little more strategic.

Maddie closes her eyes and pulls a stick from the jar. "Alright, tonight, Mary's dare is *dance with a stranger*."

Her voice rises higher with each word, her eyebrows following suit.

My lips tip up in a smirk. I added that dare months ago. Ever since I started noticing the same guy show up to open mic night at O'Malley's Pub. Tall, chestnut-brown hair, and a cloud of danger surrounding him. He watches my set every time I sing, but he never stays afterward, and he's always alone.

I thought I'd give myself the push to approach him and ask him to dance, but it looks like Mary will be tearing up the floor tonight. I look at her to gauge her reaction to the dare.

"Fun. I have just the outfit for tonight." Mary's eyes sparkle as she claps her hands together in front of her chest.

"Okay then." Maddie eyes her sister with a knowing grin. She closes her eyes again and pulls another popsicle stick from the jar. "And tonight my dare is *sing karaoke . . . in a lime-green tutu*." Maddie's eyebrows hit her hairline, and her mouth opens slightly. And I can't hold back my grin.

"Ah, I was watching a lot of *Sex and The City* re-runs when I added that dare," I offered. Maddie looks at me with her mouth open. "You know, where she wears the pink tulle skirt and looks badass walking down the city blocks? That's what I was going for, but I thought lime-green would be fun."

"Lainey, we're three fair-skinned, freckled, redheads. Lime-green is not *our* color, babe," Maddie says as she looks at me, head tilted and eyebrows drawn together like I actually need a fashion intervention. Just because I like to wear old band tees doesn't mean I don't have a good sense of fashion. I just know what I like.

"Exactly," I say with a smirk.

Mary laughs as she gets up from my bed. "Ooh, you're good, girl. Nice subtle hit on all of us—I like it. Let's eat some dinner and then get ready. I'll check what the dining hall has on their menu for tonight." Mary heads to the kitchen where we have the month's dining hall menu tacked up on a corkboard.

"But . . . we don't even have a lime-green tutu—so, ha!" Maddie yells, thrusting a finger in the air.

"Except." I cross the room to my closet, open the closet door, and shift my clothes around so I can reach the three brightly-colored items in the back. Curling my fingers around the hangers, I wrangle the items out. "Ta-da!" I shimmy the hangers, causing the tulle skirts to swish around.

Maddie looks at me for a moment before she tips her head back and laughs. "Oh my god—Mary, come here and see what your crazy cousin did!"

I hear Mary's footsteps in the hallway, and she speaks before I can see her.

"Coming! Oh, and before I forget, tonight it's spaghetti bolognese"—Mary freezes in the doorway, her mouth falling open—"and what the hell are those?!"

"Why, our outfits for tonight, of course!" I answer cheerfully.

"But only Maddie has to wear the lime-green one!" Mary whines.

Maddie doubles over on my bed in laughter. "You put two more tutu dares in the jar, didn't you?"

I smooth the tulle down on the neon-orange skirt as a smirk tips up the corners of my mouth. "Sure did. And because we love you, we're all going to wear one tonight."

I untangle the lime-green tulle skirt and toss it to Maddie. I turn to Mary, who's still standing in the doorway, and hold out the remaining two tulle skirts. "Neon orange or hot pink?"

"I can't believe I'm going to wear a neon orange tulle skirt while dancing with a stranger tonight," Mary mock grumbles.

"Excellent choice, Mary. Might I suggest wearing a solid color to make the orange really pop?" I ask with a laugh. I unclip the neon-orange tulle skirt and toss it to her.

"We're going to look ridiculous at O'Malley's tonight." Maddie sighs dejectedly.

"Nah, we'll look amazing. They love us, and Jack would never let anyone say anything bad about us," I assure her. "Besides, we just graduated, let's celebrate!"

Jack is the owner of O'Malley's Irish Pub. I met him sort of randomly a couple of years ago. I was supposed to meet my then-boyfriend there to see a band, but he never showed up, and I ended up chatting with Jack for a while. A couple months later, I showed up with Mary and Maddie in tow for their open mic night and never looked back. Now, O'Malley's has become our go-to place for a night out.

I know they know our fake IDs are bullshit, but they never call us on it. We almost always order vodka cranberries, Long Island iced teas, and Baby Guinnesses—which does not actually have Guinness in it.

I still remember the look of disgust on Mary's face when she tipped the glass back and took a huge sip of what she thought was just a small-sized Guinness.

I thought for sure she was going to spew Kahlua and Bailey's all over the bar top that day. But by some miracle, she didn't. It took her like six months to even drink a latte again—something about the smell of coffee triggering her gag reflex.

"What are you laughing about over there?" Mary asks, eyes narrow and head tilted. "Because I draw the line at footwear, Lainey."

"Actually, I remembered the time we discovered what a Baby Guinness was." I smirk, quirking an eyebrow. "Do you remember that—"

Mary fake gags before I can finish my question. "Ugh. Yes. Don't remind me, or I won't be able to look at a latte again for months," she whines.

I laugh. "Good times, good times. Now, shoo"—I flick my fingers in her direction—"and go change for dinner. We're celebrating tonight!"

"Yeah, yeah. I'm going," Mary mutters as she walks out of my room.

I hold up the neon-pink tulle skirt in front of me, twisting and turning it, and stare at my reflection in the mirror. The corners of my mouth curl into a mischievous smile.

Tonight is going to be unforgettable.

chapter two

Alaina

I SWIPE THE MASCARA wand through my lashes one last time and stare at myself in the mirror above my vintage white vanity. It's one of the few things that I have from my dad—he gave it to me on my eighth birthday.

Winged black eyeliner frames my dark-brown eyes, making the amber ring around my pupil pop against my fair skin. Freckles dot the bridge of my nose and tops of my cheeks, and no amount of concealer truly covers them up.

My dad used to pick out constellations within my freckles, and then he'd tell me the corresponding Greek story. My favorites were always the ones that ended in love stories. It's only as I got older that I realized that my dad was very loose in his retelling. The original Greek mythologies are darker, crueler, and less romantic.

I look at them now, trying to spot Ursa Major or Orion's Belt—any constellation, really. But I can't find any. I'm not sure that I believe in those types of stories anymore, anyway.

A knock sounds on my door, and I turn to see Maddie standing in my doorway. "Ready, babe?"

I mentally shake out the melancholy fog that thinking about my father always puts me in and turn to face her. "You look—"

"Ridiculous," Maddie deadpans.

"Amazing!" I squeal and clap my hands together a couple of times in glee. "Truly. Pairing the skirt with a white thin-strap tank top and wedges was a great idea!"

"I mean"—Maddie tosses her hair over her shoulder playfully—"if it's one thing I know, it's fashion." She smirks and circles her index finger in the air. "Stand up and turn around. Let's see what you're wearing to kiss a stranger tonight."

I oblige her and stand up from the little stool I was sitting on in front of my vanity. I twirl in a circle, and the hot-pink tulle skirt flares out before settling down around right above my knees. "You like?"

"I love it, Lainey. And you're lucky I love you, girl, because wearing that shirt out on a night like tonight is just asking for trouble," Maddie says.

I pluck the shoulder of my vintage white Johnny Cash tee, the one with his mug shot faded on the front. "I love this shirt. And look, I knotted it at the bottom, so it's like a crop top. I think it looks cute."

"You do look cute," Mary interjects from the hallway. I can't even see her standing behind Maddie.

"Thanks, Mary. Come in here, let's see your outfit."

"She looks amazing, and you know I love the man in black." Maddie cuts her sister a look. "I just think wearing *that* shirt on *this* day—the eve of the blood moon—is like sending a smoke signal for bad shit to come."

"Oh, not this superstitious crap again." Mary huffs and tilts her head back to stare at the ceiling.

Maddie crosses her arms and glares at her sister. "You wouldn't be saying that if you followed the signs and your horoscope like I do."

"Okay, I'll bite. What does our horoscope say for today?" Mary tips her chin in the air.

"You"—she points at Mary—"need to try something new and understand the value of commitment. And you"—she points at me—"need to prepare yourself because big life and love changes are coming your way. Work through the drama and don't be afraid to take care of yourself."

Mary rolls her eyes and throws her arms in the air, letting them flop to her sides. "What about any of that means she shouldn't wear her Johnny Cash shirt?"

"Well"—Maddie crosses her arms—"astrology is open for interpretation, but I just don't think wearing a shirt that promotes getting *arrested* when you're going to experience big life changes is a good idea."

There's something about the way Maddie says my horoscope this time that feels different. Almost like a premonition, reverberating throughout my body, soaking in and laying claim to my destiny.

"Plus, it's the thirteenth," Maddie says, her jaw tight and shoulders back. "*Friday* the thirteenth."

"Alright, Maddie. I can change if it'll make you feel better," I offer.

"C'mon, Lainey, you don't need to change. Your shirt isn't going to bring some bad omen down on us," Mary huffs with a roll of her eyes.

"Nah, it's fine. I've got the perfect shirt in mind." I spin around and go to my dresser. I open a drawer, pull out an off-the-shoulder black shirt, and hold it up. "Better?"

Maddie nods and crosses her arms, a slight blush tinting her cheeks pink. Mary throws her arms up with a huff and turns around while I whip off my Johnny Cash tee and pull on the black shirt.

I straighten the black shirt, arranging the short sleeve, so it falls just so off my shoulder. "No worries, Maddie. I don't mind." I flash her a smile over my shoulder.

She visibly relaxes a little and murmurs, "Thanks, Lainey."

"No worries. I know you believe in that stuff, and I believe in you, okay? So if you say the moon is hanging out in retrograde and Venus is shining on Jupiter—"

Maddie laughs. "I love that you tried, but none of that means anything. Mercury goes into retrograde, babe."

I shrug and smile at her. I knew that Mercury goes into retrograde. And honestly, I do enjoy reading about horoscopes and all that, but I was trying to lighten the mood, so I intentionally goofed up the terminology.

I flip my waves over my shoulder and look at both of them. "We good, girls?"

"We're good," they answer in unison.

"Ooh, you know I love it when you guys do your freaky twin thing like that." My smile is wide.

"We know," they deadpan. Again, together. And I tip my head back and laugh.

"Alright, are we ready to celebrate?"

"So ready, babe," Maddie replies.

"I'm going to tear up that dance floor tonight." Mary does a little shimmy as we all file out of my bedroom and into the hall.

"Mary, you're a vision, my friend. That neon-orange skirt is really working for you. And I love the bold choice of a patterned tank top."

Mary perks up at the compliment. "The patrons of O'Malley's aren't going to know what hit them tonight."

chapter three

Alaina

"BENNY!" I YELL as soon as I see the brunet bouncer of O'Malley's.

Hearing his name, Benny turns away from the group of guys he's chatting with to look in our direction. His face scrunches up a little before it cracks into a wide grin. He cups his hands around his mouth as he yells down the block. "Songbirds!"

The best way to describe Benny is deceptively charming. Sure, he's got boyish good looks, and he always has a kind word for us, but there's something a little off about him.

I always chalk it up to his job—doing security at O'Malley's can't be passive all the time. This is New York City, for goodness's sake—I'm sure he's had to deal with plenty of people who get out of hand.

I glance at Mary on my left and Maddie on my right. What a picture we must make—walking down the busy sidewalk in fluffy, brightly-colored tulle skirts.

I glance down, appreciating the juxtaposition between the soft, clean fabric and the stained cement sidewalk. The soft swish of the skirts and the clacking of Maddie's heels as we walk toward O'Malley's.

It's June in New York City, and the humidity hangs in the air from the impending thunderstorm. This is nothing compared to how sweltering it'll get in just a couple of weeks. The city in the summer isn't for the faint of heart. But for now, the heat is bearable.

A drop of sweat rolls down my spine as we walk the last few feet to the front door of the Irish pub. With a matte-black brick storefront, a forest-green awning, and huge twelve-paned windows on either side of the door, O'Malley's isn't what I would call flashy. It's not the type of place you'll find a bunch of young twenty-somethings in on a night out on the town.

But you will find some kind, old dudes and their ladies who come in just about every day for a pint, some guys who ride that always request the classics, and locals who stop in after work.

Except for their events—then it's a free-for-all. They host some of the best cover band concerts I've ever seen—some are so good that if you close your eyes, it's like you're listening to the real deal.

And their open mic night event is one of my favorite things in the world. Mary, Maddie, and I have been performing at O'Malley's open mic night long enough that people actually come to watch us—which is still such a weird feeling. I bite my lip as I think about a certain someone who comes to watch us sing every week.

"Woo. Would you get a look at you three," Benny crows as he checks his watch. "Nope, Halloween isn't for a few more months." Benny scans us from head to toe, lingering on Maddie a beat longer. "To what do we owe these dresses to tonight, ladies?"

"They're skirts, Benny," Mary snaps, and my eyebrows hit my hairline. Huh. Maybe this is who Mary was hoping to kiss when she put those dares in the jar.

Benny holds his hands up in surrender. "Okay, okay. Looking good, Maddie."

"In your dreams, Benny." Maddie rolls her eyes.

Mary grabs the handle to the door and pulls with more force than necessary, slamming the door against the brick. She enters O'Malley's, and Maddie follows her without a word.

Holding the door open, I flash an apologetic smile his way. "Word to the wise, Benny, you're looking at the wrong sister."

He stares at me for a moment, jaw clenched, and I see possession flash across his eyes. Before I can comment on it, he forces a smile and turns back to the guys on the sidewalk. "Sure thing, songbird."

I exhale a sigh and shake off Benny's dismissal. I'm not letting some guy ruin our celebration.

I step inside O'Malley's and inhale the familiar scent of stale beer, cigarette smoke, and a citrus air freshener.

I look around to see the owner, Jack O'Malley, behind the bar on one end and the other bartender, Levi, at the other end.

Like so many bars and pubs in this area, O'Malley's is a long, skinny rectangle, extending almost entirely to the other side of the block. Bar-height tables and chairs, a dartboard, and a handful of arcade games occupy one area of the bar toward the very back by the hallway to the restrooms. Four-top tables and chairs occupy most of the space in here, leaving just enough room to weave your way around when walking.

The bar top is one long, sweeping expanse of polished dark wood with four matching open shelves. Fancy bottles and glasses fill the shelves. Kitty-corner to the bar is the stage.

Now, this is where I'm most comfortable. The stage is rectangular and made of the same dark wood as the bar top. It's the perfect amount of room for three cousins from Boston who love to sing cover songs every week.

Aside from participating in their open mic night, the girls and I often come to sing karaoke when the mood strikes. In fact, Jack didn't even have a karaoke machine until I mentioned it in passing a couple of years ago. The next time I stepped in, I saw the machine in the corner of the stage, brand-new and ready to use. I never asked him about it, and he never said anything, but I didn't miss the twinkle in his eye when Maddie jumped up and down, clapping her hands as soon as she spotted it.

I spot the girls posted up at the other end of the bar by Levi, their skirts practically glowing in the dim light. I weave around the tables and the few people standing, and make my way to the girls. I hop on the empty stool between the two of them and lean forward so I can see Jack at the other end of the bar.

"Oi!" My voice carries down the bar and catches Jack's attention. "What's a girl gotta do to get a drink around here?" I tease, my lips twisting up in the corners.

He slaps the bar top, and with a wide grin, he booms, "Ach, our graduates are here, boys!"

In his mid-forties, Jack is objectively good-looking with rich dark-orange hair and a matching beard, light-blue eyes, and a penchant for flannel shirts. He's muscular in the way that says I could kick your ass, but I don't go to the gym religiously.

Warmth fills my soul as I watch him walk toward us. "Heya, Jack!" I yell the same thing I say every time I see him for the past two years.

"As I live and breathe, you girls get more beautiful every time I see you," Jack says, his hand on his heart. "What brings you here tonight? Here to celebrate that graduation?"

We graduated from St. Rita's All-Girl Academy on Monday. Why the school hosted a graduation event on Monday of all days is beyond me, but it didn't really matter to me. My mom texted me to tell me she couldn't make it weeks ago, so I wasn't expecting anyone there to cheer me across that stage, anyway.

I knew my Aunt Sloane would be there with her newest boyfriend to cheer the twins across the stage, and I knew she'd clap for me—and she did. But I didn't know Jack was going to show up to cheer us on. It warmed my heart in a way I wasn't expecting. Jack's become sort of a big brother to me over the years.

He's been kind and protective from the first moment I met him. I was standing outside O'Malley's, nervously checking the time on my phone every two minutes. I was supposed to meet my boyfriend, James, to watch this amazing Clash cover band playing that night, and I was mostly excited to go on another date with James. We had only been dating for a couple of months, but I'd never felt about anyone the way I felt about James. I honestly thought he was *the one*.

And if I'm being honest, I've never felt that way since.

I still cringe when I think about what happened—how James stood me up and sent me some flimsy text about how he *can't do this right now*. Residual embarrassment and heartache line my heart from the whole thing—our whirlwind relationship and his easy dismissal of me as if we didn't matter—as if *I* didn't matter.

I know it's silly, and I know I was young, but I really did love him. And maybe what's worse is that, despite everything, I'm not sure that I ever stopped.

I'll be forever grateful to Jack for that day. He got a front-row seat to James dumping me via text and was nothing but kind, even though I know he spotted the tears in my eyes, he never made a fuss about it.

I ended up joining the girls on their European vacation the next day, and when we got back to the city, they convinced me to go back to O'Malley's. It'd been a couple of months, and they were running their open mic night. I thought I might feel embarrassed or something when I went back, but Jack never mentioned it, so neither did I.

From that day on, we go to O'Malley's just about every week for open mic night. Jack's always working, and he's always kind and protective—plus, he lets us drink for free. I remember the first time we tried to order drinks.

I walk toward the bar on one side of O'Malley's, Mary and Maddie behind me. We've been coming here for a year, but we've never ordered anything alcoholic yet. Tonight, I pulled the dare order an alcoholic drink at O'Malley's *from our jar. So, I take a deep breath and rest my elbows on the bar in front of Jack. He quirks an eyebrow at me when I don't immediately say anything.*

"You're trying to drink, yeah?"

I nodded slowly, unwilling to admit to anything in case it was some sort of trap.

"Well then, better you do it here where I can keep an eye on ya." Jack crosses his arms and stares at me from across the bar. "But only you three. Don't go telling all your little friends because this exception will not apply to them."

"Alright, Jack. Uh, thanks." I flash a tentative smile his way. It still feels like a trap somehow. "We'd like three Jack and Cokes, please," I declare, placing two twenties on the bar.

"No." Jack stares at the three of us, without uncrossing his arms or moving to take the money.

I frown and feel my cheeks heat. "But you, uh, said that we could, you know, drink here."

"Aye, I did. But this is an Irish pub, little girlies, and we don't serve Tennessee whiskey. We serve Irish whiskey." Jack raises his brows at us.

Maddie elbows me in the side and hisses, "Order the Irish whiskey then, Lainey."

I clear my throat. "Uh, okay. Three Irish whiskey and Cokes?" My voice and shoulders go up at the end, and my drink order turns into a question.

"No."

My mouth drops open. "What? Why not?"

"Nah, you three aren't ready for Jameson just yet. Let's start small. Three iced teas with a splash of rum."

"Perfect," Mary chimes in, leaning forward. "Thank you."

"And your money's no good here, so don't bother," Jack says, pushing the twenties across the counter toward me. "Keep it for college."

"How about three shots to celebrate?" Maddie's question pulls me out of the memory. I look over to see she's turned on the charm by using her puppy-dog eyes on Jack.

"Ach, alright, just this once. Then it's beer for the three of you—the cheap, watered-down shit," he warns.

"Deal." Maddie smirks.

"How's it going tonight, Jack?" Mary asks as Jack places four shot glasses in front of us.

"Can't complain." He slides each of us a shot glass before picking up the fourth glass. Holding it in the air, he says, "To our newest graduates. Congratulations, girlies." Pride twinkles in his eyes, and he makes eye contact with all three of us before he downs his shot.

The three of us hold up our shot glasses, clink them together, and bring them to our lips in unison.

"You birds spend too much time together," Levi mutters when he watches us as we take our shots in complete unison.

The back of my throat burns as tequila slides down my throat. Shit, it's the good stuff, too. I place my shot glass on the bar top and slide it to Jack. "One more, to celebrate."

He throws a grin my way, and I swear it takes ten years off of his face when he smiles like that. His orange-red hair sticks out from underneath his Red Sox hat, and his light-blue eyes twinkle with mirth. He spreads his hands out on the bar top, leans in, and says, "You trying to get bolluxed tonight, girlie? You know I allow you three a lot of leeway, but you can't get shit-faced here. I'll lose my license."

Maddie laughs next to me before Jack even finishes talking, and I join in. "Lose your license? Puh-lease, Jack. We both know the cops aren't looking at O'Malley's for underage drinkers." I pin him with a mock-glare before I flick my glance to my empty shot glass pointedly.

Jack pushes off the bar top and crosses his arms across his barrel chest, stretching his Clash tee and distorting their London Calling album printed on it. "Seven songs."

"Three," Maddie counters.

"Five," Jack retorts.

"Alright, Jack, five songs and three more shots," I barter.

He lifts one dark-orange brow. "Six songs, one shot."

"Five songs and two shots," Mary says and pushes her shot glass toward Jack.

"Alright, alright. Five songs and two shots—one now and one after you play. You girlies drive a hard bargain for an old man like me." Jack lines up our shot glasses with a sly grin tipping the corner of his mouth.

I can't stop my smirk. This is a little dance the four of us play often—Jack likes to play responsible adult, but he always caves—usually after we agree to sing a few songs. He says it's good for business, but I think he just likes to sing along. And he's not the only dude in this pub that routinely sings along to Taylor Swift when we cover her songs. I snicker and turn to face away from the bar as I recall the first time I saw Jack—among several other regulars—who were loudly singing along to "We Are Never Getting Back Together."

My heart thumps a little as I scan the people in the pub tonight. I'm not even trying to pretend that I'm not looking for him—my mystery man. If I have to kiss a stranger, then I want it to be him. I've been thinking about what it would feel like to kiss him for far longer than I care to admit.

Disappointment settles in my limbs when I don't see his chestnut-brown hair at any of the tables. I knew it was a long shot, the only times I can count on seeing him is on open mic nights.

"Alright, girls, to five songs," Jack announces.

I spin around and pick up my shot, clinking my glass to Maddie's, Mary's, and Jack's.

"To five songs," we all say together.

I tip the glass to my lips and savor the burn of tequila as it slides down my throat and warms me up.

chapter four

Alaina

I FOLLOW MADDIE AS she leads the way to the stage, and Mary follows behind me. This simple formation is a metaphor for our relationship. For our entire lives, Maddie's been the first one in line, sheltering Mary and me as much as possible. She takes her role as the oldest twin very seriously.

I used to think Mary was content to let her sister lead, but lately, she's been acting a little different—more assertive. Add in her recent dares . . . I'd say our Mary is trying to spread her wings a little.

Our skirts swish and swirl as we weave around the tables on our way to the stage. Once people notice where we're going, the regulars hoot and holler.

We climb the two wooden stairs to the stage. Jack cuts the jukebox feed and flips the switch for the stage lights, momentarily blinding me. I lift my hand to shield my eyes and motion for him to turn the spotlights down.

He interprets my hand signals with ease—this isn't the first time we've done this.

I walk to the back corner of the stage and grab a tambourine and the mic stand I love to use. It's vintage bronze with a matching microphone.

As the girls and I set up, Jack cups his hands around his mouth and shouts, "Oi! Our songbirds are singing for us tonight!"

I recognize some regular faces in the small group of people as they clap and cheer. I smile and shake my head a little, my wavy dark-red hair falling forward.

After I'm all set up, I look to make sure that Maddie and Mary are ready too. With Maddie to my right and Mary to my left, I scan our outfits and wonder what kind of picture we look like tonight. I snort. I bet we look amazing—and just a touch of crazy. The perfect combination, really.

I nod at Maddie, and she steps into her mic. "Good evening, everyone! In case you haven't heard, we just graduated—"

Loud whistles, cheering, and clapping cut her off.

Maddie smirks. "Ah, so you heard then? We'll you're in for a treat. We've got a handful of songs for you tonight. We hope you like them."

Maddie takes a step back and looks around me to catch Mary's eye. At her nod, they step into their mics and smile at the crowd, and I count us in with the tap of my finger against my skirt. I sing the first line about happiness hitting her like a train.

Mary sings the next line, tapping her fingers on her skirt too. And when Maddie sings the third line, all three of us go from tapping fingers to full-on clapping—one-two-pause-three.

We sway together, left then right, and all three of us harmonize on the chorus. Singing about the dog days being over, I can't help the wide smile that overtakes my face.

We freaking graduated high school!

On this stage, with my two very best friends, singing and dancing my heart out—it feels as close to perfect as I've felt in a while. I guess those vocal lessons and dance practices weren't for nothing, after all.

The three of us dance and twirl around on the stage, clapping and leaning in to sing into the mics.

We hold the last note for four beats, staring into the darkened pub and letting the words sink into the night.

I wet my lips as the crowd cheers for us, adrenaline coursing through my limbs, making me feel light and invincible.

I can hear Jack's distinctive whistle, and I can't help the smile that spreads across my face.

"Thank you so much, everyone! That was "Dog Days Are Over" by Florence + The Machine!" Mary says, smiling wide.

I grab my mic stand and step back to look at Maddie. "Titanium?"

Maddie beams as she steps away from her mic and crosses the stage to where the upright piano sits along the back wall. She pulls out the bench and sits down, the lime-green tulle flowing all around her. From this angle, she looks like an Irish fairy princess. She kicks off her heels and warms up the keys with a few quiet notes.

I turn around and face the audience. In the last ten minutes, the crowd has doubled, and it looks like more are on their way in if the open door is anything to go by. "Hey, guys, thanks for indulging us tonight. We've got something special for you—our girl here has been practicing the keys"—I pause when a few people whoop and glance back at Maddie with a smile—"so we're going to switch it up. Hope you like it."

Maddie hits the first chord, and I sing the first line.

I close my eyes and tilt my head toward the mic, throwing myself into the song that Maddie and I have been rehearsing since my mom dropped the unsurprising bomb that she was too busy to come to graduation. I was the valedictorian of St. Rita's, and I really thought Mom would want to see it—see *me*. My throat constricts as I think about Mom declining the four tickets the school provided for each student's family.

I channel all of my grief and hope into this one song. Mary joins me for the chorus, and as we sing, I feel it. That spark that starts as a small flicker and, by the end, turns into a roaring inferno.

I'm carving out my heart with each plea from my lips, begging for someone to see me. And then it happens— everything falls away. The clink of the glasses against the bar tops, the murmur of the crowd, the noise from the street—it all fades away.

I'm submerged in heartbreak and hopelessness.

I grip the mic with both hands and deliver my heart with both hands, singing the last three lines with every fiber of my being. Mary fades out after the first line. Maddie's notes fade out until it's just my voice ringing in the still air.

I turn to the side after I end the last note, letting my long wavy hair cover the side of my face as a single tear slides down my cheek. In the silence, I glance at Mary to see she has tears in her eyes, and she starts clapping.

Her clap is the catalyst for the whole pub erupting in cheers. I wipe the tear away and turn to see everyone on their feet. Flashing a watery smile, I mouth *thank you* to the crowd. Maddie comes up behind me and squeezes my shoulders. I reach up and touch her forearm, returning her affection.

I sniffle and smile, laughing a little. "Thank you, everyone, really. Thank you. How about our girl Maddie on the piano?" I clap my hands, and the crowd whoops for her.

Jack makes his way from the bar to the side of the stage, a mini tray of shots in one hand. He pushes the tray up to us, and gruffly says, "Here. That was beautiful."

The girls and I murmur our thanks and pluck our double shot glasses from his tray. We clink them together, and as one, toss them back.

"Woo," I say into the mic with a grimace before placing my shot glass back on the tray. "Okay, guys, we've got three more songs for you tonight. Next up is another favorite. Hope you like it."

"One, two, three, four," Maddie counts us in, and then she sings with Mary about brown leaves and walking on a winter's day.

They're both so talented, absolutely killing this song, and I get goosebumps.

Two counts in, and I come in, shaking the tambourine and moving my hips to the beat. I sing about stopping in a church I passed, and the girls harmonize the second half of the phrase a half a beat behind me.

I sing the next line and look at Mary with a smile. She harmonizes with Maddie, and smiles wide, her eyes crinkling in the corners.

I flick my gaze around the bar. I want to see Jack's reaction. We've never done this song before, and while we've been singing together for years, we've only been practicing this song for a few weeks.

I see Jack behind the bar, but at the opposite end of where he was a few minutes ago. A guy stands next to him—sort of behind the bar—and my heart stutters in my chest for a moment. I miss a beat with the tambourine, but I doubt anyone picks up on it.

It's him.

My mystery man.

He's here.

And he's staring right at me. I can feel his gaze as it stays locked on me with every sway and clap to the song.

It's not even open mic night. *How did he know I was singing tonight*? I dismiss the thought immediately. Of course, he didn't somehow hear I was singing and immediately rush over. I'm sure it's just some random thing—a coincidence.

But didn't Maddie say big life and love changes are going to happen? What if *he's* one of those big life and love changes? And this is my opportunity to seize it—seize him.

Over six feet tall, his chestnut hair is tousled on top and shaved on the sides. He's too far away to see his eye color, but I'm determined to find out tonight. He always leaves in the middle of my last song, and I've never gotten the opportunity to talk to him.

That changes tonight.

As we sing the last notes of "California Dreamin'" in harmony, I decide that, for tonight, it's a sign.

I just found my stranger to kiss.

chapter five

Alaina

I STEP AWAY FROM my mic and toward Maddie. Covering her mic, I whisper into her ear, "I'm cutting out early. You two will have to finish our set."

She leans into me, tilting her head and drawing in her eyebrows. "What? Why? Are you okay?"

"Absolutely. I just need to talk to someone before he leaves."

Understanding dawns in her eyes, and she nods, a smirk tipping up her lips. "Go get 'em, girl."

Mary walks over toward us. "Everything okay?"

"Yep, just gotta have a chat with a stranger," I say with a sassy smirk.

"Ohh okay." Mary laughs. "No worries, we got this, right, sis?"

In response, Maddie leans toward her mic and says, "Thank you! Let's give Jack a round of applause. After all, it was his idea for us to sing tonight." She winks at the man in question as the crowd looks around for him, giving me the perfect opportunity to find my mystery man.

I hop off the stage and make my way toward the end of the bar where I saw him last, weaving around people watching the girls on stage. The crowd parts, and I get a glimpse of him exchanging one of those dude-handshake things with Levi and walking toward the back.

So, I follow him.

I lose sight of him as he turns the corner. There's a little hallway with three doors—two restrooms and an emergency exit. I slow my steps as I get closer to the hallway. I'm so amped up on post-performance adrenaline and Maddie's horoscope predictions that I didn't really think this through.

Shit, what am I even going to say?

Hi, I don't know you, but I feel like I do. I've watched you watching me for months. Wanna hang out?

He'll think I'm totally crazy. I bite my lip as I quickly think of another option that makes me sound less . . . I don't know, stalkerish.

Chill out, Lainey, people kiss random people all the time, I chastise myself.

It's quieter back here, but I can still hear the faint sounds of the girls singing over the thundering of my heartbeat. *Shit, why are my hands so sweaty?* Ugh. I wipe them off on my tulle skirt, fluffing it up a little when I'm done.

I dig deep, and with a new determination, I quicken my steps and turn the corner. If he went out the emergency exit, I still might be able to catch up to—

"Oomph." I grunt as I slam into something hard—and muscular. Hands clasp my shoulders, stopping me from pitching backward and steadying me on my feet. "I'm sorry. I didn't see you there . . ." My voice trails off as I stare at the perfect face of my mystery man.

His eyes are the color of the sky before it rains, dark gray with golden flecks sprinkled along the edge. This close, I can see his hair is threaded with copper highlights and darker, rich browns. He wears it styled longer on top and cropped short on the sides. He tips his head toward me, his hair falling over his eyebrow.

"You following me, little bird?"

The sound of his voice—low-timbered, rich, and smooth—hits me like a punch to the gut. I stare at his chest, a little envious of the way his black tee hugs his defined chest and arms. I trail my gaze along his body, memorizing the way he looks in case this is the only time I see him up close. I glance at his face, surprised by our proximity.

The intensity I see in his gaze is unlike anything else I've ever seen before. I feel like a dull, drab moth willingly going to the brightly-colored flame, even though I know this will end in my destruction.

I unconsciously sway even closer to him, and his crisp, citrus smell surrounds me. My fingers tingle with the need to touch him.

In a move I couldn't have predicted, he spins us, so my back faces the wall. He lets go of my shoulders, but I still feel the warmth of his palms, almost like a brand. I tip my head back, maintaining eye contact with him. The move done by any other guy would earn him a knee to the balls, but him. Not right now, at least.

"Well?"

I lick my lips, tasting the minty lip gloss I applied earlier. "I'm Alaina." The words are barely a murmur as I shiver from the intensity in his gaze.

"Aye, I know who you are, little bird."

I hold his stare and nod once. "I see you watching me every week. Why don't you ever stay until the end?"

"Places to be."

I nod like I understand. "Wife?"

The corner of his lips tips up. "No."

"Live-in girlfriend?"

His smirk grows. "Nope."

I quirk my eyebrow up. "You're single, then?"

He nods and steps closer, nearly touching me. His gaze roams along my face, and I can only hope he's memorizing my features just as much as I am his. "Is there something you want to ask me, Birdie?"

I press my back into the wall, creating a little more room between us. A swarm of butterflies cartwheels inside my belly, and I tip my chin up in faux bravado. "I'm all graduated now."

He takes a small step toward me and puts his right hand on the wall above my head, his bicep flexing in his black t-shirt. A slow flush rolls through my body at his proximity. He smells like citrus and trouble.

Is it hot in here?

"Aye, so I heard."

"It's just . . . if you were waiting for me to be out of high school—or legal, well—" I cringe before the sentence is out of my mouth, embarrassment warming my cheeks. I glance to the side, looking for my courage.

The rough pad of his finger gently traces down my cheek, and my breath hitches. "Beautiful," he murmurs.

I slowly turn my head toward him, meeting his gaze as his finger traces down my neck and follows the collar of my off-the-shoulder shirt. He traces along my collarbones, his hand spreading out to encompass my neck. His thumb slowly moves back and forth on my skin, right over my pulse that's steadily increasing with every swipe of his thumb.

My hands flex on the wall behind me, fingers digging into the drywall, looking for purchase. His lips are mesmerizing, full and pink and pouty.

I tip up my chin, straining to bridge the gap between our mouths. He takes a half-step closer, and our lips just barely touch.

"Declan," he whispers against my mouth, and I can barely hear it over my thundering pulse. "So you know what name to call out later when you're alone and thinking of me—of this."

"Of wha—"

He cuts off my words with the press of his lips, and my eyes flutter closed. For a single moment, he holds his lips against mine. Then I open my mouth, and it's all I can do not to melt into a puddle of lust right here in the back hallway of O'Malley's.

He's demanding in his kiss, and I'm more than happy to let him lead. His tongue tangles with mine in the most erotic kiss I've ever had. He slides his hand to the nape of my neck, his fingers grip my hair, and he tilts my head back. My back arches, and I grab onto the front of his tee, gripping the fabric to help ground myself. I feel lightheaded and breathless.

Declan pulls back, leaving our lips just barely separated. At my noise of protest, he swipes his thumb along my bottom lip, and I can't help it—I flick my tongue out and taste his thumb.

He groans and slowly drags his hand down, leaving it to rest on my collarbones. "Okay, little bird, okay," he murmurs against my lips.

"Dec." His name leaves my lips on a sigh. I can't believe I finally know his name after all this time. I'm silently cursing myself for not being braver a year ago when he first caught my eye—or maybe I caught *his* eye? Either way, we could've been doing this for the last year. This . . . and other things.

My heartbeat kicks up at the thought of doing *other things* with him—things I've been fantasizing about for longer than I would ever admit.

With those wicked thoughts in my head, I push up on my toes to connect our lips together again. I hook my arm around his neck and lean into him, exhilarated by the way his chest feels against mine.

His hands slide up from my waist to my ribs, and he kisses me with an intensity I lose myself in.

Just as I'm about to entertain the idea of bringing him back to my dorm, he wrenches his mouth away from mine. "What?" he snarls.

My eyes slowly open, foggy with lust. Declan's looking over his shoulder at some guy I've never seen before.

"Sorry, boss, but it's urgent." The guy looks anywhere but at Declan as he hands him a flip-phone.

"It fucking better be," he snaps, jerking the phone out of the other guy's hand. He looks at the screen of the phone, and if he wasn't pressed against every inch of me, I don't think I'd feel the tension that lines his body.

"Everything okay?" I murmur, looking at his furrowed brow.

"Fuck." The word sounds tortured from his lips. He hands the phone back to the other guy and then turns to face me. He cups my face, blocking my view of anything but him. "I've gotta go, little bird."

"W-what?" My hazy fog of lust doesn't leave me very articulate, apparently. That's pretty much the last thing I was expecting him to say.

"We're not done." He seals his words with a toe-curling kiss. And just like every other week, he disappears before I can figure out what the hell just happened.

And why his words felt more like a passionate threat than a sweet promise.

chapter six

Alaina

"OH MY GOD, Lainey! Answer your phone!" Maddie shouts as she barrels into my dorm room the next morning, sighing with exaggeration.

I fling the duvet cover off of me and squint at her. I rub the sleep out of my eyes and smooth my hair back from the messy bun I vaguely remember putting it in last night. "What's going on?"

Maddie points at my vibrating and ringing phone on my nightstand. "That has been ringing for the last fifteen minutes! Honestly, how can you sleep through that?"

I grab my phone and unplug it from the charger just as it stops ringing. Looking at my screen, I see five missed calls from my mom. "Shit. It's my mom."

"Oh, shit." Maddie visibly loses some of her steam, her shoulders losing some of that tension she had when she barreled in here. "Want me to stay?"

"Nah, I'm good."

"Babe. It's seven o'clock on a Saturday"—Maddie hesitates for a moment—"on the fourteenth."

"Yeah." I sigh and scoot up my bed to lean against the headboard. A yawn escapes me as I try to muster up some energy to call her back.

My mom is complicated on a good day. But every May fourteenth, she's . . . unrecognizable. Today is my dad's birthday, and since we don't talk about him *ever*, you'd think the day would go unnoticed by her. Instead, she does something rash that usually has me calling in a favor to some friends back home.

Last year, she impulsively got a back tattoo, a belly button ring, and a pixie cut. I had to call Aunt Sloane, and after she tracked her down, she was able to talk some sense into her. Unfortunately, she didn't get to Mom until *after* her tattoo, so she has some misspelled Chinese symbols and a flamingo decorating her shoulder blade. I had secretly hoped that it would serve as a good lesson for her. And then maybe we could start talking about Dad.

It's been ten years since I've seen him. Ten years is a long time to go without a dad.

Honestly, the day my dad left, I didn't just lose him—I lost my mom too. And while she might physically show up for ceremonies or dance recitals, she's been emotionally checked-out for a decade.

A swarm of shame coats my belly like it does every time I think about why my dad left. Before I can go down the same depressing path, Maddie clears her throat.

"Alright, babe. Since I'm up, I'll go grab us some lattes from around the corner," Maddie offers with a small smile.

"Thanks, Maddie. You're the best. Is Mary up?"

"Nope. That girl can sleep through anything." She playfully rolls her eyes.

"Okay—" My phone rings, interrupting me. "I'm going to take this," I say as I hold up my phone.

Maddie nods and closes my bedroom door as she leaves.

I take a deep breath and paste a smile on my face. "Morning, Mom."

"Alaina, hello. It's your mother." A small smirk flits across my face when I hear my mother greet me the same way she has been since I was old enough to have my own phone. She pauses long enough that I double-check the call is still connected.

"Is everything okay?"

"What? Yes, of course. Why wouldn't it be?" Her words are sharp, and without giving me a chance to respond, she continues, "I have news. I'd like you to spend the summer with me. I booked you a train ticket for this morning at eleven."

"R-really?" I look around my room, expecting someone to pop out of my closet and yell *gotcha*! "Wow. I mean, that's great, Mom. Yeah, I'd love to spend time with you. I'll have to see if I can get my summer classes swapped with online courses, and I'll have to let the coffee shop know. Oh, and cancel my volunteer hours at the studio." I scoot forward, my mind whirling with possibilities. "But, yeah, I can definitely make it work."

"Sure, sure. I'll text you the address," Mom says to me before she says something that's muffled.

I get out of bed and walk over to my closet. Holding the phone between my neck and my ear, I reach up and grab my suitcase from the top shelf. "Come on, Mom, I know it's been a few years since I've been home, but I remember our address." I chuckle a little. "Do you think you could pick me up at the train station? We can stop at our favorite bakery on the way home, maybe get Dad's favorite . . . to, I don't know, celebrate a little."

Every year, I bring up celebrating my dad's birthday, and every year, Mom says no, but that's usually after she made her May-fourteenth rash decision. But this year—this year, I'll actually get to *be with her* on May fourteenth. I haven't been with her for his birthday in forever. I swallow and nod a few times at the possibility.

Maybe this year will be different, I think as I allow hope to fill a tiny part of me.

I hear some rustling over the phone. "Place those over there, dear. Yes, thank you." I hear more rustling before her voice comes through the line clearly. "What? No. I can't pick you up. I have several appointments today that I can't miss. I'll have someone pick you up."

I put my suitcase on my bed and unzip it. Shaking my head, I internally chastise myself for even suggesting it. "Of course, Mom. I should've known you had to work. You don't have to do that. I'll get a cab."

"Nonsense. I'll have one of the boys pick you up. They're nice boys."

I pause with my favorite sweatshirt hovering over the suitcase and scrunch up my nose. "What boys? I hope you don't mean Tommy O'Connelly and his friends. Mom, they're *not* nice boys."

"Hmm? Oh, no. I mean your new stepbrothers."

My body locks up, and the breath in my lungs freezes. *Stepbrothers?* That can't be right. I must've misheard her. Has she missed more appointments? I worry the side of my lip as I recall the last time I talked to Dr. Carruthers, Mom's psychiatrist.

Usually, there's a big line about doctor-patient confidentiality that's never crossed, but over the years, he became a trusted family friend. So, if Mom misses more than three appointments in a row, he has his assistant send me a text to check-in to make sure nothing happened to Mom. I know it's not entirely ethical, but I reason that since no one is divulging patient information, it's okay. I'm just trying to look out for my mom. Just like I've done for most of my life.

"Mom."

"Please place my armoire next to the closet." Her muffled words confuse me even more. I pinch the bridge of my nose and release a breath I didn't realize I was holding.

"Mom. When's the last time you saw Dr. Carruthers?"

"Oh, you know I don't like visiting with him too often. He's a quack, you know. Eileen O'Neill told me last week that she doesn't even think he's Irish! Can you believe that?! And he doesn't even have any decent coffee." She huffs into the phone, and I can just picture her crossing her arm tightly across her chest. "Besides," she says with a sniff. "I don't need to see him anymore. I have Cormac now."

I cross my room and sit down on the edge of my bed and rub the tension headache forming in my forehead. I'm going to have to spend the rest of my day calling in favors back home for someone to check on her until I can get back there.

A few years ago, on May fourteenth, I got a call from our neighbor at the time, Mrs. Walsh. Mom had an impromptu garage sale consisting of all my dad's things. After calling Mom a dozen times and going right to voicemail, I called around to some of my childhood friends. By the time I got a hold of Tammi O'Neill and she got to our house, Mom had sold almost everything. Tammi grabbed Dad's Polaroid camera and his vinyl collection for me. It cost me two hundred bucks, but it was worth it.

"What's going on, Mom? What are you doing right now? Did you move again?"

"Hmm? Oh, it's just the best thing, dear. I moved!"

"What? Why?" I stare out the window without really seeing anything.

"Well, of course, I moved! And it's the cutest little cottage—so charming. I'm not going to live in a different house than my husband. That just doesn't make sense." She tsks. "Honestly, Alaina, what kind of nonsense are they teaching you at the school?"

"Wh-what do you mean your husband?!" A weight falls into the pit of my stomach, making me feel both weighed down and lightheaded.

"Keep up, Alaina. I'm getting married! Isn't that wonderful?" Her voice is so cheerful it actually hurts my ears.

I don't respond. I can't respond. She can't get married again. *Right?* What about Dad?

I must've said that question out loud because she says, "What about your father? He hasn't been here for a long time, Alaina. He lost his right to have a say ten years ago."

"B-but you're still married to Dad! You—you can't just marry someone else!" I yell and flinch as soon as the words are out of my mouth. I've never yelled at her before.

She clucks her tongue. "Alaina Murphy McElroy!" Hearing my entire name shocks me out of my stupor. "I can, and I will. Cormac said he'll make sure everything is perfect for my big day." I can hear the smile in her voice, and it turns my stomach.

"Who the hell is Cormac?!" I all but yell at her. My head spins so fast that I think I'm going to be sick.

"Hmm? Cormac is my fiancé. Pay attention, dear. And he has three boys around your age too, isn't that wonderful? I know you've always wanted siblings."

"What?" The pitch of voice is comically high, and I can feel my eyebrows practically in my hairline.

I asked for a baby sister once. Shelly Walsh's mom just had her baby sister, and Shelly came to school bragging about how you were only cool if you had siblings. Shelly had the prettiest blonde hair and brought the best classroom treats; of course, I wanted to be just like her—I was six.

"I said, Cormac Fitzgerald is my fiancé. Keep up, dear. Now, I'm not sure if his boys have the same mother because I thought I heard Eileen once say that she heard that Cormac just came home with one of his boys one day—without his mother." I hear the judgment in her voice, and for one tiny, weak moment, I consider telling her she shouldn't throw stones at glass houses. "But that doesn't matter, I suppose, because they have me now."

"Cormac Fitzgerald? The Cormac Fitzgerald?" I feel like I got hit in the head. There is a weird ringing noise reverberating through my skull, making it hard to think. I can't get enough air in my lungs, and my chest feels tight. Am I having a heart attack?

"Mom, you can't just up and marry one of the most prominent bachelors of Boston!" I felt the hysteria rising through my body like a tidal wave. I stand upright quick enough that all the blood—and panic—rushes to my head. I grip the end of my bed to steady myself. Oh my God, what has she done?! She's going to get herself killed! Everyone knows there's something shady about Cormac Fitzgerald. He practically rules Boston—and with an iron fist, and anyone who disagrees, well, they disappear. And if rumors are to be believed, he has ties to the mob.

"Don't be ridiculous, Alaina. This is what we always wanted. Anyway, I'm off, dear. Lots to do in the next few weeks. See you soon!"

"Wait—" She ends the call before I can even finish.

I pull my phone away from my ear and stare around my room with wide eyes. What the hell am I going to do now?

I TRACE THE TIP of my finger over the worn grooves of my vanity. The same vanity that I've had for the last eleven years. I rub the smudge of eyeliner off the edge as I pack my makeup in my travel bag. It's not pristine anymore, but it has character and history. And it's one of my most-treasured things. My dad gave it to me for my seventh birthday.

I run into my parents' room and push open their door. "It's my birthday!"

My mommy groans and tosses the comforter over her head. "Too early, Alaina. Go back to sleep."

Mommy doesn't like to get up too early on the weekends, but I couldn't wait in my room a moment longer. It's my birthday, *and I'm sure I'll get to open presents today. I go to my daddy's side of the bed and notice that he's not there.*

I bet he's making my birthday breakfast!

It's a family tradition to have a birthday pancake breakfast with whipped cream and chocolate chips. I round the bed and go to my mommy's side. I peel back the corner of the comforter and give her a kiss on her forehead. "See ya later, Mommy!" I whisper-shout, bouncing on my toes a little.

She cracks an eyelid open and reaches out to squeeze my hand. "Happy birthday, honey. I just need another hour, and then we can do presents, okay?"

I nod a few times. "Absolutely. I'm going to find Dad. I'm going to ask for extra whipped cream."

"Okay, honey, enjoy your birthday breakfast. I'll be out soon."

With a wide grin, I spin around and dash through the house until I reach the kitchen. I skid to a stop at the sight of a plate full of chocolate chip birthday pancakes with enough whipped cream to fill a bucket!

"Happy birthday, Lainey!" My daddy picks me up and spins me around, planting kisses on the top of my head. "How's my seven-year-old today?"

"WOW, DADDY. THAT looks so good! Can I eat it now?"

"Sure thing, kiddo, but first, check out the present in the living room."

I wiggle a little, and he lets me down. I can't say no to a present—who would? I follow Daddy into the living room, and there, sitting in the middle with a giant red bow, is a makeup desk for big girls. I squeal and clap my hands a few times, running over to it. "Wow! A makeup desk! Shelly's older sister has one of these, and she says only big girls get to use them. Oh boy, she's going to love this!"

"It's called a vanity. And you have a few years until you can use makeup, so until then, you can use it for other things." He opens the side cabinet door. "You can store your necklaces here"—he closes the door and pulls out one of four drawers—"or store your nail polish and other jewelry here. You can even do little craft projects on here if you want. I made it just for you, Lainey."

"I love it. Thank you, Daddy!" I wrap my arms around his middle and squeeze, so he knows just how much I love it.

"Babe. I've been calling your name for like five minutes," Maddie says as she walks into my room with two lattes. "How was the conversation—whoa."

I shift on my stool and look at her, accepting the latte from her outstretched hand. "Thanks," I murmur.

"Are you okay? You look pale—paler than usual, I mean." She pivots to look around, her eyebrows rise when she spots my open suitcase on my bed. "What's going on?" She looks at me with furrowed brows and a crease in the middle of her forehead. Gosh, she'd hate that. I've never met an eighteen-year-old more concerned with wrinkles—thanks to Aunt Sloane, no doubt.

My aunt has been searching for the fountain of youth at the bottom of every serum, elixir, chemical peel, and pill bottle for decades. She's been obsessed for as long as I can remember. Every school break, she comes to the city for a week or two, and all of us stay in a fancy hotel suite with her. She treats us to spa days and shopping sprees, lunches at the nicest restaurants and evenings on the top of exclusive clubs. I remember the first time she included me on her school-break girls' week—that's what she calls it.

We had a week off around Halloween for parent-teacher conferences. I always thought it was a joke—a conference for the parents of a bunch of kids at a boarding school? What's the point? Most of the girls that attended St. Rita's didn't live anywhere near the actual school. And those of us lucky enough to have parents living close-by, well, there was a reason we attended a boarding school, wasn't there?

Aunt Sloane came to her conferences for Maddie and Mary and found me afterward, sitting in the common area of our dorm room. She told me to pack a bag and be ready in ten. Seeing as my only plan was to spend the next week alone in pj's, bingeing on our DVDs of *The Vampire Diaries*, I was ready to go in eight.

That year we all got massages, facials, seaweed wraps, haircuts and blowouts, and mani-pedis. It was just the four of us—joking, smiling, and laughing—and I felt like I was part of their family. I mean, I am—we're related, but this felt different—special. It was one of the best days of my life.

We haven't had a girls' week in six months or so, ever since Aunt Sloane got a new boyfriend. A new, *younger* boyfriend. I haven't met him yet, but Maddie found him on Aunt Sloane's Instagram account last month—wearing only tiny shorts and lounging in their living room. Let's just say that he's easy on the eyes and closer to our age than hers. So I get why she hasn't been to the city in a while.

Realizing that I've been staring at Maddie for too long, I shake my head and blink a few times. "I'm sorry, what did you say?"

"Mary! Get your ass in here. Something's going on!" she yells. She tosses her arm around my shoulders and steers me toward the end of my bed. Pushing the suitcase back, she sits us down.

I don't even hear any footsteps, but suddenly, Mary is standing in front of me. "Lainey? What's going on? Why are you packing?"

I open my mouth to answer, but nothing comes out right away. I just can't believe my mom's getting married—and she tells me on my dad's birthday.

Mary worries her bottom lip, flicking her gaze between Maddie and me. "Maybe we should call Mom. Or Aunt Lana."

"N-no." I clear my throat and look at Mary first, then Maddie. "No, don't call Aunt Sloane, and my mom's busy moving . . . and planning her wedding."

"She's what?!" Maddie says at the same time Mary does.

A feel the wry smile slide across my face, and I take a sip of my latte. "You guys know I love it when you do your twin thing." I sigh. "She just called to let me know that she's getting married. To the notorious bachelor of Boston, Cormac Fitzgerald." At their slacked jaws and wide eyes, I just nod. "I know. That was my reaction too."

Mary rocks back and sits on the floor in front of my bed. "Start from the beginning."

chapter seven

Wolf

"'LO?"

"Good, you're up. I'm still in the city. Just got a call from Da. You need to pick up some chick from the train station," my brother, Rush, blurts out.

"Rush?" I wipe a hand down my face, trying to wake up a little. "Fuck, what time is it?"

"It's noon. You need to be at the Boston train station by three."

"Fuck off, I'm still at the Blue Knights' clubhouse. I just got to sleep a few hours ago"—a yawn escapes me, and I rub at my eyes—"so, I'm not even in Boston."

"I would do it myself, but Sully went for coffee with his grandma early this morning, so I stayed back to go with him."

I sit up and release a breath. Years ago, when we discovered that we had a traitor in our ranks, my brothers and I started talking in coded phrases. Rush just told me our other brother, Sully, got tangled up in an altercation early this morning. Now it's just a question of how bad. "Shit. Okay. Should I bring some donuts?" *Is there a body—should I send in the cleaners?*

"Nah. We've got enough here. Just get the girl."

"Okay, okay. Description?"

Rush sighs. "All I know is she's got dark-red hair. You'll have to figure it out once you get there."

I've done more with less. "Okay. Where should I bring her once I pick her up?"

"Home." Rush's tone is flat, and I hear the noise of the city in the background.

"Home? Who's home?" I lean my head back against the back of the couch and try to stop the room from spinning.

"Sober up, asshole. *Our* home."

I smirk at the annoyance in his voice. I can just picture him pinching the bridge of his nose—it's his tell whenever Sully and I irritate him. "Yeah, yeah. Our house, got it."

"Good. Don't be late."

I grimace as I widen my legs, rearranging my dick. Sleeping in jeans is the fucking worst. "Late? Bro, I think you're confusing me with our brother." I scoff. "Who is this girl, anyway? And why can't she take a cab back to the house?"

"Lana's daughter."

I pause to let that sink into my alcohol-addled brain. "Shit. Am I still drunk? I didn't even know she had a daughter." I grimace.

"Neither did I, and I really don't like surprises—or being played. If I find out that little weaselly fucker gave us bad intel, I'm going to—damn it, Sully, I told you to wait for me. I gotta go, Wolf. Watch the girl, and we'll talk tonight."

"Yeah, okay. Later."

"Oh, and brother? It goes without saying that she's off-limits until we can figure this out, yeah?"

"Got it." I grit the words out between clenched teeth.

I end the call and push my black hair back, scrubbing my hands down my face. I need a goddamn haircut and a shave.

Fuck, Lana has a daughter? There's no way our guy missed that. Shit—there's no way *Da* missed that. So either he knew and didn't tell us, or he just found out, and I'm not sure which option is better.

Rush is definitely going to freak out over some-thing—*someone*—slipping through his web. Dude loves background checks more than anyone I've ever met. I get why he's so intense about it, but it's odd that we didn't hear about some daughter until now. Weirder still that she didn't pop up on Rush's data expedition.

Everything about this feels off. Even just the fact that Da moved someone into the house two weeks ago without so much as telling us beforehand is suspect.

Sure, the house is a legit mansion where I could go days—weeks—without seeing another person, but still. You don't just move some random woman into a house you share without talking about it first.

Fuck, I need some coffee and aspirin. Thinking about Da and his motivations is giving me a fucking headache.

I glance around and see a few of the Blue Knights passed out around the couches in their game room. I scrub my hands over my face and push off the couch. If I leave now, I should be able to get home and shower the booze off.

Whenever I visit the Blue Knights' clubhouse, I always end up on my ass. Those guys drink Fireball like it's water, and after four or five hours, I usually bail and head home. But last night, I ended up passing out on one of their disgusting couches. Those fuckers have seen more ass than the Red Light District. Half of building this friendship with the Blue Knights is showing up on Friday nights to hang with them. We always end up swapping intel four shots in. Nothing big, but enough to let the other one know we're building trust.

And trust is important when you're in the family business. The Brotherhood could survive on its own, but it won't thrive. And between Da's vision and Rush's new ideas, we're expanding, slowly, of course. It's lonely at the top and forever watching your six is not how I want to spend the rest of my days.

So, that's why we started our long game last year. Rush is the guy you want coordinating your plans and cyberstalking every possible outcome—and then some—but he's not the guy you send to befriend the local one-percenters.

We're strategically creating a network of families we can trust—a relationship beneficial to everyone involved and one you'd think twice about eliminating for a higher offer.

I lightly slap my cheeks to wake up and push off the couch, my pant leg sticking to the leather a little. Fucking gross. Now I'm going to have to throw these away.

On my way out, I see Diesel, the Blue Knights' VP, sitting on a barstool. The news is playing on the TV mounted above the bar, and a coffee mug sits half full in front of him. Knowing him, there's a generous splash of whiskey in there with his coffee. I clap him on the shoulder as I pass him. "Later, man. Thanks for the hospitality last night."

"Sure thing, Wolf. You and your boys are always welcome here," Diesel replies as he takes a drag from his cigarette.

"Appreciate that. I'm out."

Diesel raises a hand in acknowledgment. And that right there is why Da asked me to come here and not Rush or Sully. These guys know me as the Lone Wolf of the Brotherhood—a party-lovin' sniper who never misses. But that's only a partial truth.

I am the best sniper in the Brotherhood.

But I'm also a wolf in sheep's clothing. I blend and adapt. And sheep never see me coming until my blade is sticking out of their throats.

Hopefully, it won't come to that with the Blue Knights. I kind of like Diesel and some of his boys. Be a shame to carve a red smile on them.

Outside the clubhouse, I spot even more members passed out on lawn furniture, half-naked women draped over them. I walk across the gravel parking lot to my car. A few members crack an eye and throw up a hand in acknowledgment. I tip my chin at each one, but I don't say anything. I don't think I could speak right now—my head feels like someone took a meat cleaver to it.

Over the last year, not only did I cement the relationship between the Brotherhood and the Blue Knights, but I actually got to know some of these dudes. A few are total pricks, but most of them are decent.

Diesel and his boys are one-percenters, but they live by a similar code: no families and no skin.

We don't wipe out an entire family because some asshole gambled his savings account away. Sure, we'll break some kneecaps and maybe some torture when necessary, but never his family just because they're *his* family. And we don't deal in skin—and we don't allow skin to be trafficked in our ports. Luckily for the Blue Knights, they agree with us on these two rules.

And in our life, these relationships between two like-minded families can be the difference between life or death.

So while Rush and Sully fuck off to the city every Friday, I'm here, at the Blue Knights' clubhouse. It's not so bad, really, but at some point, I'd like my Fridays back.

If for nothing else than to tail Rush. That asshole comes back from the city every week, nearly giddy, which is fucking weird. Every time I ask him about it, he's cagey as fuck—even more than his usual paranoid ass.

So one of these days, I'm going to follow Rush and see what he's really doing. I have a feeling he's got a little bird hidden away in the city.

Which would mean he fucked up the pact we made two years ago. The pact that says we share. After seeing the destruction caused by four brothers—the entire junior Brotherhood council—fighting over the same woman and turning their backs on one another—and all of us—we agreed that we'd never put ourselves in that same situation. And after seeing the war that one of those brothers started when he turned *rat*, we all agreed to a pact.

And when Rush, Sully, and I exterminated the rats and *became* the junior council, we promised each other we'd fall for the same woman or no woman at all.

For the past two years, we've all dabbled in pussy, but it's never serious, and no one has dated. We haven't even brought it up again, but I sure as fuck haven't forgotten. It seems like I might have to remind my brother.

I unlock my car and head to the nearest coffee shop, rolling down the windows for some fresh air. And I can't help the smile that spreads across my face as I think of all the ways I can remind Rush. We might have to make use out of the boxing ring in the basement.

chapter eight

Alaina

I PULL UP MY GPS on my phone and check our progress. Looks like we'll be arriving at the train station in ten minutes. If I'd had more time to pack, I would've made a special playlist for the long ride. But after I recited the phone call to the girls, I barely had enough time to pack.

And how do you pack for somewhere you've never been for an undetermined amount of time? I agonized for ten minutes, just staring blankly at my closet.

I haven't lived with my mom since I was eight.

"Mommy, guess what?" I ran into the living room of our new apartment after school. "We got a new assignment today. We get to make family trees! Look, I already started mine." I proudly held up a piece of construction paper with a big tree outlined. My name was at the bottom, and I carefully wrote Mommy and Daddy above my name. My bestest friends and

cousins were on a branch next to time with my Aunt Sloane and Uncle Collin written above them.

Mommy rolled over on the couch, cracked an eye open, and peered at me. She's been in the living room a lot, ever since Daddy went away. She always slept in the living room when Daddy had to leave for work. She said that she wanted to be the first one to see him when he came home. But Daddy left so long ago, and we even had to switch houses. Sometimes, I'd get scared that he wouldn't be able to find us, but then I'd remind myself that Daddy's really good at finding things. He's helped me find Belle, my stuffed pink bunny, so many times. "Hmm?"

"I drew a branch connecting you and Aunt Sloane because you guys are sisters!" I beamed at her. "But I don't know your parents' first names, and Miss Baker said we should use real names."

She sat up quickly and snatched the paper from my hand fast enough that I got a paper cut. "Ouch." I squeezed it tight, hoping it didn't bleed. Paper cuts always stung.

"Go pack your favorite things in your travel suitcase. I forgot to tell you we're going to visit your grandparents today. Don't forget your pink bunny; we don't want to leave our things behind." Mommy stood up quickly, grabbed her phone, and started calling someone.

Two days later, after a plane ride to South Carolina, we learned that my grandparents were killed in a car accident on the way to get us from the airport.

The following week, Mom sent me to St. Rita's.

As Taylor Swift sings in my ears, I close my eyes and think about everything we found online about Cormac Fitzgerald. Which is to say, not much. While I quickly packed whatever I thought I might need for the summer, Mary and Maddie were on their laptops, searching for more information.

He's a prominent figure in Boston, and while he's often photographed at philanthropic events, he's never photographed with women—or his children. Apparently, he keeps his personal life very private.

Ah, yes. Cormac Fitzgerald has three children, but we couldn't find a single article or image of them online anywhere. And while I didn't have a ton of time to do research, I couldn't even find their *names*. The amount of power Cormac must have to issue and uphold that gag order is . . . frightening.

There were way more conspiracy articles about Cormac and what he really does when he's not posing for the cameras than actual facts. There are rumors that he's part of a faction of the Irish mafia—Summer Knoll. They say that he holds meetings for the other members of the mafia at his house, but it's so hush-hush that the most I could find were threads full of rumors, some wilder than the others.

One thread I found had over 300 comments with alleged rumors. I only read a couple of them before I had to shut down my computer to leave for the train. One particular rumor alleged that Cormac keeps an old well on his property, and if someone stands against him, he throws them in the well—still alive, until they starve to death.

I shudder and roll my eyes, both freaked out and annoyed that I actually put any stock into such obvious speculation.

Once the train pulls up to the station in Boston, I wait for the handful of passengers to file down the center aisle before I slide out of my seat. Sliding my arms through the straps of my backpack, I walk down the narrow aisle and wheel my suitcase behind me, duffle bag perched on the top.

Stepping off the train and onto the platform, I take a deep breath, a tentative smile on my face. That's quickly wiped off my face when I choke on some smog wafting from the front of the train.

Waving my hand in front of my face, I get myself under control and take my first look around. This is the first time I've ever been to the train station here, and I haven't called Boston home in so long that it feels foreign to me. It looks . . . just like any train station. My shoulders drop for a moment, but I paste a smile on my face, and they hitch up again.

Blue awnings dot the platform, providing shelter and shade for benches perched against the concrete divider walls. Two sets of train tracks are to my right—including my commuter, and two sets are on the other side of the platform which makes sense considering this station has several routes and destinations going out each day.

Maybe Mom and I can take a day trip back to the city soon. See some sights together or grab a show—really, just spending some one-on-one time together would be amazing. And traveling via train was a lot more comfortable than you might think.

My backpack straps dig into my shoulder, weighed down by a change of clothes, my laptop, and a few books. I blow a loose strand of hair out of my face and slip my sunglasses over my eyes.

I don't know what I was expecting, but definitely something more, I don't know, welcoming. Or magical. Maybe some small, secret part of me hoped that Mom would show up and greet me like the woman twenty feet away greets the girl who sat two rows behind me—a big, handwritten silly sign, three balloons, and over-the-top affection.

But instead, some guy I've never met before is picking me up. For all I know, he could be a total creep. I don't exactly trust Mom's judgment, especially not today. She's impulsive and erratic.

I'm hit with a realization that would've knocked me on my butt if I wasn't holding onto my suitcase—holy shit, am I turning into my mom?

Who the hell just packs up everything and leaves their home after a phone call like that? Granted, it was a phone call from my mom, but still. It feels very impulsive and erratic—just how I describe Mom.

I shake that thought aside and look around again. *I only came because she called me, I wouldn't just pack up and move for some random person*, I reason with myself.

The platform is clearing out, so with a deep breath, I roll my suitcase toward the stairs and follow the signs for short-term parking and pickup.

I spy a restroom on the bottom level and duck inside to freshen up. Ignoring the overwhelming stench of urine and the overflowing garbage can, I do my best to tame my wild waves, finger-combing them and tossing them over one shoulder. I dig around in my backpack until I find my travel makeup bag and pull it out, setting in on the countertop. I reapply some deodorant, roll my perfume on my left wrist and rub my wrists together, and swipe some pink-tinted lip gloss across my lips.

Staring at my reflection in the warped mirror, I lean forward and look into my own eyes. "You can do this, Lainey. Here's your chance to live with Mom. You'll be in college soon, and then you'll never live at home again. Don't waste it."

When I'm sufficiently freshened-up and feeling positive after my impromptu pep talk, I wheel my suitcase out of the bathroom and walk down the covered walkway to the parking lot and designated pickup spot. Tattered paper rustles as the wind whips through the walkway, drawing my eye to the wall with colorful flyers. I eye laminated train routes that leave from this station, particularly the train that goes upstate New York. Hmm . . . Mom and I can easily take that train to the city for a few days.

Once I emerge from the walkway, I pause to look around for my supposed ride. I don't see anyone that looks like they're waiting for someone, so I wheel my suitcase over to a bench underneath the overhang to the right. I peel off my long-sleeve shirt and stuff it into my teal backpack. I was sitting by an AC vent on the train, so I needed the extra layer, but it's definitely unnecessary out here.

I gather my long wavy hair and sweep it across one shoulder, allowing the warm breeze to drift across my neck.

I eye a few people waiting in the pickup area. Two guys around my age talk in low tones to one another, and they both have bags at their feet—passengers. There's a middle-aged man talking on his phone, and he's looking around while he talks. He must be here to pick someone up, but I don't think he's here for me.

"Alright, come on, Red."

Startled, I turn around at the sound of his voice.

Over six feet tall, black hair tousled like he just rolled out of bed, and a cocky smirk that says *I left a woman in the bed I just rolled out of.* Black brows that arch over espresso-brown eyes and thick, dark lashes that any woman would be jealous of.

His jawline is sharp, and there's a bump on the bridge of his nose—he definitely broke his nose in his life. I idly wonder what happened that ended up with him getting punched.

He is stunning and quite possibly one of the most attractive people I've ever seen. And I once met Henry Cavill at a hole-in-the-wall restaurant in SoHo.

Butterflies take flight in my belly, and I feel a flush roll through my body that has nothing to do with the warm breeze.

Tattoos cover nearly both of his arms, mostly Irish symbols, flowers, and what looks like an old gun. I spot another tattoo peeking out of the collar of his tee, drawing my gaze up his neck and to his lush lips.

A cigarette hangs from the corner of his mouth. "You alright?"

"Hm? Oh, yes." With effort, I tear my gaze away from his mouth. Pink and full, the bottom one is just a tad fuller than the top. Honestly, it should be illegal for a guy to have such perfect lips. "I'm waiting for someone."

Geez, Alaina, you kiss one guy, and suddenly, you're checking out every hot guy you see, I mentally chastise myself.

He pinches the cigarette between his thumb and index finger and takes a drag. He exhales, and the smoke curls into the air around him. Jesus. He looks like some sort of James Dean type, all bad boy vibes and sex appeal.

He's a predator, and right now, he's looking at me like I'm prey—*his* prey.

I meet his gaze again, and the intensity shining back shocks me. "Okay, then," I mumble and turn my body away from him to continue looking for one of Cormac's boys—even though I have *no idea* what any of them look like. I'm not even sure what to expect, but based on Cormac's public functions, maybe a polo-wearing preppy boy.

I pull out my phone from my back pocket and send Mom a text asking what Cormac's son looks like. Out of the corner of my eye, I see the guy take another drag from his cigarette as he walks toward the garbage can. Stubbing it out in the attached ashtray, he looks over his shoulder at me, his face giving nothing away.

"Come on, Red, your mom's waiting."

My eyebrows hit my hairline as I scan him from head to toe, trying hard to keep my face blank. "You're my ride?"

He turns around to face me. "Sure am. Now let's get moving. I got places to be." Without waiting for a response, he walks backward toward the parking lot.

"Wait."

At the sound of my voice, he pauses and raises a brow.

"How do I know you are who you say you are? You could be a psychopath or a kidnapper or . . . *something*." My heartbeat kicks up a notch, and I'm embarrassed to admit to myself that I'm not sure if it's in fear—or lust.

"Babe. If I wanted to kidnap you, I would just do it. I wouldn't have a fucking chat with you beforehand." His expression deadpans.

I cross my arms and jut out my chin. "I'm not getting murdered today, thank you very much. I've seen enough *Dateline* to know that once you go to a secondary location, your chances decrease by like seventy percent. And all the true sociopaths are stupid good-looking. It's how they lower their victim's defenses."

He chuckles a little, a smirk ticking up the corner of his mouth.

When he doesn't say anything, I get all flustered and snap, "What?"

"So, you think I'm good-looking, huh?" He chuckles as he pulls his phone out of his pocket and takes two steps closer.

My cheeks flush with embarrassment, and I shift my weight to my other foot. "Wha—yes—no, I mean—" I take a deep breath. "If this is your weird way of coming onto me, it sucks." My lips flatten into a thin line.

He raises an unimpressed eyebrow. "If I'm tryin' to chat you up, you'll know it, Red." Ringing fills the air as he holds up his phone to show me the call is connected to the speakerphone.

"Hello?" My mother's voice is unmistakable.

"It's Wolf." His voice is flat, and it's such a change from how it was five seconds ago that it stuns me silent for a moment.

"Oh, hello, dear. Is everything okay?"

"Tell your daughter you sent me to collect her." Wolf's tone is cold and curt.

I look at him with a new understanding. His tone tells me more than his words, and it adds another layer of suspicion for this whole ordeal.

"Sure, sure. Alaina, dear, can you hear me?"

I clear my throat and take a couple steps toward the guy—Wolf—and closer to the phone. "I can hear you, Mom."

"Oh, good. This is one of Cormac's boys, so he'll take you home. See you soon, dear!" She ends the call before I can respond.

Wolf pockets his phone and reaches down to grab my suitcase. Without a word, I follow him to a sleek flat-black car.

Once my bags are stowed, I climb into the passenger seat and run my hands over the soft tan leather. I settle in and look around the interior as Wolf drives.

"You know anything about cars?"

I smile and shake my head a little. "Not really. I live in the city, so I don't spend a lot of time in cars, but it looks nice."

The corner of his mouth tips up in response. He drives with his left hand on the top of the steering wheel and his right hand on the gearshift. His tattooed fingers flex around the gearshift, and I tilt my head, trying to read them. I can only make out L and I, and there's something vaguely familiar about it. I scan his profile, looking for any other familiarities. It must remind me of one of the guys from O'Malley's.

"So, Wolf, huh?"

He stares at the road, shifting gears as we coast to a red light.

"That's an interesting name. Is it a family one?"

"You could say that, Red."

"It's Alaina," I correct him.

He shrugs in response, never taking his eyes off the road.

"So, what kind of car is this?"

"Special edition Jaguar XJ."

"Cool." I nod like I know what he's talking about. It's silent for a few minutes, and I scramble to think of something to say. He's not making it very easy to engage in conversation, but I don't mind the challenge. "So, do you—"

He reaches forward to turn the volume up, effectively cutting me off mid-sentence. "Electric Love" plays from the speakers, and I lean my head back against the seat.

I glance at Wolf and see a smirk playing along his lips. I sing along to the words and alternate between watching Wolf and the scenery for the rest of the car ride.

chapter nine

Alaina

ARCADE FIRE CROONS through the speakers as we pull into a gated driveway. A security guard comes out of a little building outside the gate and walks over to the driver's side door.

"Good evening, Mr. Fitzgerald," the security guard greets us as he leans down and peers into the car. "Ah, and a lady tonight. Good evening, miss."

Wolf laughs. "Come on, Dave. I've told you, Mr. Fitzgerald is my da. Wolf is fine. And this"—he gestures to me—"is Red. She'll be staying here."

I look at Dave with a smile. "Please, call me Alaina."

"Welcome to the Summer Knoll Estate, miss. I'm Dave, head of security."

"Nice to meet you," I murmur as my mind whirls. Did he say this was the *Summer Knoll Estate*?

What did I just walk into?

Dave steps away, and a moment later, the gates open, and Wolf drives us up the long, winding driveway.

"Jesus. This must be ridiculous to shovel in the winter." The thought escapes my lips before I can stuff it back in.

Wolf chuckles and glances at me but doesn't reply. He pulls around the semicircle driveway and stops right in front of the front door.

I swallow the lump of trepidation in my throat as I stare at this monstrosity my mom called "a cute cottage house." This was—this was a certified mansion.

Three stories tall, light-colored brick with white siding and expertly trimmed bushes and bright flowers—this mansion looks like it came right from the pages of some magazine like HGTV. It's wide enough that I can't even see the end of it from this vantage point, but I think I glimpsed a pool in the fenced-in backyard when we were driving up. I bet there's at least a ten-car garage around the back too.

Green ivy crawls up the brick and continues to climb toward the roof, gathering in the top corners and spreading out to frame it.

A small carriage house sits on the opposite side of the property with two black cars parked outside the attached garage.

A knock on the window breaks me out of my musings. "Come on."

I nod, and with a deep breath, get out of the car. I follow Wolf up the stairs to the front porch, and with a deep breath to shove down my fear, I square my shoulders and step over the threshold.

An older man dressed in a tailored suit greets us inside the foyer. "Welcome back, Mr. Fitzgerald."

Wolf nods as he sets my suitcase down next to me and walks toward the wide staircase in the middle of the room.

"Your dad requests you for dinner at six thirty sharp."

Wolf pauses on the second step. "Okay, Claude" he says before he jogs up to the second-story without a second glance.

I'm not that surprised that he didn't stick around to make sure I was okay; it's not like he was giving off the warm and fuzzies, but I kind of thought he'd at least tell me where my room was before he disappeared. I guess I can cross him off my list of possible coconspirators. I suppose I don't need anyone else's help to figure out just what exactly is going on here, but I thought if I had one of the sons in my corner, it would be easier for me.

Jesus, if the foyer is this big, I can't imagine how big the rest of the place is. To the left of the foyer looks like a sitting room with a fireplace and a leather couch and matching overstuffed chair. It's an open concept, so I can see quite a bit just standing in one spot. To the right is a room lined with mostly empty bookshelves and a stiff-looking chair in one corner.

A throat clears, capturing my attention. My cheeks warm as I turn around to face the man in front of me. What did Wolf call him—Claude?

I thrust my hand out. "Hi, I'm Alaina. It's nice to meet you."

"Hello, Miss McElroy, it's a pleasure to meet you"—he shakes my hand—"I'm Claude Fontaine, the manager of Summer Knoll Estate," he says with a smile. "Here, let me show you to your room." Claude grabs my suitcase and duffel bag and starts up the staircase.

"Thank you." I grab my backpack and hurry after him. At the top of the stairs, we turn left down the hallway and pass six huge sets of closed doors—*double* doors. I'm trying really hard not to let it show just how mesmerized I am. "Who stays in all these rooms?"

"Three rooms are the boys' bedrooms, two are guest bedrooms, and one is a bathroom. But don't worry, Miss McElroy, you have an en suite bathroom in your room." He stops in front of the only open doorway, gesturing for me to go in front of him. "Here we are, miss."

"Wow . . ." I drift to the middle of the spacious room and spin in a circle. My breath catches at the sheer luxury of it. The plush cream-colored carpet is soft, and a light-gray patterned rug in the center of the room, partially tucked underneath the bed, is cozy. A huge flatscreen TV hangs above the white brick fireplace across from the bed, and a white chandelier with what I think are actual crystals hangs from the ceiling, softly illuminating the room. The walls are painted a soft pink, like a muted cotton candy, and surprisingly, I like it. I'm not usually a big fan of pastels, but there's something so feminine about it.

I wonder who usually sleeps in this guest room?

I spot a balcony beyond the French doors to the right of the bed—I think it might overlook the backyard.

I sigh as I take in the high ceilings, framed with crown moulding, the light-gray headboard, and soft-white blankets.

"It's a beautiful room, isn't it?"

I jump a little at the sound of his voice. I'd forgotten he was here. I turn to see Claude by the doorway, a small smile on his face.

"It's perfect." My voice is quiet, but even I can hear the wistfulness in it.

"Oh, Claude, before I forget, do you know where my mother is?" I pull out my phone and see that I don't have any missed texts or calls from her.

"I believe she went shopping for the day, but she'll be back before dinner. Your presence is requested for dinner at six thirty sharp in the formal dining room," Claude says, not unkindly.

"Oh, okay. Six thirty, got it. Thanks again, Claude. I appreciate it."

"No problem, Miss McElroy—"

"Please, call me Alaina."

He nods with a small smile playing across his lips. "As you wish. Alaina. If you need anything before then, here's the intercom system." Claude points to the small white rectangular box on the wall next to the door. "I'll have Wolf go over it more in detail with you, but here are the basics. There's one in every bedroom as well as the kitchen, library, pool, and theatre. You can connect to the guards' station here"—he points to the blue button at the top of the device—"and each room by typing in their three-digit code. Yours is seven-three-three. This button"—he points to the big red button next to the blue one—"is only for emergencies. And not the 'I spilled my drink on the carpet' emergency." Claude stares at me for a moment, his eyes tight and mouth turned down.

"Emergencies only, got it." I nod, trying to figure out why the hell there's such a complicated security system in my bedroom. What could happen in my room that needs a direct line to the security station and another line for emergencies only?

"Wait. Shouldn't I just call nine-one-one if it's an emergency?"

Claude stares at me for a moment. "No. They'd never get to you in time. Your best bet is the boys, then the guards—in that order."

I blink a few times, and I feel my eyes going wide, but I don't have time to gather myself enough for a response before Claude turns around and leaves my bedroom.

I don't even know what I would've said to him, so it's probably a good thing that he didn't wait for one. What kind of situation should I prepare for if nine-one-one can't—or won't—reach me in time?

Jesus—what if those conspiracy theories were actually right?

Did I just move in with the actual mob?

chapter ten

Alaina

ONCE CLAUDE CLOSES the door, I swear I feel a ripple in the air, like something changing my fate. I shake off my willies; it's all that talk of omens and horoscopes from Maddie last night.

I set my backpack on the end of the bed and explore the room. I still can't get over how big it is—it's even bigger than I expected—and I adjusted my expectations once I saw the fountain in front of the house.

Everything but the walls is done in soft grays and whites. The twin nightstands and long dresser are distressed white wood, but not the kind of distressed that comes from love and use—the kind that you pay a ton of money for. A pang pierces my heart when I think of my well-loved vanity from my dad in this pristine room. I'm sure that's a great metaphor for me in this house.

White-framed abstract art hangs on either side of the TV, and a floor-length oval mirror sits in the corner by the French doors. I cross the room and draw the gauzy white curtains away from the glass doors.

My breath leaves me in a puff as I take in the view. I was right—it's the backyard. If your backyard was a national park. A pool takes up a large portion of the backyard—it even has a waterfall and a slide. A hot tub sits to the right of the pool, and it looks like an actual pool house is beyond that. I spot a basketball hoop and a large vegetable garden to the right.

Beyond the fence is green as far as the eye can see.

Wow.

Just wow.

It sure doesn't feel like I'm standing in Boston. It feels like I'm in some sort of fairy tale. If fairy tales came with hot guys with tattoos and bad attitudes who drive too fast.

Okay, so that actually doesn't sound *all* that bad. I roll my eyes at myself and huff a self-deprecating laugh.

I spin around and take in the room again, mind whirling on what this means for me—and for Mom.

Everything about this is too much, and I'm scared for my mom. I'm not even sure I want to know what she did to catch the eye of the man who owns all of . . . this.

But if I don't help her, who will?

I grab my phone and send her another text.

Me: Hey, Mom! I'm here! Call me when you get here!

After five minutes go by without a reply, I toss my phone on one of the nightstands and decide to unpack. I didn't bring a ton of things, but Mom always said I was really good at cleaning and organizing, so I suppose I have time to put those skills to good use.

After I get unpacked, I change into a flared black skirt and white V-neck tee. I don't want to dress up too much, but I don't want to underdress either. It's hard to know what to wear when you're seeing your mom for the first time in a year—and meeting her fiancé for the first time.

When I don't hear from Mom, I video call the girls to show them my room. They ooh and ahh over the room—especially the en suite bathroom with its claw-foot bathtub and rainforest four-head shower. We don't talk long since they have to finish packing for their trip to Europe.

At six twenty, I walk down the hallway slowly, listening for any noise in the rooms. Either they're soundproof, or they're empty. I wonder which one is Wolf's.

I wipe my sweaty palms on my skirt and walk downstairs. I don't know exactly where I'm going, but I'm sure I can find it—or find someone from the staff who can direct me.

I wonder what it would be like to grow up with a staff of people who do—well, I'm not exactly sure what they do around your house, but they must do something. Like, does Wolf do his own laundry?

I flush as soon as the thought flits across my brain. If I wasn't thinking about Wolf in his underwear before, then I'm definitely thinking about it now.

I take a deep breath and try to think about anything else so I don't have to face him red-faced.

I follow the sounds of pots and pans clanking down the hallway and spot my mom at the sink with her back to me.

"Mom, hey!" At the sound of my voice, she turns around. A smile lights up her face, and she walks toward me, wiping her hands on the yellow ruffled half apron tied around her maxi skirt.

"Alaina, dear. So lovely to see you." She leans in and gives me a kiss on each cheek, never quite hugging me.

"It's so good to see you, Mom. You look great." I scan her from head to toe; she looks elegant and polished. "I texted you when I got here." I work hard to keep my voice even.

"Oh, well,"—she picks a piece of invisible lint off her shirt, never meeting my eyes for longer than a moment—"I wasn't home then, dear. And then when I got home, I had to put away and organize all my purchases, and then I had to hop right into the kitchen." She waves her hand in the air behind her, indicating the island behind her.

"Right." I swallow and force my smile. "Well, this looks incredible." I eye the homemade lasagna and manicotti, two different salads, and two types of freshly baked bread laid out on the island. "I didn't know you could cook like this." Heaviness settles on my shoulders, weighing me down.

"Yes, well . . ." Mom runs her fingers over her hair, smoothing nonexistent flyaways into her chic chignon. Her red hair is a few shades lighter than mine, but we're the same height and similar build. Good genes on the McElroy side of the family tree. "My mother taught me to cook when I was your age." She turns toward the island and starts moving the dishes around a little bit.

"Well, I'd love to learn how to cook—"

"Sarah does most of the cooking here."

"Oh, okay," I murmur. My eyes feel hot, and I take a deep breath to rally.

I look around the spacious kitchen. It's so large, I wouldn't be surprised if it runs the entire length of the house. Everything is done in stainless steel and matte blacks—the wide cooktop stove, the double ovens, the two dishwashers, and the biggest refrigerator I've ever seen tucked behind a faux cabinet.

The island is long enough to fit six stools comfortably on one side, and the other side has a small sink and a mini cooktop stove. There is a built-in breakfast nook on the other end of the kitchen, though the word *nook* feels a little misleading. One side is built into the wall with bench seating, and the other has eight black chairs.

With so much seating, they must host a lot of parties or family events. I wonder if I'll be here long enough to see any.

I turn around to see my mom still fussing with the food. "Can I help bring the food in?"

"Hmm? Oh, sure. Isn't this just lovely, Alaina?" Mom grabs the pan of lasagna, and I grab a salad and follow behind her as she goes down another hallway.

"Mom, what's going on though? Why are we here?" I ask her as we pass what looks like an office and a living room.

"What do you mean? We live here now." Her tone is sharp, and I quicken my steps to get next to her.

"Mom, I live in the city, remember? I'm going to college at St. Rita's with Maddie and Mary."

She throws a glare over her shoulder at me. "Of course, I remember, Alaina."

"Okay. But I still don't understand why you're here. How did you even meet this guy?" We reach what must be the formal dining room. The table seats twenty people, at least. I follow Mom to one end of the table and carefully place the salad down. I touch her arm, stalling her movements. Lowering my voice, I ask, "Mom, are you in danger?"

"Do you honestly think I'd bring my only daughter to a place that was dangerous?" she snaps.

I flinch from the anger in her voice and drop my hand. I stare at the black table, my eyes unfocused. "This is the first time you've asked me to live with you in ten years, Mom, so I don't really know what to think."

"Yes, well . . ." she trails off as she busies herself with setting the table.

"Why didn't you come to graduation?"

She sighs. "You've been taking college classes for over a year now, Alaina. I didn't think it mattered much."

"Right, but I was valedictorian, and I just don't—I don't understand why—"

"I had plans," Mom snaps, finally looking at me. "Not everything is always about you."

I recoil, her words a blow to my very soul, and the tiny part of my hopeful heart that thought this was our chance to bond shrivels up.

"Got it," I murmur and spin around to get the rest of the food from the kitchen. When I get back into the dining room, I don't meet my mom's eyes. I can't, not when the hurt is still so fresh.

At six thirty sharp, Wolf saunters into the dining room and takes a seat toward the middle of the table.

"Wolf, dear, so lovely of you to join us," my mom greets him in a sickly sweet voice from her seat to the left of the head of the table. He doesn't reply, just clenches his jaw and looks at me from underneath those dark, sooty lashes of his.

Why is it always guys that have the longest, darkest lashes?

When Wolf doesn't take his gaze off of me, I figure it wouldn't hurt to try again to make a friend, so I pull out the chair across from him.

"That's not your seat." His voice stops me. I crane my neck around to see the back of the chair. Maybe I missed an engraving or name or something. "That's my brother's seat."

"I'm sorry, I didn't realize," I murmur. I push the chair in and go to pull out the one next to it.

"Nope. That's my other brother's seat." Wolf's lips tip up in the corners, turning his lush lips into a cruel smirk.

"Okay." I push the chair in and try with the next chair.

"That one's taken too, Red," Wolf says with faux-cheer, linking his hands behind his head.

I glance at my mother to see if she's going to step in. She's staring at the bottom of her full wine glass, so I guess that's my answer.

I grit my teeth and move to the next chair, resting my hand on the back of it. "How about this one?"

"Nah, that's taken too."

Just as I reach the opposite end of the table, a man walks into the room. With black hair cropped short and broad shoulders, his very presence commands the room. I flick my glance between the two men. Even though I see a physical resemblance, it's the cloud of danger surrounding both of them that really makes the familial connection apparent.

He walks straight to my mother and kisses the top of her head. She tilts her chin up and murmurs something to him, but his gaze stays on me.

"This your girl, Lana?"

My mom sips her wine and says with a wave of her hand, "Cormac, meet Alaina. Alaina, Cormac."

"What're you doing at that end of the table? Come on up here and sit next to my boy so I can get a good look at you."

His tone brokers no argument, so I slowly walk around the table, choosing the seat next to Wolf. I glance at him, but he's just staring at Cormac with his brows drawn.

"It's nice to meet you, sir," I say as I pull out my chair and sit down.

"Well, I'll be damned . . . the resemblance is uncanny," Cormac muses. "And please, call me Cormac."

I nod my head in agreement.

"Where are your brothers?" Cormac looks at Wolf, his brow raised.

"Dunno, Da"—Wolf shrugs—"they went to the coffee shop with Grandma earlier today, but I thought they'd be home by now."

Cormac checks his watch and sighs, his brow furrowing with the movement. "I'll give them five more minutes, then we start without them. Lana made this delicious meal for us tonight, and I, for one, am not going to let it go to waste." The smile he sends my mom is wide and genuine.

Her cheeks pink in response. "I'm happy to cook for you every night, Cormac, you know that. And I'm just so delighted that Wolf could join us tonight."

Jealousy swirls in my gut as I watch my mom dote on Cormac, pouring his beer from the bottle into a pint glass. "So, Alaina, your mom tells me you were the valedictorian? And that you're already in college?"

I see Wolf stiffen out of the corner of my eye.

"Yes, I just graduated, but I've been taking college-credit courses for over a year, so I'm technically going into sophomore year at St. Rita's." I reflexively smooth my skirt underneath the table.

"Ambitious. I like it. Maybe some of your love for academia will rub off on my son here," Cormac says with a chuckle.

I turn my head to see Wolf clench his jaw and narrow his eyes.

"Told you three years ago when I graduated, Da. I don't need college. I'm already in the family business," Wolf says with a sneer.

Cormac glares at his son but doesn't reply.

"What do you guys do?" I ask as I take a sip of water, my eyes on Wolf.

"Construction."

"Recycling."

They answer at the same time.

I glance between the two of them, blinking in confusion. "The recycling of construction materials?"

"Sure, Red. We recycle construction materials." Wolf stares at me blankly.

"Alright, it's six forty, let's eat," Cormac declares as he serves himself a double helping of lasagna.

"I'm happy to help if you need it," I murmur so only Wolf can hear. "With tutoring or whatever, I mean."

When he doesn't answer, I turn to face him. His eyes narrow as he sneers at me. "I don't need your help. Pass the food, Red."

chapter eleven

Wolf

DAD PUSHES HIS plate away and leans back in his chair. "Delicious, Lana. Thank you."

"It was my pleasure, Cormac." Lana beams at Da, and it's all I can do not to gag into my lasagna. It's too good to waste on whatever the fuck is happening at the end of the table.

Red has been mostly quiet during dinner, only talking when Da asked her a question. Interesting that her ma didn't ask her much. Red keeps staring at me out of the corner of her eye like she's trying to be sneaky and I'm not sitting two feet away from her.

"Alaina?"

Her head whips to the side. "Hmm?"

"I said, I'm heading to the city for a few days. I need to find a wedding dress!" Lana's overly excited, and it grates on my fucking nerves.

Red smiles, but it looks a little forced around the edges. Shit, I smother my grin behind my hand, smoothing it against my stubble. I never did get a shave in yet today. *Sully'd be proud of how quickly I can read her.* That fucker can read anyone faster and more accurately than anyone I've ever met.

"Oh, that sounds like fun. I'd love to come with you, Mom. And you know, I was thinking that we could take the train into the city for a few days. Wouldn't that be fun? The train I took here today was really nice, and I think you'd like it." Red leans in, staring at her ma with hope shining in her eyes.

No one says anything in response to Red's babbling, and I sense the air shift. I put my fork down and sit back in my chair, content to watch this play out.

Lana grabs her necklace and twists it around. "Oh, dear, I meant Cormac and I are heading to the city." She fingers the pearls at her neck. "He has some business to do, and I'm meeting Auntie Sloane at Kleinfeld."

"Kleinfeld?!" Red sets her fork down and leans back into her chair. "Mom, that's . . . those dresses are—"

"Gorgeous." Lana sighs.

"Expensive," Red says at the same time.

I don't know where the fuck Da found this bitch, but Rush better come through with more intel, because I cannot take nightly dinners with all this. I shift in my seat, widening my legs and leaning back. The strange family dynamic between these two is making me uncomfortable. And fuck me, because why the fuck should I care about two redheaded strangers—even if Da is fucking one of 'em. I pulled a dude's nails off one by one last month, and I didn't even flinch.

I eye Lana, scanning her with a critical eye. I can see the appeal—red hair, nice curves, cooks a decent dinner. But

Penelope Black

she has what Sully calls *the crazy*. It's not one particular feature, more like they're always one word away from going category five on your ass.

Sully always did know how to pick 'em though. I smirk as I remember one of the last girls he brought home. She hid out in the house for two weeks before the staff found her sleeping in a closet somewhere. That chick was fucking crazy. I tried to warn him, but he argued that he was tired of one-night stands and quick fucks in the bathroom of some dive.

I snort, *as if there's ever such a thing as being tired of too much uncomplicated pussy.*

Every girl I'm with knows the score, and no one has hurt feelings when I leave. I never even exchange numbers with anyone—there's no point. I never go back for seconds. Most birds are just excited to say they bagged someone from the Brotherhood.

Lana's right eye twitches as she stares at Red for a moment. "You leave our finances to me, dear."

Red's cheeks flush, and I'm mesmerized by the way the pretty pink stains her cheeks. I wonder what other parts of her blush like that and how long it would take to see it.

"Of course," Red replies and stares at her half-eaten plate of food.

"Great." Lana claps her hands twice like some fucking elementary-school teacher. "Now that's settled. We're leaving early tomorrow morning. Cormac's boys will be here to show you around."

I grunt. This is news to me. I lean back and balance the chair on two legs as I stare at Da with my eyebrows raised.

"So, I'll see you in a few days," Lana says, her words ringing with dismissal.

90

Red scoots back her chair and picks up her dishes. Without meeting anyone's gaze, she says, "Thank you for dinner. It was nice meeting you, Cormac, Wolf."

She hightails it out of the dining room and down the hallway, presumably to the kitchen. I spare her a moment of thought before I turn my gaze back to Da and Lana—the latter is grinning like the cat that got the canary, and my patience snaps.

I blow out a breath and lean forward, slamming the chair's front legs down. "What's your endgame, Lana?" I all but growl at the woman at the end of the table.

Her eyebrows scrunch up as she sets down her wineglass. "What do you mean, dear?"

"Cut the shit."

"Wolf!" Da barks.

"Oh, come on!" I throw out my hands to the side. "What the hell is going on here? We've never eaten in this room in my entire *life*."

He raises an eyebrow. "Your point, son?"

"My *point*, Da, is that we don't even know this bitch, and then—"

Dad slams his hand on the table. "Don't call her a bitch."

"If it walks like a duck . . ." I let the cruel smirk I've been holding in spread across my face. I don't take my eyes off my da, but I see Lana flinch in my peripheral.

I don't know what the fuck is going on here, but I do know that it's not adding up. I'm not naïve enough to think my dad isn't getting his dick wet, but in all the seventeen years I've been living with him, he hasn't so much as dated. And now, all of a sudden, he's marrying some bitch we've never even seen before two weeks ago? I don't fucking think so. Rush is right—there's something else going on here.

"You're pushing it, boyo," my dad growls out.

Just to piss him off, I shrug my shoulders like I don't give a fuck. I mean, I don't really give a fuck about her, but usually the unreasonable asshole routine is more Rush's style. I'm more of the easy-going asshole type. And Sully's the angsty asshole. But since *neither* one of my brothers are here, I gotta step it up.

"Fill me in here, Da."

He sighs and covers his mouth with his hand, smoothing his beard—his tell that he's stressed. "Give us a minute, Lana."

"Of course," she murmurs as she grabs her wine glass and stands up. "I'll just go start packing."

Da waits until she's out of the room before he gives me his attention. "Ten minutes ago, I got a text from Jimmy. His wife and some other wives were at a restaurant when there was a drive-by. They targeted their table."

"Shiiiit." That was the last thing I thought he was going to say. "Casualties? And do they know who did it?"

"No fatalities, thankfully. I don't think Manhattan would survive their wrath. A few were hit—superficial wounds."

"Yeah, no shit. You're telling me you wouldn't do the same if that was your wife?" I eye him, and he smirks. He knows I'm trying to pry answers from him. I shrug.

"They didn't catch the people who did it. All they know it was a black SUV."

I drum my fingers on my leg. "You have any theories?"

"Nah. But it's the third attack on our Irish brothers in—"

"Third?" I snap.

"Aye. A few different soldiers from the small faction just outside the city got popped. No details." He shrugs.

I nod. "So what are you thinking?"

"Not sure. I need more information, so Sully is heading upstate to be our eyes and ears there."

"Fuck." I lean forward, resting my forearms against the table, and hang my head for a moment. Looking up at him, I ask, "For how long? And why didn't you tell me this has been going on?"

He levels me with a look before exhaling. "I'm not sure. A couple weeks, at least. I need someone we can trust up there to find out what the fuck is going on."

"Yeah, and who's going to watch Sully's six?" I cross my arms across my chest. "You can't send him alone. If I get on the road now, I can be there in—"

"I need you here, son. There's something else at play here, and my gut is telling me this is only the beginning." His lips purse as he smoothes his beard. "There are some rules we don't cross—ever. We don't go after families—wives and children are never on the table. And I know the Italians and Blue Knights agree with us. For the attacks to escalate from a few soldiers to the wife of the President of the Westies? It's demanding my attention."

"So, what are you thinking? Russians? Chinese? Cartel?" I pause. "Or someone defecting?"

He nods. "That or some fucker watched one too many episodes of *Sopranos* and decided he wants to play with the big boys." He releases a breath and pins me with a look. "That's why I need you here."

I scoff. "What the fuck, Da? You want me to sit and play house while you send Sully on a suicide mission? And where the fuck is Rush?" My chest heaves with frustration.

Dad looks at me calmly, that goddamn impenetrable mask on. "You done?"

I tip my head back and stare at the ceiling for a moment, my muscles coiled with frustration. "Yep. I'm done." No matter how angry I am, he's still the president of the Brotherhood.

"Rush should be here tomorrow. He's tying up loose ends in the city from Sully's coffee date this morning." He smirks when he says it. He always got a laugh from our code words. "And I need you here, watching over the house." He stares at me for a moment. "And protecting everyone inside it."

I roll my eyes. "Claude taught me how to shoot when I was eight, and Sarah gave me my first set of throwing knives. They know how to take care of themselves." I expel a breath and uncross my arms. "But, yeah, okay. I'll guard the homestead."

My jaw tics, and my stomach roils as thoughts of being left behind fill me.

He nods a few times, smoothing his beard with one hand. "I know I can count on you and Rush. We're on the precipice of war, but there's a new opponent, and they have the advantage right now. I don't like it. Check the armory and make sure we're still fully stocked. I already spoke with Claude; he's changing our codes and running our data through another encryption. And he sent home all non-essential personnel. The Brotherhood is putting their families on lockdown, and the same goes for here: no one in and no one out for the next week until I get a better handle on what the situation is."

More than anything, this bit of information causes alarm.

"And one more thing." He pauses. "Stay away from Alaina."

My eyebrows hit my hairline. "Well, how the fuck am I supposed to keep her safe if I have to stay away from her?"

His reaction only firms up our theory that there's more that dear ol' Da isn't telling us—and that shit just isn't how it works. Not when I'm the next VP in the Brotherhood.

"I haven't been a kid for a very long time," I grit the words through my clenched jaw. "Whatever it is, it'll be easier if I go into it with all the facts."

He stares at me for a beat, his gaze roaming my features. "I know that, boyo. But some things are instinctual—like protecting your sons."

"*Protect us*?" I scoff. "My first kill was at thirteen years old. I think *protecting us* went out the window a long time ago." I hate the note of bitterness in my voice. Truth is, I'm not bitter.

He sighs. "I know I haven't always done right by you boys, but I—"

"It's fine, Da. You did the best you could. It couldn't have been easy with all of us. Shit, I was three-year-old when you adopted me, and Rush was one. Then less than a year later, some bitch you fucked dropped Sully off as a baby and split."

Yeah, even I can hear the bitterness in my voice, but it's not directed at him. I place all that anger solely on my parents—the pieces of shit junkies who couldn't get their shit together enough to take care of their son—me. And definitely on Sully's mom—who the fuck drops off a baby at some guy's house and leaves without a backward glance?

Apparently, Cormac fucked this bitch a couple of times, and then she shows up over a year later with a baby. The timing was off, and after a paternity test, it was confirmed that Sully isn't Cormac's biologically. But that never stopped him from raising us both as his own.

Every day, I'm thankful that it was Cormac's house my parents took me to. Of course, my dad is Cormac's brother, so it makes sense that we came over one day. But it didn't make sense for him to just up and leave without me. I shudder thinking about how different my life would be had my parents not given me up. I doubt I'd even be alive.

"I wouldn't trade you boys for anything. You're a good man, Wolf, and you'll be a helluva VP when the time comes. But we're not there yet, so you have to trust me on this one. I'll pull you in as soon as I can, but until then: protect Alaina."

It's not until later that night when I'm trying to fall asleep and can't get a certain redhead out of my mind that I realize my da never answered me.

Who the fuck is Lana, and maybe more importantly, what the fuck am I gonna do about Red?

chapter twelve

Alaina

I WAKE UP TO the sun streaming in the French doors, and for a moment, I don't remember where I am. I flip onto my back and snuggle into the fluffy down comforter while I try to sort through the last twenty-four hours.

I'm not sure what I was expecting, but I guess when my mom asked me to live with her, I thought it meant actually living with her. Not me staying in this gigantic house with a bunch of people I don't know while my mom leaves. To go to the city I just came from.

With a sigh, I decide that I'll bake some chocolate chip cookies. You can't be bummed out if you have freshly-baked chocolate chip cookies. I'm thankful I memorized Grandma Eileen's recipes when I was a kid, because my mom stopped making them after she died.

I used to think that my mom was so overcome with grief after my dad left and her parents suddenly died that she just didn't have enough left of herself to give anyone—even me. But after seeing her dote on Cormac and Wolf last night at dinner, I'm starting to think that it's *me* she has trouble with.

With that depressing thought swirling around, I reach over and grab my phone off the charger. No new messages. Not that surprising, since the only two people who really talk to me should be on a plane right about now.

I fire a quick group text to Mary and Maddie.

Me: Have a safe flight today! I miss you both already xx

With a solid plan for the day, I hop out of bed, grab some clothes, and head to the en suite bathroom. The shower is massive with tiled walls and floors and a clear glass shower door. It has an electronic panel and four showerheads, and I'd be lying if I said I haven't been dying to check it out.

I make sure all my shower stuff is on the bench inside the shower and spend a few minutes figuring out the panel. A giddy sort of thrill runs through me when I discover speakers in the shower and a Bluetooth connection. I hook up my phone and cue up a playlist of songs I've been practicing and step in.

I smirk when I think about how loud I can sing at any time of the day without interrupting anyone here. Even though the three of us all enjoy singing, Mary would often whine about my early-morning shower singalongs. I doubt anyone can even hear me in this house—if anyone was home.

A groan leaves my lips as the warm water hits my skin. I increase the temperature and the strength and sigh as the bathroom gets steamy. This might be the best shower I've ever had.

When my fingers resemble prunes, I shut off the shower, still singing the lyrics to "Titanium," and dry off. I slip on my panties and clasp my bra when I notice that I grabbed my skirt, but not my shirt. I guess another perk of having your own bathroom is that I could walk from my shower directly to my closet to get dressed.

I'm totally doing that next time.

Sliding on my cornflower-blue skirt, I use the towel to press the water from my hair as I walk into my room. A scream lodges in my throat when I see a shirtless Wolf just casually laying on my bed with his arms behind his head and his eyes closed.

"What the hell are you doing in here!" I shriek as I press the wet towel to my front, shielding my tits from his view. With his black joggers low on his hips and his muscles on display, he looks like a Greek god. All ripped muscles just begging to be touched. Sweet Jesus, he has that thing that really ripped guys have—the *vee.*

Maddie is gonna die when I tell her about it.

He cracks an eye open and raises an eyebrow. "Relax, Red, it's nothing I haven't seen before."

I bristle and flush. "Well, you haven't seen *me* before."

He opens both eyes and honest to god smolders. "Is that an invitation?"

"No," I growl out and point to the door with one hand. "Get out."

"No can do, baby girl. Da said I'm your man for the next few days until your ma gets back."

My heart stutters, and I'm not sure if it's because he said he's my man or if it's the reminder that my mom so easily dismissed me. "Well, can you do . . . that from in the hallway?" My chest is heaving from surprise . . . and lust, if I'm being honest. It's just, he looks like a goddamn fantasy all sprawled out on my bed—the colorful tattoos contrasting against the light-gray blankets.

"Nah, your bed is much more comfortable than the hallway." He pats the space next to him, and I flush as I remember the dream I had last night. I was at O'Malley's, and my mystery man—Declan—didn't stop after one kiss. We didn't stop *at all*. He had me pinned against the wall with my legs wrapped around his waist, grinding against him. And just as he was sliding his cock into me, he lifted his head, and suddenly, it was espresso-brown eyes staring into mine—Wolf's espresso-brown eyes. His features twisted in pleasure, and` just as I was about to come, I woke up.

I've had sexy dreams before, but I've never experienced something that felt as real as that. I was so worked up that I slipped my hand into my panties, and less than a minute later, my legs were shaking.

A masculine groan breaks me out of the sexy-dream spell I was reliving . . . as I was staring at that goddamn vee.

"C'mon, Red. Don't look at me like that."

I flash my gaze to his and shift my weight to the other foot. "Like what?"

The smile that tips up the corner of his lips is downright sinful. Or maybe that's just where my mind is right now.

Get it together, Alaina.

I clear my throat and look to my closet. "I need to get dressed." When he makes no move to leave or avert his eyes, I grunt. "Now."

When I just stare at him, he huffs. "Fine, fine, I'll close my eyes."

"Uh, thanks?"

His smirk is all the reply I get. I grab my racerback tank top that fell on the floor and hustle back to the bathroom to get dressed. Ten minutes go by, and just when I think he actually left my room, his voice startles me.

"How long have you been singing?"

One part of me—the stubborn, petty part that I shove down—wants to ignore him, but the other part of me—the part that had politeness drilled into her head since birth—wins.

"I've been taking vocal lessons for as long as I can remember."

"You're talented." His voice is closer than it was a moment ago, and I turn to see him leaning against the doorway.

I pause with the mascara wand halfway to my eyelashes and meet his gaze in the mirror. "Thank you."

"Are you in a band or something?"

"No, but I sing with my cousins every week at an open mic night in the city."

"Any place I would know?"

I twist my mascara closed and turn toward him, leaning a hip on the counter and looking him over. This Wolf feels different from the one from before, but this feels like an olive branch. "I don't know. Do you go to the city often?"

"Sometimes, but not as often as my brothers."

"Brothers?" I quirk a brow.

"Rush and Sully."

"Do they live here too?"

"Sometimes."

"Okay . . ." I raise both brows. "Do you live here only sometimes too?"

He stares at me for a moment. "When I'm not somewhere else, I'm here."

"That's . . . cryptic," I say, frowning. "Should I be expecting your brothers here this summer?"

He pushes off the door frame to stand to his full height and crosses his arms across his chest, his biceps flexing with the motion. I try not to stare, I really do, but they're so distracting—*he's* so distracting.

His jaw hardens. "Why? If you're trying to bag one of the Fitzgeralds, I'm your best bet," he says with a sneer. "Sully's hung up on his ex he dated years ago, and Rush has a little birdie stashed away." He pauses, his eyes narrow as he stares over my shoulder for a moment. "Which is against the fucking rules," he murmurs more to himself than me.

I quirk a brow and straighten my shoulders. "I was just curious."

"Yeah, sure, that's what they all say." He sneers.

"Look, I don't know what your problem is, but I'm just here for the summer to connect with my mom—"

He snorts. "Yeah, and how's that working out?"

My shoulders hitch, and I nod, turning to face the mirror again. "I've gotta finish getting ready, so . . ."

It takes a minute, but Wolf spins on his heel and stalks out of my bedroom. I release a breath and finish applying my lip gloss.

I've got a cookie date with the kitchen.

chapter thirteen

Alaina

DESPITE WOLF'S PROMISE of sticking to me like glue this morning, I haven't seen him since our conversation in my bathroom. Which suits me just fine, honestly.

I found my way to the kitchen and caught Sarah on her way out. She gave me a quick tour, pointing out the pantries, snack cabinets, hidden appliances, and the bulk storage pantry. More importantly, she gave me free rein to use anything I want.

My Grandma Eileen used to tell me that you don't go into someone's kitchen and mess with their order of things or make a mess—as far as she was concerned, it was the biggest insult. I was seven at the time, so I'm sure it was more of a warning not to make a mess. But it was one of the last times I saw her, and I've sort of applied this philosophy to my moral code.

Given that I've spent most of my life in a dorm room suite—even if it's a luxurious one—I've never had a full kitchen before, let alone a kitchen like this. It looks more befitting of a hotel or high-end resort.

I spin in a circle and whistle under my breath, taking in the high cabinets and crystal knobs and handles. I can't contain the smile that spreads across my face when I imagine all the use I'm going to get out of this kitchen. I'm not sure how much longer I'll be here, especially if Mom isn't even around. I mean, that's the whole reason I came—to spend time with her—so my time here might be limited. Best I take advantage of this gorgeous kitchen while I can.

After I get all the ingredients for my grandma's recipe, I plug my phone into the speaker system next to the refrigerator and play my baking playlist on shuffle.

Fleetwood Mac fills the kitchen, and I sing my way through some of my favorite songs as I whisk, stir, and sift ingredients.

Hours later, I have two dozen chocolate chip cookies—one dozen with walnuts and one dozen without—a batch of blueberry muffins and vanilla scones. All of which are my grandma's best recipes.

I arrange the baked goods under the domed pastry stands I found in the bulk cabinet as I sing along to "The Chain." It always fascinated me how Fleetwood Mac's best record came after they were all broken up, like their heartbreak fueled their best songwriting or something. You would think that their best albums would be from when they were all together and happy, but that's not how it worked out.

I think back to the time after my last ex-boyfriend, Dean, and I broke up, and I don't remember feeling much of anything. Not relief or joy or grief—nothing. I didn't have any emotion to channel into anything, let alone something that ended up making one of the best albums in history.

But after James you could've, the little voice inside my head taunts. My heart aches just like it does every time I think about my first love—and my first broken heart.

Luckily, Stevie Nicks distracts me, and I pause to pull out my air guitar for the breakdown and really give it my all, whipping my hair to the side.

My cheeks are flushed, and I laugh. I haven't had this much fun baking since I was a kid.

"Go Your Own Way" starts next, and I laugh even more, joy squeezing my heart. I have some fuzzy memories of Grandma Eileen singing this song.

I crank up the volume and sing along to Stevie and Lindsey, shaking my hips and closing my eyes. I even whip out my air guitar again and really go after it.

Gratitude for the short time I had my grandma fills me to the brim, and I send up a prayer of thanks to the moon even though I can't see it.

I shake my ass to the guitar breakdown in the last minute of the song as I wipe down the counters when Wolf saunters in.

He's sweaty and breathing heavy, dressed only in gym shorts, and I physically have to stop my jaw from dropping. I know I saw him shirtless earlier today, but I didn't get to appreciate it properly since he scared the hell out of me. I follow a bead of sweat with my gaze as it slides down his pecs, over his tattoos, and down each ridge of his six—no, eight—pack. *Sweet Jesus.*

He beelines for the fridge and pulls out a Gatorade, tips it back, and drinks it in one go. Wiping his mouth with his hand, he caps the bottle and stares at me across the island.

"Wanna watch a movie?" he asks as he reaches over to grab a muffin out of the container on the island.

He couldn't have surprised me more than if he started tap dancing and doing the Charleston. "A movie?"

"Yes, a movie. Ever heard of them," he says around a mouthful of muffin. "God, these are good." He groans in appreciation.

"Of course, I have." I bristle at his insinuation and flush at his moan. My brain wants to be offended by his hot and cold behavior, but my libido couldn't care less—she's practically panting. "But I'm just confused why you want to watch one. With me."

"I'm bored. And my brothers aren't here," he says as he finishes the muffin. "Damn, that was good. Shit, cookies too? Sarah's spoiling us."

I shrug and wipe down the counters again. "Why don't you call someone else then? I have to study. And I made all this stuff."

"Damn, really? These are really good. If you keep making this kind of stuff, I'll never let you leave," he mumbles as he eats the chocolate chip cookies with walnuts.

My cheeks heat at the insinuation, and then I feel my face lose all color when I realize one very important detail.

"Don't eat that! It has nuts in it!" I reach across the island and slap the cookie out of his hand. The look of horror on his face has panic and adrenaline soaring through my body. "Oh my god, are you allergic to walnuts!"

He stares at me, eyes wide, and grabs his neck with both hands. He makes this horrible choking noise, and I feel tears in my eyes. "Holy shit, holy shit, holy shit." With trembling hands, I snatch my phone and run around the island to stand next to him. "Okay, hold on. I'll call nine-one-one!"

My hands flutter around him as I begin to dial. Before I can get to the second number, the choking turns into chuckles. After a second, the chuckles turn into full-on laughter.

I glance at him to see the hand that was at his throat now covers his smiling mouth, his eyes crinkling in the corners. It takes me longer than I care to admit to realize that he's not choking, and he's totally full of shit.

"Oh, Red," he says in between laughs. "You should see your face right now."

The relief that I didn't just kill Wolf accidentally consumes me, and my breath hitches. Tears prick my eyes, and I blink, sending them down my cheeks. "I-I th-thought I killed you."

He sobers quickly. "Oh shit." He takes a step toward me, half-caging me against the island. "Shh, Red, no. I was only kidding. I'm totally fine, see?" He holds one hand out to the side, the other firmly planted on the island behind me.

"I-I don't know why I'm c-crying. I w-was j-j-just so scared."

"Oh, baby girl, it's alright. It's just the adrenaline crash." He slowly runs his hand down my arm. "You'll be fine in a minute. Here, eat this. The sugar will help."

And if I wasn't in the middle of a meltdown, I'd appreciate the way his long, tattooed fingers brush against my lips as he feeds me the other half of his chocolate-chip-walnut cookie.

I eat the cookie, staring at the swallows tattooed on his chest and trying to get my trembling limbs under control. I've always had the worst adrenaline crashes—crying, shaking, nausea. After a few minutes, the worst of it has passed.

He brings his hands to my face and sweeps his thumbs along my cheekbones, wiping away my tears. I glance at him from underneath my lashes, and I get lost in his eyes. They're endless pools of the deepest brown, promising things I'm not sure I'm ready to agree to.

"I'm sorry. For almost killing you. And the crying," I whisper, holding his gaze.

"No, I'm sorry, Red. I was just messing around. I'm used to pranks and stupid shit with my brothers. You good?"

I clear my throat and nod. "I'm okay."

"Okay," he murmurs as he searches my face. After a moment, he steps back, letting his hands slowly slide down my neck. "I'll catch you later for that movie, Red, yeah?" Wolf flashes what I'm noticing is his trademark smirk—it's smug and sexy and makes me lose my focus every time he flashes it my way.

"Yeah," I breathe.

Holy shit, I am totally crushing on my possible *stepbrother.*

A FEW HOURS LATER, Maddie finally returns my video call.

"Finally," I groan out, answering the video call. "What took you guys so long? I sent that SOS text like two hours ago. And where's Mary?"

"Babe. You know my service here is shit. And I think Mary's dating someone!"

Maddie's shrill tone is enough to distract me from my current train of thought, and I sit up. "Wait—why do you think that? And why do you sound mad about it?

Shouldn't we be encouraging her to date?" I shake my head slightly.

"I'm not mad that she's *dating*. I'm mad that she's *lying* about dating!" Maddie waves her hand around.

"Okaaaay . . . start from the beginning."

"Fine. We both know that she's adding all those dares to the jar with a specific person in mind, but every time I ask her who the guy is, she clams up and denies it! So, here are my theories: he's married, he's a teacher—"

"Babe, we go to an all-girls academy," I deadpan.

"No, we went to an all-girls academy. Now we're enrolled in an all-girls college—like it's nineteen-fucking-fifty, might I add—but they let male faculty teach at the college level, unlike the high school level." She tips her chin up and smirks.

"Okay. What's your other theory? That's only two, and you'd never bring less than three *anything*, so let's hear it."

She bites her lip. "Well, that's the thing. I can't think of another option. And you're right, you know how I feel about the power of the number three."

I resist the urge to roll my eyes. If I didn't love her more than just about anything, I'm not sure I'd reel myself in so often. I don't really believe in all that hippie stuff, but she does, and that was enough for me. "Okay. I have a theory. What if she's just dating some random guy, and she wants to take it slow before she introduces us?" I raise both my brows.

She taps her chin. "Maybe. Or maybe she's sleeping with one of our exes."

I laugh. "That's one of the most ridiculous things you've ever said! First of all, she'd never do that to us. Girl code. And second, what exes? If you're talking about Dean, then I seriously doubt that. That guy was the worst—and the only reason I even went on a few dates with him was to stop thinking about—"

"James," she finishes for me.

"Yeah. James." I clear my throat. "And there's no way she's seeing James. The guy is a ghost."

"Yeah." She turns those sad eyes on me, and I fight the urge to end the call.

It's been a long time since I talked about James. Sure, I still think about him. I think that's true for most first loves though. I just wonder what happened to him and why he left me like that.

Mostly, I just think about how all the men in my life leave.

"So, to answer your question. No, I don't think she's seeing an ex of mine. And I seriously doubt your twin sister—your best friend, after me, of course"—I flash her a cheeky grin—"would date any of your exes. Even though some of them are stupid hot." I waggle my eyebrows, and she laughs.

"That's true, I guess. I just want her to talk to me."

"She will," I assure her.

After a moment, she blurts, "So, did you find out any more info on the secret afiamay?"

I grip the phone in one hand and cover my mouth with the other, smothering the laugh that wants to break out. "The what? How long have you been holding that question in?"

"You know, the afia-may. The m-o-b. And too long. I thought of it like two hours after you left," she says with a laugh.

I laugh through my hand and raise a brow. "Babe. Why are you speaking pig Latin?"

"I don't know, I was trying to speak in code or something. I just watched some episodes of *The Sopranos*—super informative, by the way. You should totally watch it! But they never called it *you know what*, because phones are tapped and stuff."

"It's not Voldemort." I roll my eyes. "But to answer your question, no, not really. The internet is not the wealth of information that I thought it would be." I shrug. "I suppose I could do some recon. I have the house to myself—well, except for a few staff members . . . and Wolf."

She whistles. "The stepbrother?"

I nod. "Yeah, one of them, at least. There are two others, but I don't know where they are. I'm not even sure if I'll meet them."

"Because the house you're staying at is so big?" She rolls her eyes playfully.

"You don't even know the half of it. Wait until you see the bathroom in my bedroom in person! It's insane!"

"So, what's the problem? Just slip the stepbrother a little tongue to distract him from your sleuthing ways," she says with a saucy smirk.

"What! You literally just said the problem out loud—stepbrother!" I argue.

"So what?" She shrugs. "You're not even related—and even if your mom marries his dad, you still wouldn't actually be related."

I sigh in response and lean my head back against the wall. "Maybe," I murmur.

She gets close to the screen and stage-whispers, "One to ten, Lainey?"

I get close to the screen and stage-whisper back, "Twenty."

Then we both start giggling, and it turns into one of those things where we can't stop for a few minutes. The girls and I have been doing this silly thing since we were in sixth grade and realized that boys were actually cute.

One means *no chance of dating*, and ten means *yes, you want to date him*. But twenty is like the ultimate—there is nothing higher.

She whistles again. "Dang, girl, a twenty? I don't think you've given anyone a twenty since . . ."

She doesn't have to finish her comment, we both know she was going to say James. "Yeah."

"It's the stepbrother thing, isn't it? I knew it! It's totally hot in the forbidden way." She snaps her fingers and laughs.

"I don't know, Maddie. He's super hot, tattoos everywhere, but he's kind of an asshole." I lift a shoulder.

"Babe, you know I say this with so much love, but you kinda love the asshole type. So I'm not really surprised that you're into this guy," Maddie says, affection shimmering in her eyes.

I chuckle. "Keeping it real, huh?"

"Always, cousin. Always." She tosses me a cheeky grin. "So, what're you going to do about the stepbrother?"

I bite my lip as I think about it. I smirk as I say, "Did I mention he has an eight-pack . . . and *the vee*?"

Her mouth drops open. "Holy—I'm not even going to ask you how you know this. But all I'll say is this: photos or it didn't happen!" She waggles her eyebrows at me.

I nod a couple of times. "We'll see. So, you think I should make a move?"

"Hell yes, I do! Plus, I like that it's kind of sticking it to your mom too." Her mouth forms a line when she mentions my mom.

I ignore her comment about Mom entirely. "It's just . . ." I sigh.

"That he could be your stepbrother," she finishes.

"Exactly." I pause. "And Declan."

"Ah, the hottie from O'Malley's, right? The one who's been low-key obsessed with you for forever?" She clucks her tongue at me.

I laugh. "Obsessed? I don't think so, babe."

"You know I love you, Lainey, but you are so oblivious. This dude shows up every week while we're singing—"

"Maybe he's just a fan of open mic night?" I interrupt.

She snorts. "Sure, babe, sure. That's why he only stays for our set and leaves before we're even done."

"Yeah, that is strange, right? I asked him, you know. Why he always leaves before the end."

"What did he say?"

"That *he has places to be*," I mimic him with a poorly impersonated, low-pitched voice.

"Sounds like a player. I bet he has a girl. Honestly, he's too hot *not* to have someone waiting for him." Maddie scoffs.

"I know, but he said he didn't." I shrug. "Besides, I'm not even sure when—if—I'll see him again. I'm here for the next couple of months and—"

"And you'll be back in the city for school, right?" The thread of anxiety in her voice takes me by surprise.

"Absolutely. I'm not missing college."

"Oh, thank god. Because I love my sister, but I cannot live with just her for the next four years." She laughs.

I smile. "Nah, you're not getting rid of me that easily. It's just . . . I thought . . . I thought when my mom asked me to stay with her this summer that we'd actually spend some time together, and I don't know . . . bond or something. God, I feel stupid saying it out loud." I sigh and look down.

"Babe, no. Don't feel stupid. I think it's normal to want that with her, and it's her loss if she can't see how amazing and brilliant you are." The sincerity in her voice is like a hug to my soul.

My heart feels a little lighter. "You're the best, Maddie. Love you."

"Love you too, babe. Now go find that man and climb him like a tree." She makes kissy noises and laughs. "Pics or he doesn't exist!"

"Maybe," I say between laughs. "Tell Mary I love her when you see her! And have fun seeing the sights! Keep me updated on your adventures."

"Will do! Later, babe!"

"Bye!" I end the call feeling lighter than I have since I stepped off the train.

chapter fourteen

Wolf

STEPPING OUT OF the shower, I hear my phone ringing. I wrap a towel around my waist and reach for it on the bathroom counter.

"Wolf." Da speaks as soon as I answer.

With just one word, my attention zeroes in on him. I listen for background noise, but it's either quiet where he is, or he's covering the mic.

"Aye. What's going on? Rush? Sully?" My voice is low and even. It's been years since I felt any genuine panic at hearing the commanding tone of voice when he randomly calls. When he greets me with "boyo," I know it's either personal or nothing serious, but when he greets me with "Wolf" and that sharp edge to his voice, I know it's Brotherhood related or bad news. It took me a couple of years, but I don't even blink anymore.

"Sully's by Nolan, and as far as I know, he's fine. And Rush should be home tomorrow. But I'm headed across the pond to visit with family."

I pause, trying to decipher the code he's telling me. He's going to Ireland, but why? And who's he around that he can't outright tell me?

"Is this an impromptu family reunion?" *Did he get called in by the OG council?*

My da is the head of our family, and he shares the US with Lenny Bryne. He handles the east coast, and Lenny handles the west. There have been a couple times that I know of where Cillian Kelly, the boss of the OG Brotherhood in Ireland, called all family heads in for a goddamn tea party—literally. They sipped tea and plotted world domination. And then there was that time a few years ago, where he called everyone in and then removed the heads of half the men in the room. He's a crazy motherfucker and nearly impossible to read.

"Does this have to do with Jimmy?" I'm not sure I'd believe him if he said it was. There's no way Cillian cares about a drive-by and a few soldiers meeting their makers.

"I'm not sure yet."

"Are you bringing your bird with you?" *Are you bringing Lana?*

"Aye. So I need you to do a few things for me, Wolf."

"Name it."

"Take care of our little birdie while I'm gone."

"Consider it done, Da." I take a breath, trying to add another piece to the puzzle. "I don't like it. Something doesn't feel right."

"Aye. The timing is all off."

"Take some friends on this family reunion, yeah?" *Take backup.*

"I am, don't worry 'bout me, boyo. I can handle myself just fine."

"Aye. Hard to handle yourself if you're dead, Da," I deadpan. "Ambushes are never fair fights."

"Don't I know it. But I'm done playing games, and I'm getting impatient waiting for the next move. We have too many players on the board, some of which we haven't met yet."

"Are you thinking someone's playing on more than one team?" *Do we have another rat?*

"Not sure yet, but I intend to find out."

I nod. I'm not surprised. Cormac Fitzgerald, the Butcher of the Brotherhood, never met a puzzle he didn't want to solve. And this has all the makings of a messy puzzle— one that ends with the Butcher living up to his name. "How long will you be visiting?"

"A few weeks, probably. No one in or out. Trust only blood. Take care, son."

"Aye. You too, Da."

I end the call and stare at myself in the mirror, cataloguing every scar, burn, and the two bullet-shaped reminders from the last time someone played double agent.

Sweat drips down my back, and I swat away mosquitoes as my brothers and I carefully make our way around the overgrown plot of land in the abandoned industrial park in Brooklyn.

According to our resident technical genius, Buzz, the warehouse 100 feet away is where we'll find our stolen merchandise.

"That motherfucker better be right about this," Rush grumbles next to me.

"Face it, brother, Buzz found our shit before you did." I flash him a condescending smirk that I know pisses him off. He takes it as a personal affront when someone finds intel before he does.

He flips me off and glares at me. "Fuck that—"

The first notes of some song pierce the air. I spin and jump over a rotted log to land right next to my brother, Sully.

"What the fuck, dude?! Turn that shit off before you get us killed!" I hiss at him. I glance around us, looking for movement.

"Shit. Sorry." He holds the power button down to turn off his phone.

Rush stops abruptly in front of us, and Sully walks right into him and grunts. "Something's not right."

Sully rubs his nose as he looks to the left and then to the right. "What do you mean?"

"I mean, why is it so quiet?" Rush whispers.

I step next to Sully and scoff. "Look around you, man." I open my arms wide. "We're sneaking around in these shitty woods at eight o'clock on a Friday."

"Exactly." Rush glares at me. "Where the fuck is all the noise? I don't hear a single goddamn cricket or branch moving."

"No shit, man. We don't want them to hear us." My eyes widen to emphasize my point. "What's up with you?"

Sully slowly turns in a circle. "He's right, Wolf. It's too quiet."

Rush tilts his head. "Do you guys hear that?"

I look to the left and then to the right. "What?"

"Shh!" I take a step forward and cock my head.

"Is that . . . buzz—"

"It sounds like . . . ticking?" I interrupt Rush, my eyebrows furrowing.

"Why the fuck—"

"That's ticking!" I yell, interrupting Sully as my pulse roars in my ears, and adrenaline floods my veins. "We gotta get the fuck outta here!" Before I even finish talking, I turn around and grab my brothers' shoulders and start to fucking run.

"It's a fucking trap! Get back! Get back, Da!" Rush screams into his phone as we haul ass over fallen branches, uncaring about the noise we're making.

I'm not meeting my maker today. I've got shit to do in this life, and when I find out who set this fucking trap, I'm going to make them wish for death.

We make it halfway back before the ticking stops.

And then the world fucking explodes.

It was a trap.

The whole goddamn thing was a trap.

The stolen shipments, the industrial park, the tip— everything was a setup. It took us a few days to figure out how the fuck they pulled it off, but once Rush traced the breadcrumbs Buzz found, he uncovered a world of shit.

The entire junior council was fighting over some bird, and our president, Pete, decided to turn rat. Unlucky for him, the Russians don't know the meaning of the word loyalty, so they saw an opportunity and took it. Instead of a hit on two members, they buried ten bombs around the perimeter of the warehouse—exactly where our guys were waiting for the signal. And they had snipers on the roof, which backfired since not only could they not accurately see through the smoke and flames, but some of the bombs set off a chain reaction, and part of the abandoned warehouse went up in flames.

Sometimes when I close my eyes, I can still hear the high-pitched ringing noise that's somehow muted and deafening at the same time and feel the grit in my eyes and the heat from the explosion.

I circle the bullet-wound scar on my shoulder hidden in my skull tattoo. One of those cowardly fucks got me when I went to check on Sully and Rush. It wasn't my first time being shot, but it taught me a valuable lesson that day.

Family over everything.

We lost five members that day. More if you include the rats involved. But I don't, since I'm the one that cut out their tongues. It didn't end well for those sad excuses for brothers, just like it won't end well for whoever is behind this.

Everyone knows once you join the Brotherhood, you're in for life.

Blood in, blood out.

chapter fifteen

Alaina

AFTER THE VIDEO call with Maddie, I'm still riding that high that only a pep talk from your best friend can give you.

I meander to the kitchen, hoping to run into Wolf, but instead, I find a note from Sarah.

Dinner's in the warming drawer and meals for the next two days are in the fridge.

Alaina—help yourself to the kitchen!

—Sarah

I trace her name at the bottom of the note, warmth filling my heart. I know it's her job—I *know* that—but it feels . . . nice to be looked after like that. Really nice.

I chuckle as I reread the note. I guess I shouldn't be surprised that this place has something as fancy as a warming drawer, but I've literally never met anyone who's had one. That's not really saying much since I've been living in a dorm room for longer than I haven't.

I suppose it's a useful feature in a house like this, with so many people coming and going. I wonder if I'll get to meet the rest of Cormac's boys. Though, if they're anything like Wolf, I'm not sure that I'll have any sort of *brotherly* feelings toward them. I flush when I think about Wolf lounging on my bed like he had every right to be there. I'd be lying if I said I didn't think about what it would be like had he walked in the bathroom—and in the shower—with me instead.

I bite my lip as a daydream of a naked and wet Wolf flashes across my mind. All six feet of sexy, tattooed, and hard muscles on display.

I shake my head to dislodge the fantasy. And that's all it'll ever be—a fantasy. No matter how attractive he is, there's no way I can date someone who's going to be my stepbrother. *Right?*

But there's a lot of gray between dating and hooking up, a little voice which sounds a lot like Maddie taunts.

That's true. I mean, I'm not going to marry the guy. Just kiss him. A lot. And maybe some other stuff too.

Jesus, I need to get a hold of myself. I'm over here giving myself whiplash with my internal debate and fantasizing about the dude as if it's even a possibility. He's probably got legions of girls following him around. I exhale a breath at that thought.

Shit, I bet he does. There's no way a guy like that doesn't have a girl.

Mood soured, it takes me a few guesses to figure out which drawer is the warming drawer. Everything in the kitchen is all sleek lines and dark wood—even the refrigerator is concealed behind faux wood cabinets, making it look like it's built-in to the surrounding cabinetry.

I grab the covered plate of spaghetti from the drawer and decide to eat at the island. It seems silly to use the formal dining room for just me—plus, it didn't really feel *lived-in* when we ate in there last night.

I can't keep the groan in as I eat a forkful of Sarah's spaghetti. I'm going to have to ask her for this recipe. Mary would love it.

Looking around the kitchen as I eat, I don't see any clues that scream they're Irish mafia. I'm not exactly sure what sort of clues I'm looking for, but I'm hoping it's one of those things I'll know when I see it.

I look out the French doors that lead to the enormous backyard. The pool catches my eye—I bet it would be fun. I might have to check that out tomorrow. Sarah said to make myself at home, so I'm sure that includes using the pool.

I wonder what Wolf's up to as I finish my dinner. Earlier, he mentioned watching a movie together, but it's six thirty now, and I haven't heard so much as a peep in the house in the last hour.

I'm sure he has better things to do than hang out with his new *maybe* stepsister. I bet he already had plans and just got caught up and forgot.

Which is totally fine, I tell myself as my stomach knots uncomfortably. Am I kind of bummed that I won't be able to hang out with a hot guy today? Sure. I may or may not have schemed with Maddie to do the scary movie test.

The idea is if you're watching a scary movie, and you cover your eyes or duck behind his shoulder, and he comforts you, he's into you. And if he doesn't, then he's not into you.

I still think it's juvenile, but Maddie swears by it, so I thought I'd give it a try. It's not like I have much else to do in a giant house by myself. I suppose I could explore the city, but I was kind of holding out hope to do that with my mom. I guess I could get a head start on my summer courses, but classes don't start for another three weeks, so I have plenty of time.

I finish my dinner, take my plate to the sink, and wash it. I leave it to dry on the drying rack next to the sink.

I spot Sarah's note out of the corner of my eye, and I decide to write her a nice note back to thank her for dinner, but I need a pen. It's those damn southern manners.

I open some drawers, starting with the ones nearby. Cutlery, knives, utensils, but no pens. There's gotta be a junk drawer, right? Someplace where they just shove random things that don't have a permanent home but still need to be kept. I'm just looking for any sort of writing utensil—I'd take a crayon at this point.

I find not one but four junk drawers on the other side of the island, close to the breakfast nook.

Jackpot.

I open the top two, and they're so different that I pause for a moment to stare at them. The one on the left has a few blank notepads, a handful of pens, a tape measure, tape, and a stapler. I grab a pencil and look in the right drawer. It's like a hoarder's wet dream. Takeout menus, old receipts, scribbled notes, pens, old Christmas candy, packets of soy sauce, headphones, and—*holy shit, is that a gun?*

I use a pencil to lift some papers up and stare at a handgun. SIG Sauer is etched along the top, and I'm assuming that's the type of gun. Jesus, I really better start watching some mafia movies.

Why is there a gun in their junk drawer in the middle of the kitchen?

I guess it's possible that someone set it down on the island, and they were tidying up before company came over, so someone just shoved it in the first available junk drawer, right?

I roll my eyes at my flimsy, made-up excuse.

I drop the pencil, and the paper covers the gun again. I slowly close both drawers and open the next two. One is completely empty, and the last one is more like the hoarder's paradise above it—minus the gun. I poke around, but I don't find anything worth noting.

I close all the drawers and go sit on a stool at the island and think about everything I know. Which isn't much.

I need more proof.

It's time to go sleuthing.

chapter sixteen

Alaina

I TAP MY INDEX finger against my lips as I stare into the backyard. If I were part of the Irish mafia, where would I hide all of my important stuff—the kind of stuff that could be used for blackmail if it got into the wrong hands?

I snap my fingers—a safe!

Common sense quickly replaces my exhilaration. Unless I absorbed some lock-picking skills by osmosis watching *Ocean's Eleven* last week, I can't get into a safe.

"Think, Lainey, think."

I figure I've got about an hour, maybe two, before my luck runs out. Either Wolf will actually find me expecting to watch a movie, or I'll run into someone from the staff.

Shoulders back and chin high, I start with the first floor. I remember seeing a few rooms that might shed some light on who exactly these people are. I practice my believable excuses in case I run into anyone: I'm lost,

I got turned around, I was looking for Wolf, I couldn't find the library. Okay, so they mostly center around me being lost. But that's believable, *right*?

I walk down the hallway toward the west side of the house, and the first door I open leads to the basement. After a deep breath and a quick look around to make sure I'm alone, I flip the switch and lights illuminate the basement.

I descend the stairs and try to keep my jaw off the floor. "Wow." The one-syllable word stretches into three as I take in this entire basement—if you can even call it that.

It's big enough to house a family of five—if that family also loved to play pool, darts, foosball. Warm, dark neutrals decorate the space down here, and again, there's enough seating for twenty people easily.

Two black leather sectional sofas frame the fireplace, and one of the biggest TVs I've ever seen hangs above it. All the games are in an area to the left of the sectionals, and an l-shaped bar and six stools are to the right. I whistle under my breath when I see enough bottles of alcohol to get an elephant drunk.

They must really like to entertain.

Or, it's for their mafia friends, a little voice says.

I spy a jukebox next to the bar and head over to check it out. Maybe I'll get lucky, and there will be a song titled "I'm in the mob." I laugh at my own stupidity. There'd never be a song titled that—snitches get stitches and all that.

"Holy shit," I whisper when I get close enough to the jukebox. It's a vintage machine, not one of those copycat ones made in the last ten years.

I press a button, and the whole thing lights up, illuminating a ton of 80s vinyl. A black coffee mug full of nickels is on the chair next to the jukebox. I pluck a few out and place them in the coin slot before picking my song choices.

As David Bowie sings, I step behind the bar, careful not to touch too much. Not that I'm worried about fingerprints or anything, but I don't want to be stupid about it either. The last thing I need is to leave it all messed up, so they know someone was down here snooping.

I don't see anything out of the ordinary—just lots and lots of bottles of Jameson and some soda in a mini refrigerator.

I walk around the basement and check out the game area when an art print catches my eye. My brows furrow when I realize it's that obnoxious Dogs Playing Poker print. It doesn't feel like it goes with the rest of the house.

I cross the room to stand in front of the print as the song switches and Marvin Gaye sings about mountains being high enough. I tentatively hook a finger around the edge of the frame and pull it toward me. A rush of adrenaline floods my system, and my mouth falls open when the whole frame swings toward me to reveal a built-in safe.

"Holy shit."

It's dark-gray with a black keypad and a small handle. Okay, so I was right, there is a safe. *Deep breaths, Lainey, deep breaths*, I tell myself as I rock a little from side to side.

I freeze when I realize that I have no way of figuring out the code. With my hands steepled in front of my face, I push up onto my tiptoes to get a better look. Without touching anything, I tilt my head to look at it from different angles, and that's when I see it.

Part of what looks like a manilla envelope is sticking out of the bottom corner of the safe.

"I wonder . . ." I rock back on my heels and pat my pockets down, hoping to find a stray bobby pin or something. I have a crazy idea that tells me I've definitely been watching too much TV lately.

I don't have anything on me besides my phone, and I'm not willing to risk running into anyone by going up two stories to my room. My pulse kicks up a notch, feeling more like a ticking clock than anything. I scan the basement, looking for anything I can use.

Ah-ha! The bar! I jog to the bar and grab the long, metal bottle opener, a wine bottle opener, and a couple of thick cardboard coasters and bring them back to the safe.

I exhale a deep breath and attempt to calm my nerves. I open the wine bottle opener and wedge the flat metal end between the envelope and the door. With one hand, I wiggle the opener back and forth a little, and with the other, I tug on the manila envelope. My eyebrows hit my hairline when the door pops open.

I know I'm not that strong, so either someone didn't close it, or they have a really shitty safe. Judging by everything else about this house, my money is on the former.

I set the openers and coasters down on the floor and peer into the safe.

"What the hell . . ."

Stacks and stacks and stacks of bundled-up hundred dollar bills sit in tidy piles, two guns on one side, and the manilla envelope on the other. I carefully extract the envelope and open it. A twinge of guilt pierces my moral compass, but I quickly snuff it out when I remember that I have no idea what kind of people my mom got tangled up with.

It looks like some sort of log—fifty or so sheets of loose-leaf paper with numbers and dates going back ten years. I flip through them, but I can't make sense of any of it. The numbers could be lottery numbers or addresses for all I can tell.

My shoulders droop when I realize that there's nothing in these papers that helps me. I snap a photo of one page to show the girls and see if they have any ideas and then stuff the pages back into the envelope. I carefully place it back inside the safe where it was and gently shut the door.

I fix the painting so it covers the safe and quickly put everything back where I found it just as the Queen song ends and the jukebox goes dark. I take one last look around the basement, making sure everything is exactly as I found it before I head upstairs.

chapter seventeen

Alaina

SINCE I HAVEN'T seen Wolf, I'm going to assume he is otherwise occupied, so I stop in the kitchen and grab a few snacks and a bottle of fancy iced tea for my own movie night.

I guess I worked up an appetite after all that snooping around, I think with a smirk.

I'm not adventurous enough to try out their home theatre, and I've never had a TV in my bedroom like this before. I might as well take advantage of it while I'm here.

Jogging up the stairs, I pause at the top and strain my ears. I could've sworn I heard a thump. When I don't hear it again, I chalk it up to my imagination. I'm probably jumpy from my discoveries today.

Once I've changed into some short cotton shorts and a tank top, I make the perfect movie night nest with blankets and pillows in the middle of my bed. Snacks are within reaching distance, and I cue up Netflix. Turns out, they have a Fitzgerald house Netflix account, and each room has its own profile.

I'm tempted to look at Wolf's and see what his favorites are and how they match up to mine, but that feels like it borders on creepy. Plus, that's not really how I want to get to know him.

I click on the Pink Room profile and spend the next twenty minutes looking for something to watch. I finally settle on *A Star is Born* with Lady Gaga and Bradley Cooper. I haven't seen it yet, but I've heard it's amazing. And I'm in the mood to get sucked into a great drama.

One of the girls in my choir class sang "Shallow" for her final project. Since it was a solo, it didn't have quite the same impact as a duet, but it was still beautiful. She sang the hell out of it too.

Thirty minutes into the movie, my door flies open, and a tall silhouette fills the doorway, backlit by the dim light in the hallway. A small scream tears from my throat, and I throw my open bag of M&M's toward the door. As far as defenses go, it's terrible. Brightly-colored M&M's hit my would-be attacker in the shin and roll away.

It takes me a moment to calm down the thundering of my heart enough to hear Wolf roaring with laughter. He bends over and scoops a few M&M's off the ground and pops them into his mouth.

"Oh, Red, you are gonna be so much fun." Wolf walks into my room dressed in gym shorts and a black tee and kicks my door shut. He stops next to my bed and stares at me for a moment, eyes twinkling before turning to see Ally and Jackson kiss. "This isn't really what I had in mind, but alright. Slide over." He kicks off his all-black Vans and shoves my blankets to the side, and climbs in next to me.

It's a king-sized platform bed, so there's plenty of room for both of us to sit comfortably—and then some. And I just sit there, frozen.

Where the hell did all my bravado go.

I feel hyperaware of every movement—mine, his, hell, even the characters in the movie have me on edge.

Wolf settles in close to me, close enough that our arms brush when he reaches for a snack, and I snap out of my frozen stupor.

"Have you seen this before?" he murmurs, his breath tickling the fine hairs on the back of my neck.

I look at him, expecting him to be facing me, but his eyes are fixed on the screen. Looking back at the TV, I answer, "No, but I've heard it's really good. We can watch something else if you want." I shrug one shoulder.

"Nah. Let's watch this." He pops another M&M in his mouth, eyes on the TV.

So for the next hour, that's what we do. We watch a movie together without talking. I alternate my attention between the movie and Wolf, stealing glances at him out of the corner of my eye. I swear, I feel his hot gaze slowly caress my exposed skin, but whenever I look, he's casually sitting there, eyes on the TV.

Sometime during the movie, we shift. He slouches down with his arms behind his head, and I sit stiffly against the headboard, too busy overthinking everything.

But by the end of the movie, I've nearly forgotten him as I sit with my legs crossed, leaning forward, hand covering my mouth. Tears slowly roll down my cheeks, splashing on my bare knees. I take a stuttering breath as my heart aches for these characters.

"You alright over there?" Wolf's voice is low and gravelly.

I sniff and nod, never taking my eyes off Ally singing the final song.

I feel the bed move, and then I feel his warm hand on my back. He leans forward to catch my eye. "You cryin', Red?"

I sniffle. "It's just so, so sad." My words come out thick with tears. "And tragic. And heartbreaking. And soul-crushing."

He lets out an amused chuckle. "You're like a thesaurus. Those all mean pretty much the same thing."

"I know." I wipe a tear from underneath my eye. "I don't know why I'm crying so much. It's just so . . ."

"Sad?" He quirks a brow, and I flash him a small smile. "It is sad, Red. He was sick. And he needed help," Wolf says, voice soft, pain etched in each word.

I nod a few times. "They had the magical kind of love though. The kind that transcends this life and continues on in the stars. And it was tragically short."

His hand stills on my back. "You do know that these are actors, right? They don't have any kind of magical love."

I shift to meet his gaze and see a smirk on his face. His hand slides down my back with the movement. "Of course I know that. But it doesn't make it any less sad. To have that sort of connection with someone and have it ripped away from you like that is heartbreaking."

Something shifts across his face, and for a split second, I see longing so profound it steals my breath. Just as quickly as it appears, it leaves, and his mask of quiet amusement is back.

"Don't you want a love like that?"

I'm not sure what compels me to blurt that out. Maybe it's the longing I swear I caught a glimpse of, or the fact that he shut it down so quickly. But I'm dying to know his answer.

His lips part, and even though he's looking right at me, it feels like he's not really seeing *me*. "A love that ends in tragedy? Nah." He punctuates his deflection with a forced smirk, and now I'm positive I saw longing on his face a moment ago.

"No, not one that ends in tragedy, but a love story for the ages. And maybe this movie isn't the best example, but my point still stands. A love story that gets told to generation after generation until it turns into a fabled story mapped out in the stars." I hold a hand to my heart and hold his gaze, letting him see the deep-seated longing.

I'm playing a dangerous game by handing him my vulnerability so openly, but a tiny part of me hopes he'll rise to the challenge.

He swallows, and his gaze hardens as he looks at me. "That's not going to happen, Red. Not with me."

I wince, embarrassment flushing my cheeks. "What? No. I mean, of course. I wasn't—"

"Look," he interrupts, "I think you're hot as fuck, but I don't do relationships, okay? It's nothing personal."

"Yep." I nod. "Got it." I nod again and turn to face the TV, watching the credits scroll. "I wasn't asking you to be my boyfriend or whatever. I was just making conversation," I grumble, willing the flush to cool down. "Besides, you're not even my type." I sniff and raise my chin, refusing to look at him to see his reaction.

"Ahh, there's that famous redhead fire. 'Not my type,' she says!" He laughs. "Come on, let's not kid ourselves." When I don't rise to his bait, he drops it. "Let's watch something funny. I think you could use a laugh."

I take a deep breath and wipe under my eyes one more time, catching a few mascara smudges.

"Alright." I lean back against the headboard and get comfortable.

Wolf grabs the remote control, and after a moment, hits play on season one of a sitcom. Two minutes in, and I'm already giggling and cringing at the main character's actions. Ten minutes in, and Wolf links our pinkie fingers together, sending a kaleidoscope of butterflies fluttering around. I sneak a glance at him and see a sly smile spreading across his face.

And that's exactly how we spend the next couple of hours—linked fingers and laughing.

Sometime later, I wake up, startled to realize that I must've fallen asleep. The *Are you still watching?* screen softly glows in the darkness of my bedroom.

My bladder screams as the pressure increases, and I slide out of bed—or try to. A heavy weight pins me down, and it takes me a moment to realize that it's an arm. A tattooed, toned arm.

Holy shit, Wolf is spooning me. *Okay, don't freak out*, I coach myself, *just be cool and slip out of bed before you pee your pants.*

I take a deep breath, and his scent surrounds me. Jesus, he even *smells* attractive. Like sandalwood and temptation.

Slowly, I lift his hand from where it's curled against my stomach and quietly shift out from underneath his arm. I see some letters inked onto his fingers, but it's too dark to make them out.

A stray thought about my ex-boyfriend's inked fingers flits through my mind. I guess I do have a type.

Focus, Lainey.

Once I clear his arm, I untangle my legs from his and swing them over the bed, careful not to jostle him. Something tells me he would bolt the moment he realizes he fell asleep.

He mumbles something about firecrackers before rolling into the empty space where I was laying, curling his arm around my pillow and snuggling it.

I'm almost annoyed with how unassumingly attractive he is to me right now.

With a huff, I quickly make my way to the en suite bathroom, leaving the lights off. Once I relieve my bladder, I stare at myself in the mirror. My face is all shadows and angles, highlighted by the nearly full moon shining in through the open blinds by the shower.

"What are you doing here, Lainey?" My words are barely a whisper, but the accusation is loud in my mind.

What am I doing here? I'm in a strange city, in a strange house, in bed with a strange guy, waiting for my mom to—what—pay attention to me? God, I sound pathetic when I lay it out like that.

The silvery glow of the moon spotlights one pattern of freckles—Orion's Belt. A pang of sadness hits me in the chest when I think about Dad tracing these very freckles when I was young.

And that's exactly why I'm here.

I owe it to Dad.

Even if I'm stashed away in this big house all alone, waiting for the moment she needs me. Like a forgotten toy.

"I miss you, Dad," I whisper to the moon. He used to tell me that no matter where he was in the world, he would look to the moon and send his love to me. All I had to do was look up at the moon to feel it.

"Please come home, Dad. I need you." A single tear rolls down my cheek as I plead with the moon.

I swipe it off my cheek as I hear Wolf mumble, "Not the platypus, man."

I chuckle quietly, a smile curling up the corners of my mouth. I climb back into my bed, facing him and leaving some space between us. He reaches an arm out and palms my butt, pulling me closer.

I put my palms on his bare chest—when the hell did he take his shirt off? "Wolf," I whisper.

"Shh, Red, just go back to sleep," he mumbles as he tucks me closer to his chest.

His sandalwood scent and warmth surround me, and after a few minutes, his breathing evens out. It takes me another ten minutes before I'm relaxed enough to fall asleep.

I guess I'm not completely alone, after all.

chapter eighteen

Wolf

I WAKE UP ON my side, surrounded by gray and the scent of sweet peaches, and nursing a serious case of blue balls. It takes me a moment to realize I'm not in my room. The sunlight pours in through the open French doors on the opposite side in my room.

Blinking away the last images of the dream I just had, I struggle to wipe the fog of sleep from my mind. I'm warm and comfortable, and it feels too good to leave.

Wavy dark-red hair tickles my neck, and one of the sweetest asses I've ever felt presses against my dick. I stop myself before I thrust against her.

I must've fallen asleep sometime after the second season we watched last night. I lift my head up to look at Alaina, and I get an eyeful of all that soft, creamy skin dotted with those sexy little freckles.

Fuck, I groan. I don't know what the fuck is going on with me if I'm thinking freckles—of all things—are this hot. I need to get laid.

And Red here would be a perfect way to scratch that particular itch.

If she wasn't going to be my fucking stepsister, that is.

I lightly trace a pattern on her shoulder in front of me, mesmerized by the way they seem to flow into patterns seamlessly.

I doubt she's even going to be my stepsister. Rush was right, there's something fucking weird going on with Da. He's never moved a woman in here—and definitely not her kid. I bet he needs something from Lana, and once he gets what he needs, he'll cut her loose.

Which means I'm on borrowed time with Red.

I stop tracing her freckles and roll onto my back.

She shifts in her sleep, turning toward me and sighing when she settles on my chest, and my brain short-circuits when I see some serious sideboob.

I grit my teeth and curse Rush for putting her on the no-fly list. I'm going to have some words with that motherfucker today. I need an update on her background—and Lana's. And a better reason not to roll her over and slide into that hot pussy I can feel against me.

Scrubbing my hand over my face, I recall the greatest Boston players ever, in chronological order. By the time I get to Ortiz, I'm calmer. Once I'm able to think clearer, I pull my arm out from under Red and get out of bed. She never so much as cracks an eyelid.

I pause at the doorway and glance over my shoulder at her. She rolled over, so she's on her back, her face tilted toward the spot I was laying, and something clenches in my chest.

Something foreign.

I grit my teeth and shove that bullshit way down deep where it won't see the light of day anytime soon.

I close Red's door softly as I leave her room and head toward the kitchen.

Time for coffee. I've got a phone call to make, and I have a feeling I'll need the caffeine.

I SLIDE OPEN THE patio doors, and with my fresh coffee in hand, I step outside. Breathing in the crisp morning air, I make my way to the loungers by the pool.

I sit on the edge of my favorite one and sip my coffee while I stare at the water, wishing it was the ocean I was looking at. The pool is nice, and the slide was a nice touch last year, but nothing beats the soothing sound of waves crashing against the shoreline.

Or the unforgiving waves beholden to no man.

I often wonder what that would be like—to be free and make my own rules. I suppose I'll know what it'll feel like soon enough.

Setting my phone and my cup down, I pull out a cigarette and light it. I know it's a filthy habit, but my hands are far filthier—bloodier—so I might as well enjoy life while I can.

Once we convince the Brotherhood council that we're more than capable of ruling the junior chapters with just the three of us, we can start acting in an official capacity.

We've been doing shit behind closed doors for nearly two years—ever since they inducted us as the acting junior council—but since we're unwilling to bring up some random soldier for a fourth, we've been iced.

I take a drag and think about my first act of business.

Two days had gone by since the abandoned warehouse turned into a war zone, and now that we were all patched up, I was up.

My first act as VP of the Brotherhood's junior council, and the final step to VP of the Brotherhood's council—but that won't be for years. Not until Da and the rest of his council members are ready to retire.

I shake my head to clear it of all the Brotherhood politics and focus on the bleeding guy in front of me. He's tied to a metal chair in the middle of a concrete room. Even if he wasn't gagged, no one would hear his screams. We're in the basement of the carriage house on Summer Knoll.

I crack my knuckles and pace a few steps in front of him. "Normally we don't shit where we eat—but I don't need to tell you this, do I, brother?" The term tastes like ash on my tongue. "Aye, but then you're not really a brother, are you, Timmy?" I tap the end of my sharpened blade against my chin as I continue to pace in front of one of the rats responsible for what happened in Brooklyn.

Timmy mumbles something incoherent, but his gaze follows me as I continue pacing.

"Alright." I stop in front of him, eyeing the drain beneath his chair. "We can do this the easy way or the hard way. So, what'll it be?" There's murder in his eyes as he looks at me. "Ah, hard way then. Suit yourself." I learned long ago that adopting an unaffected—cheery even—demeanor while interrogating or torturing for information always unsettles the other person.

So now I do it for everyone.

I glance behind me to see Rush and Sully leaning against the wall and watching the show.

And Timmy didn't disappoint. He put on quite the show for everyone as I pried out each fingernail, a few teeth, and ultimately his tongue.

I stub out my smoke in the ashtray on the table, sip my coffee, and call my brother.

"What."

"Brother! How's the city?"

"You called me at—" I hear some rustling. "Eight o'clock in the morning to ask how the city is? Fuck off, Wolf. I just crawled into bed two hours ago."

"What kept you out so late? Dinner with grandma again?"

"Yeah. She had the fish fry." *She's somewhere in the middle of the Atlantic.* Or as I like to say, she's sleeping with the fishes. I snicker. I know it's fucking cliché, but that's why it's so funny.

"Mm, and how was it?"

"Crispy," he deadpans. He knows I'm just fucking with him now. We don't have any code phrases about how the fish fry was.

I snicker. "Alright, man. Coming home today?"

Rush sighs and I hear more rustling on his end. "That's the plan. Sully should be settled up north."

"Good, good. Listen, did you have a chance to do some digging on Lana and her daughter? Something's off here, man, but I don't have all the pieces yet."

"Shit." He draws the word out for three syllables. "Hang on." I hear more rustling. "You're on speaker. I'm checking in with my contact. I didn't have time to do my own search, but I trust this guy. He's good and discrete."

I sip my coffee and lean back in the lounger, keeping an eye on the patio door. The last thing I need is for Red to wander out here and overhear this conversation.

"Okay, so he sent me his findings. Lemme just open it and see what he found . . ."

"Rush?" I check the phone to make sure I didn't drop the call.

"What the fuck?"

I sit up, and my muscles tense with the quick movement. "What did he find out?"

"Nothing. He found nothing. There's not a single photo or a name or a goddamn extracurricular activity—there's jack shit." His voice rises with each word.

My brows rose. "What the hell does that mean?"

Rush exhales into the speaker. "It means, brother, that she's a fucking ghost. There's no record of her anywhere. Someone went through serious lengths to erase her from record."

I whistle under my breath. "That must've taken some serious dough—and manpower. Do you know anyone who could do that? Fuck, do you think she's in WITSEC?"

"I don't know, man. The better question is what the hell happened to her life," Rush murmurs. "Maybe we have to approach this another way."

Unease prickles down my spine. "What do you mean?"

"You've met her, right?"

"Yeah . . ." Apprehension fills me. There's something off about Rush's voice that has my hackles rising.

"Well, how is she? Do you think you could seduce information out of her by tonight?"

I sputter the sip of coffee I just swallowed. "What the fuck, man?"

"What the fuck *what*? Since when do you turn down pussy? At least this time, you'd be getting more than just your dick wet." Rush scoffs.

"I'm not sure if I should be flattered that you think I can have her on her back, information flowing in the next five hours, or offended that you'd think I'd have to stoop to that to get the info."

"Relax, Wolf. I didn't think you'd mind. But if it's that big of a deal, just wait until I get home, and I'll seduce the info out of her."

My shoulders tense, and I force a humorous laugh. "Fuck you, man. You lost your opportunity when you asked me to pick her up from the train station."

"Yeah, yeah. We'll see when I get home. I'll be there later tonight."

"Alright, later, brother."

"Later, Wolf."

chapter nineteen

Wolf

LATER THAT AFTERNOON, I follow the sounds of James Gandolfini as Tony Soprano—but like a fucked-up version of him. *Why the fuck is he saying* fluff *so much?*

"What did you say? Fluff me—fluff me, you said? Fluff you, you motherfluffer!"

I round the corner of the hallway that opens up to the theatre room, and sure enough, Tony Soprano's face fills the projector screen.

I creep up behind Alaina as Tony fires a gun, and I wait for it to get quiet again. "What are you doing?" I say right behind her, rushing my words together.

She shrieks and jumps a foot off the couch, turning and throwing her popcorn bowl behind her. Luckily for me, she has terrible aim.

I laugh and hold my stomach. "The look on your face is priceless, Red."

"What the hell, Wolf! Why do you keep scaring me like that?" She grabs a throw pillow and whips it at me.

I easily sidestep it and hop over the back of the couch, landing next to her. She huffs and flings another throw pillow at me—this time hitting her target: my face.

"Alright, I deserved that one. But honestly, Red, you make it too easy. You're at the back of the house, and you've got this turned up to like 100." I take the offending pillow and tuck it under my right arm.

"There's no one here! And the remote control with the volume wasn't working for me, so . . ." She shrugs. "And you're picking that up." She flicks her gaze to the scattered popcorn behind us.

I settle back into the couch and turn my head to look at her fully. "You think you can boss me around, baby girl?" I tsk.

The prettiest pink darkens her cheekbones, and she crosses her arms over her chest. "I'm not trying to boss you around," she mutters.

"Good. Because it won't work. I don't get on my knees for anyone. So it's best not to even try. Understand?" I run my thumb over her cheekbones to soften my words. Not because I didn't mean them—I'll never get on my knees for anyone again.

"I don't—I wasn't"—she meets my eyes, and I see twin embers in their depths—"that's not what I was doing, Wolf."

Ahh, there she is. I knew underneath those pleated skirts and "yes, sirs," there was a firecracker waiting to be lit. Heaven help the bastard who sets her off. I hope I get a front-row seat to that show though.

"But you shouldn't make people clean up your mess." The tiny thread of steel in her voice is admirable, if misplaced.

Dropping my hand from her cheek, I say. "Ah, but that's where you're wrong. The world was created to survive—thrive, even—with order. And without hierarchy, there's chaos.

"That's . . . I don't even know what to say to that." She blinks a few times and tilts her head. "And you see yourself—where? At the top of the food chain?"

I toy with the ends of her soft hair. "Aye, Red. I'm pretty close to the top. And in this world, either you work for someone or someone works for you, yeah? And I've never been good at taking directions"—I pause to look at her face. Pleasure moves through me slowly, snaking around my limbs, when I find her gaze on mine—"unless I'm in the bedroom. Then I can be easily persuaded to follow." I stare into her eyes, letting her see the hunger shining in them.

After a moment, I break the connection and snatch a handful of popcorn. "Why the fuck are we watching this dubbed bullshit?" I gesture toward the TV.

She shrugs one shoulder. "It asked for passwords to watch HBO, but I found *The Sopranos* on one of those free channels on TV. You get used to the inventive swear words after a few episodes."

I laugh. The idea of these characters not saying fuck every other word is laughable. But she's right, it is entertaining.

We're quiet for a moment as Tony Soprano kills Big Pussy on screen. A quiet chuckle slips out before I can stifle it.

She turns to look at me, brow raised. "What's funny about killing Big . . . you know, that guy?" The light flush on her skin is so goddamn alluring that I think I might've had it wrong all these years. Maybe I should've been looking at the *innocent* ones to take home instead.

"Hm? What guy?"

"That one—right there." She points to the screen as they bind Big Pussy's body in chains and toss him overboard.

I can't tell her that I laughed because I know that shooting someone three times in close quarters like that is a real bitch to clean up. There was blood still in the tiny grooves of the boat's cabin for months. Da called it a learning experience when he made Rush, Sully, and I clean that job up. So I settle on a smirk instead and switch directions.

"What's the matter, Red? Can't say a man's name now?"

She rolls her eyes. "That's not even his real name. That's his . . . code name or whatever."

"It's alright, I don't expect a girl like you to—"

She shifts to face me, a scowl marring her beautiful face. "What the hell does that mean?"

I smother my grin with my hand. I haven't had this much fun riling anyone up in too long. "What do you think it means?"

"I can say it, you know." She stares at me for a moment, shoulders tight.

I raise an eyebrow in challenge.

"Pussy. See? Pussy, pussy, pussy."

"You done?" Watching her lips wrap around the word pussy is giving me ideas that I'm not sure I can act on. Da said to protect her *and* stay away from her, and Rush said she was off-limits at first, but now he's pushing for me to fuck her for insider intel on what the fuck her mom's deal is. Technically, I would be keeping the closest eye on her while protecting the house like Dad asked.

I'm the first to admit that my moral compass is dead, but fucking her for intel doesn't sit right with me. Not after seeing the pretty pink blush spill down her neck all the way to the tops of those perfect tits.

Her chest heaves as she maintains eye contact with me, her gaze traveling lower, slowly taking in my inked chest and abs, and settling on the growing outline of my dick. I guess I'm not the only one affected by her declaration of pussy.

I smirk. "See something you like?"

She flashes her gaze to mine, not replying with words. But those beautiful doe eyes of hers tell me everything she's not ready to say yet.

Mostly *yes, more, please.*

I won't fuck her just because Rush wants me to, but I'll definitely fuck her just to feel that tight pussy hugging my cock. I rake my teeth over my bottom lip, envisioning that blush all over her body.

Without a word, I lean forward and take the popcorn bowl from between us and set it on the coffee table. I sit back and extend my hand out, a silent question. It's her choice. Her gaze flicks between my hand and my eyes, and whatever she sees there must be what she's looking for.

She places her hand in mine, and I pull her toward me on the couch.

"We go at your pace, Red, okay?"

She nods and gets up on her knees, leaning into me and brushing her lips across mine softly. Jesus Christ, her lips are so soft—I bet everything about her is soft and warm.

She's a fucking angel wrapped in white and so goddamn tempting.

I groan when she opens her mouth and teases me with her tongue. When her tongue tangles with mine, my control slips, and I bring her closer with my hand on the back of her neck.

She slides closer and throws her leg over mine, so she's straddling me. Her skirt flares out around us, and the image sears itself into my brain. Just thinking about fucking her in nothing but this preppy little skirt gets me even harder.

"You good?" I breathe the words into her neck.

"Yes." She moans the word as she sinks down on me and swivels her hips. A groan leaves her lips before she slides her hand into my hair and grips it tight. The bite of pain makes my dick swell, and I can't help the involuntary flex of my hips. Fuck, I knew she'd be soft everywhere.

She seals her lips to mine as she rubs her hot pussy right over my cock—and the only thing between us is two flimsy pieces of cotton. It's a real testament to my patience.

With my hands spanning her ribcage, I guide her movements, enjoying the little noises of pleasure she makes with every swivel of her hips, mimicking the movement of her tongue.

My phone vibrates against my leg, but I ignore it in favor of the bombshell currently grinding on me.

She leans back, hands on my shoulders and lips brushing mine with every word. "Your pocket's vibrating."

"Fuck 'em. I'm busy." I grip the nape of her neck and crush her mouth to mine. A few moments later, the vibrating starts again. I tear my head to the side and reach into my pocket for my goddamn phone, intent on throwing it across the room. "Fuck."

It's Rush.

He's called five times.

I sigh and hit accept. Before I can even say hello, he's yelling.

"Why don't you answer your motherfucking phone, motherfucker?"

His panic is clear, and knowing my brother as well as I do, I know something went sideways. "What's wrong?"

"What's wrong, he says. Answer your motherfucking phone when I call next time, asshole!" He's panting, and I hear sirens in the background.

There's no way Alaina doesn't hear him, but she doesn't say anything. *Good girl*, I think. And she doesn't move from my lap. Of course, I haven't eased up my grip on her hip yet either.

"Okay, okay. Talk to me, Rush."

"Mama Rosa's is in flames."

"Where are you? Are you hurt?" My voice is calm as I lock down the shock coursing through my veins, a skill I developed years ago. I tap Alaina's thigh, and she slides off my lap to sit next to me.

"I'm fine. I was stopping to pick up a couple of pies to bring home tonight, and when I was about a block away, I heard it."

"Fuck. How bad?"

"Pretty bad, but at least the eight floors above didn't go up in flames. And word on the street is a tea party was happening at the time."

A tea party? Anyone who blows up a place with a bunch of bosses is making some serious moves. Fuck. I lean forward and stare at the floor, trying to connect the dots. There's something here, but I can't quite connect the pieces yet.

"Is everything okay?" Red murmurs, reaching out and tentatively touching my back.

"It's fine," I reply absentmindedly as I get off the couch. I rearrange my dick and walk toward the hallway.

"Who the fuck is that?" Rush demands.

"It's no one. Just the TV man. Tell me what you need," I placate him.

Alaina

I'M ROOTED TO the couch, Wolf's cutting words swirling around my head. *"It's no one."*

I fight against the embarrassment that threatens to take root. I don't want to jump to conclusions. For all I know, it wasn't even a question about me.

I follow quietly behind Wolf as he leaves the theatre room and goes into the hallway. I feel a little guilty about eavesdropping, but I reason with myself that something's obviously going on.

I'm not stupid enough to think that one make-out session makes us a couple or anything, but I am living here, at least temporarily, and I want to know what's going on. And just because he's an amazing kisser doesn't mean that I forgot about my mission to get some information on his dad.

I creep down the hallway, staying close to the wall. There's no way he wouldn't see me if he turns around, but luck is on my side tonight.

I don't catch the first few things he says, but then he steps inside one of the formal living rooms, so I stop outside the doorway and lean against the wall.

"Fuck, man. Did you talk to Sully? Maybe"—he pauses—"yeah, yeah, okay."

I hear Wolf release a breath. "Does Da know yet? Because I'm tellin' you, man, three hits on the Irish and now the Italians? Someone's making serious plays here. It's fucked-up."

I freeze, my breath stalling. Three *hits*? Like con-tracted killing?! I tip my head back against the wall and close my eyes.

Fuck, okay, it could mean nothing. You've definitely watched two seasons of the Sopranos today, so you're all hopped up on Hollywood's version of the mafia. Chill out, Lainey, I tell myself. Nothing like a good pep talk to talk yourself off the edge of panic.

Another pause, and then Wolf says, "Alright. See you in two days. Be safe, asshole."

When I don't hear anything else, I slowly make my way back to the theatre room. I pause the *Sopranos* episode but grab my phone and the popcorn to take to the kitchen.

I don't know what to think, but I do know that Wolf is right about one thing: something seriously fucked-up is going on.

chapter twenty

Alaina

THE NEXT MORNING, I wake up bright and early. I had a hard time sleeping last night, and my dreams felt like an episode of the *Sopranos*.

I push the softest comforter known to man off of me and reach for my phone. Given the time difference, I usually have a few texts from the girls by the time I wake up. Sure enough, there's a text from Mary and a photo of her and Maddie eating ice cream on the beach.

Mary: Wish you were here!

I smile and quickly type out a reply.

Me: Me too! Miss you guys!

Maddie must have her phone right in front of her because I see the three dots bouncing on the bottom right away.

Maddie: how's Operation Stepbrother going *waggles eyebrows*

Me: I took your advice and went for it.

As soon as I hit send, my phone rings with an incoming video call. I answer to see Mary's and Maddie's smiling faces.

"Hello, my favorite cousins," I greet them with a smile.

"Girl, are you still in bed?" Mary questions.

"Who cares if she's still in bed. I want the details! Spill! Is he a good kisser? Jesus, please tell me he doesn't kiss like that fool you dated last year," Maddie says, fake-gagging.

"Oh, come on! It was two dates—I didn't even really like him. *You guys* are the ones who encouraged me to go out with him."

"Well, how were we supposed to know he kissed like a, and I quote, 'fish out of water,'" Maddie deadpans.

I can't contain my laughter. "Ugh, that guy was the worst kisser *ever*. His tongue just kept limply flopping around—and it was so wet and just gross."

"Yeah, yeah, we all remember your vivid description of that guy. Stop stalling and answer my question, babe."

I sigh with a smirk on my face. "Yes, alright? He's a good kisser—a great one. And yes, I'm in bed. It's only seven here."

"Nice, babe! Air five!"

I hold my hand up for an air five, and then we all giggle. "Dang. I miss you guys already. I don't know how

I'm going to last the whole summer without seeing your beautiful faces."

Mary glances at Maddie, her eyebrows drawn together. "Didn't your mom tell you?"

I sit up straighter at her tone. "Tell me what?"

"Babe," Maddie says slowly. "We're coming home soon."

I laugh. "Oh, gosh. You guys scared me! That's great news. When are you coming back?"

"We'll be home for your birthday," Mary says quietly.

"That's amazing! Then we can celebrate together! Ooh, let's go to O'Malley's! I'll catch a train to the city. I'm sure Jack will turn a blind eye like usual." My head spins as I think of new plans. I'd never tell them, but I was disappointed that I wasn't going to be spending my birthday with them. We've always celebrated our birthdays together ever since we were young.

They both grimace.

"Wait. Why are you guys coming home early? And why aren't you happy about it?"

Mary blows out a breath before she squares her shoulders and looks right at me. "Okay. So, we're coming home for a few weeks because Mom is meeting Aunt Lana in London to go dress shopping for a few weeks."

My brow furrows, and I shake my head. My chest feels tight, like someone is squeezing me too hard. "But . . . but that doesn't make any sense. Mom said she's only going to Kleinfeld's in the city for a dress, and she should be back tomorrow."

"I don't know, babe. I guess she didn't find anything," Maddie says in a low voice. "I'm sorry, Lainey." The pity in her voice heats my cheeks and sours my stomach.

I wave a hand in front of me. "It's fine. I wasn't"—I clear my throat—"I wasn't sure I was going to celebrate my birthday with her anyway, so this—this just makes it easier for me."

"It's her loss, Lainey," Mary says softly.

I nod. "Yep. It always is," I murmur with a bitter smile, my eyes filling with tears. My shoulders drop before I hitch them up again. I sniff and blink my eyes a few times, making sure that none of the tears fall. "Okay, tell me: have you found any conquests yet, Maddie?" I ask with a forced smile.

We liked to tease Maddie about her man-eater ways, and she always took it good-naturedly. She looked at me for a moment before a smirk curled her lips. "I have my eye on a few prospects."

I laugh. "Tell me all about them."

And for the next thirty minutes, I laugh with my best friends as Maddie tells us in detail about each guy she's met in the two days they've been there.

And by the end of the conversation, it's a little easier to breathe.

For ten years, I always assumed that my mother was too busy to make time for me, but now—now I *know* that she just doesn't want to.

I GIVE MYSELF EXACTLY ten minutes to wallow before I make myself get out of bed and start the day. Since I spent most of the previous day binge-watching *Sopranos*, I think I'll try looking around again. After the phone call last night, I feel like there's definitely something else going on. And if I'm honest, I'm kind of starting to believe the rumors about them being in the Irish mafia.

Except for that first day, I haven't seen another person—besides Wolf—in the house, so I feel pretty good about casually snooping without getting caught.

I throw on a short, flirty yellow skirt and a band tee and make my way to the kitchen. As usual, I don't encounter anyone on my way, and I try to look around discreetly for any cameras.

I should've been more careful in the basement, but I can't do anything about it now. If there were cameras, I'm totally screwed. But since no one said anything yet, I can only assume that there aren't cameras down there. I can't be sure it's the same for the rest of the house though, so I need to be smart about it.

I gather ingredients for grilled cheese and start cooking it on the stove when I hear footsteps hurrying around somewhere, but I don't see anyone. I wouldn't be surprised if it's someone on the other side of this mostly empty house—I mean, mansion. The thing is so huge that I imagine any sort of noise bounces off all the walls and amplifies.

I turn back to the stove and flip my grilled cheese. My mouth waters at the smell of delicious melted cheese. They had four different kinds of cheese in the fridge, so I used them all. Whoever said cheese isn't a breakfast food never had extra toasted grilled cheese before. It's not for your everyday breakfast, but for those days where you need a little comfort to start your day.

"Miss McElroy."

"Ahh!" I turn around and hold up my spatula like a sword in front of me. "Dave, it's you. You scared the pants off me!" I place a hand on my racing heart and will it to slow down.

"My apologies, Miss—"

"Alaina, please," I interrupt with a smile.

He nods. "Alaina. My apologies for startling you, but I wanted to let you know that we've tightened security, so if you need anything, please reach out. Remember, there is a security panel in every room. You know how to use it, right?"

"Yes, I remember. But why is security tight now? Did something happen? Should I be worried?"

I cringe at the panic in my voice, but I can't help it. I feel like I'm stranded on a strange island with amazing amenities at my fingertips—including a fuckhot guy, even if he may or may not be my stepbrother soon—but it's still an island. And I'm definitely feeling more alone here than in the city.

"Nothing to worry about, just a safety precaution while Mr. Fitzgerald is away," he says, his mouth in a straight line.

"Okay . . ." Well, that's not reassuring at all. The smell of toasted cheese hits my senses, and I turn around to shut off the burner and flip my sandwich onto the plate. When I turn back around, Dave is gone.

I eat my breakfast at the island and side-eye the room with each bite, half expecting Dave to just show up out of nowhere. Unease flickers in my belly when I really think about what Dave said. *Tightened security*? Was that his nice way of giving me a heads-up that he saw me open the safe? My heart drops.

No. No, don't be ridiculous, I reason with myself.

But just to be on the safe side, I shelve any idea of looking around for clues for the rest of the day.

I wash my dishes and set them in the rack to dry, looking out the window over the sink. I think I'll take a swim to clear my head.

chapter twenty-one

Alaina

I SLIP MY OVERSIZED black sunglasses over my eyes as I step into the backyard. Country club would be a better term for it. The patio area right off the French doors is massive, with what looks like a full outdoor kitchen and enough chairs to seat at least a dozen people. It's partially covered by a pergola with light green fabric woven in between each slat.

To the left is a basketball court that looks to be the size of a real court. On the other side of the pool is the pool house with one of those garage-door window walls.

Straight ahead is the most perfect pool. Shaped like a figure eight with a hot tub right outside next to the far end, the multi-colored tiles on the deck are in shades of black and gray, and the side closest to me is a zero-entry with a tiled floor. A couple of mini waterfalls are wedged in the space between the hot tub and pool and gives it a very cohesive, tropical paradise feel.

Ten poolside loungers and a few side tables frame the space closest to the pool house. A couple of umbrellas are stationed around the pool area, though none of them are opened.

I feel like I'm in an alternate reality here—or on some reality prank show. I spin around slowly, half expecting someone to jump out from behind the hedges and yell "gotcha!"

I walk over to one of the loungers by an umbrella and put my phone down. I toe off my sandals and slip off the Clash tee that I tossed on over my swimsuit as a coverup.

I still can't believe that I let Maddie talk me into getting this swimsuit. We walked into Nordstrom last month, and I had every intention of getting just a plain black swimsuit. Black never goes out of style. I don't usually get anything fancy anyway, since I so rarely have the opportunity to swim anywhere. But since we thought I might join them on their European adventure, I got a few new swimsuits. And since I'm in Boston instead of the beaches of Greece, I wore my favorite one.

It's still black, but it's gorgeous. It's technically called a monokini, but it looks like someone added a line of fabric between the bikini top and the bikini bottoms. The top dips low enough to show some cleavage, and it has straps that crisscross and wrap around my lower back. It'll probably be a pain to take on and off when I have to pee, but it's a small price to pay when it makes me feel this good. This confident.

I snap a photo of myself sitting on the lounger and send it to the girls in our group chat.

Me: Pretending I'm at the beach with you guys! xoxo

Mary must've been on her phone because she sends me five fire emojis instantly.

Mary: You look amazing, Lainey! Where are you?

Me: Thank you! I'm in the backyard—and it's unbelievable! I'll have to video chat you guys and show you!

Maddie: Total smoke show, babe! Yes! Raincheck on the video chat date—we're off to get drinks with some locals we met last night.

Disappointment fills me for a moment before I squash it down. I'm happy they're having fun. A tiny part of me just wishes that I was there with them.

Me: Tell me details tomorrow!

Maddie: Will do! Later, babe!

A small smile plays around my lips as I finger the small strings that attach the top bikini to the bottoms and think about Maddie and Mary tearing up whatever town they're staying in. Those girls know how to cause chaos when necessary, and if you ask Maddie, it's *always* necessary.

I'm determined to make the best of my time here, so after I apply a liberal amount of sunscreen, I scroll through my extensive collection of playlists and look for the perfect one for today.

After another glance around to make sure I'm alone, I hit play on my Sunny Days playlist and walk toward the zero-entry end of the pool. I walk into the water. It feels cool now, but I know by mid-afternoon, it'll feel refreshing. By the time the water reaches my stomach, I take a breath and dive all the way under. When I come up for air, a laugh leaves me as I slide the water off my face.

I'd forgotten how much I enjoy just letting go—is this what carefree feels like?

I mean, sure, I've got a crush on my soon-to-be step-brother, my mother ignores me, and I'm possibly living in a mob boss's house, but I suppose, other than that, yeah, I feel pretty carefree.

I kick back to float on my back and close my eyes, exhaling my worries. Everything sounds different when you're partially submerged under water—even Florence Welch's voice sounds different, more masculine.

I feel droplets of water hit my face, and I open my eyes to see Wolf's upside down face. I startle and lose my balance, and my floating posture collapses.

"I've been looking for you, Red." His cocky smirk both irritates me and turns me on. He's sitting on the edge of the pool with his legs in the water. Wearing only black swim trunks, all six feet of tan, tattooed skin is on display.

Spinning around, I give him my most unimpressed glare, though I doubt he really gets the full effect because of the sunglasses. "What's with the pranks, Wolf?"

He throws his head back and laughs. The sunshine catches on his tousled hair, highlighting the inky-blue undertone. "Oh, baby girl, these are barely even classified as pranks. If you think this is a prank, then I'm not sure you can handle what my brothers and I normally do."

His condescending tone grates on my nerves, and that part of me that always rises to a challenge surges forward.

"Oh yeah? Like what? Pretending to be allergic to some-thing when you're not?" I quirk my brow in challenge.

He chuckles and leans back, placing his palms flat on the ground behind him. "Nah. That wouldn't work on

Rush. He's too much of a control freak, so there'd be no way to get anything past him. And Sully would sooner die than go to a hospital."

I search his face for a moment. "Is he afraid of hospitals? Sully, I mean." Something about Sully sounds familiar to me, but maybe I've been watching too much TV.

"Everyone's afraid of something," Wolf murmurs, his brows drawn in.

"What are you afraid of then?" I tread water as I wait for his answer. I expect something silly like bears or flying, and instead, he knocks me on my ass.

Espresso-brown eyes connect with mine. "Rejection."

"That's . . . not what I was expecting you to say." I can feel my eyebrows at my hairline.

He shrugs, never breaking eye contact with me. "When you grow up how I did, you develop a certain affinity for the truth."

"What do you mean? How did you grow up?"

"A truth for a truth, Red. What are you afraid of?"

Music softly plays in the background while I debate on how deep my truth should be. Let's test the water first—pun not intended.

"Snakes." At his intense stare, I sink into the water, so it's up to my chin. I take a deep breath and exhale slowly. "And . . . that I'm the reason my dad left all those years ago."

He nods but doesn't comment further. Leaning forward, he slips into the pool and swims underwater toward me. When he's a couple of feet away, he emerges and smoothes his wet hair off his face. Sweet Jesus, he looks like Poseidon or Aquaman, all broody intensity and muscles in places I didn't even know existed.

I follow a droplet of water that falls from his pouty bottom lip to his chin and slides down his neck with my gaze, and I swear my nipples tighten in response.

"I spend more time in this pool than anywhere in the house, except maybe the theatre room."

When I don't say anything right away, he murmurs, "A truth for a truth."

I meet his gaze and give him a safer truth. "I room with my twin cousins nine months out of each year. The other three months, I usually have the dorm to myself."

Wolf sinks into the water up to his mouth, his gaze intense and almost predatory.

"I spend one month every summer in Ocean Beach surfing. Usually, my brothers come with me."

"But not this summer?" I sway in the water, enjoying the way it curls around my body with each movement.

"Not this summer," he confirms. "There are things that need my attention here." His gaze never strays from mine.

"Like the wedding?" I wince at the sarcasm in my voice.

"Among other things."

I clench my jaw at his vague answer. I thought this was a truth game? Maybe I should up the stakes. "Ever been in love, Wolf?"

I force myself not to flinch away from his hard stare. I don't know exactly why I asked that—I mean, I do want to know if he's ever been in love, but I'm not sure why I chose *this* moment to blurt that out. It's too late now to take it back even if I wanted to. Which I don't.

A cruel smirk twists his lips, turning his handsome face into something I don't immediately recognize. "Love?" He scoffs. "I'll do you one better—I've never had a girlfriend." His words say one thing, but his tone is a challenge.

"Never?" I gasp, disbelief coloring my voice. "As in not one girl? Wait, are you—" I clamp my mouth shut, but the damage is already done.

He tips his head back and laughs like I just told the punchline to the funniest joke he's ever heard. I know he's not a virgin, I mean, Jesus, look at him. All wet and sun-kissed with those inky-black lashes and that pouty bottom lip—he's a lethal combination, and no girl would be able to resist that pull.

Hell, I can't even resist it—*him*—and I have some very good reasons.

I feel my cheeks flush, and I grit my teeth, fighting the glare I want to unleash on him. When his laugh peters out, I grit out, "You done yet?"

With mirth and amusement shining in his espresso eyes, the flecks of silver and slate-gray shining, he says, "Oh, no, baby girl. I'm just getting started. And to answer your question, no. No girl has ever had the pleasure of being my girlfriend. But don't worry, Red, I've never had any complaints about *anything*."

I feel my cheeks heat at his insinuation and sink further into the water. I tried to shock him, but it ended up backfiring.

"Come on," Wolf says as he swims to one side of the pool.

I follow him and sit next to him on the built-in bench seat. I lean my head back on the lip of the pool and let the sunshine warm my face.

"You could map constellations on those things," Wolf murmurs.

My heart skips a beat, and I crack an eye open to peer at him. "What did you say?"

He slowly brings his finger to my cheekbone, giving me plenty of time to move. But I don't. He slowly trails his finger over my cheek and down my neck in a random pattern, and then it clicks.

He's tracing my freckles.

I stare at his eyes as he stares at the path his finger is taking.

"Have you ever let anyone trace your constellations, Red?" His voice is low and rough.

I slowly shake my head and swallow. "No one."

"Mmm," he says as he leans toward me.

I hold my breath as he places a soft kiss on my shoulder, right where I know a cluster of freckles loosely resembles Ursa Minor.

"So beautiful," he breathes against my skin.

I tip my chin toward him, ready and waiting for his lips to land on mine. I'm breathless with anticipation, fingers tingling.

With a sigh, he sits back and drapes his arms across the ledge behind him. I stop myself from groaning at the loss of contact.

He tips his head back and closes his eyes. "A truth for a truth, Red."

"I haven't lived with my mom since I was eight." I hold my breath when I scan his face for a reaction to my truth. When he doesn't so much as twitch, I continue, "And when she asked me to move in with her this summer, I thought . . . I don't know what I thought." I sigh. "But I didn't expect"—I gesture to the mansion in front of us—"this."

He tilts his head toward me and pins me with his intense gaze. "Cormac isn't my dad biologically, he's my uncle."

My mouth parts with his admission. "Okay . . ." I pause, thinking about giving him an out and blurting out another truth, but then I remember my truths, and

I ask what I really want to know. "Where are your parents then?"

"Lily is dead, and Seamus is in prison." He's so matter of fact, not a single emotion is visible on his handsome face. "They stopped by for Rush's first birthday, and halfway through the party, they left and never came back. A few years ago, Rush was able to track their movements and figure out what happened." He shrugs as if he's not bothered by it, but my heart aches for him.

"Wolf, I . . ."—I turn and reach for his hand, skimming the water's surface and lace my fingers with his—"I'm sorry," I whisper.

"Don't be, Red. Cormac is my da in all the ways that count. He's raised me since I was three, and I couldn't have asked for a better role model." Despite the cocky smirk on his face, his voice rings with sincerity. "Besides, now you know you're not really banging your stepbrother," he says with a dirty little smile.

I can't help the laugh that bubbles up. With a smirk, I cut my arm across the water, creating a mini wave that splashes him right in the face. "I wasn't worried about it."

He wipes the water from his face with both hands and grins, a manic predatory sort of grin that does all sorts of things to me. "A dirty bird, I like it."

He stares at my mouth with a possessive hunger in his gaze, and I tremble in response. A slow smile spreads across my face as I push off the wall a split second before he lunges for me. He grabs me around the waist and hoists me in the air. I'm laughing too hard to protest too much, and he launches me into the air. I have just enough time to hold my breath before I hit the water with a huge splash.

My toes just graze the pool floor before I swim to the surface. I toss my head back and smooth my wet hair back, so it's off my face and notice I lost my sunglasses somewhere.

I can't keep the smile from my face as I look to Wolf, who's ten feet away and grinning like a lunatic. A super hot, tattooed, soaking wet lunatic.

"You ready, baby girl?"

"I'm ready, Wolf."

A sense of déjà vu hits me, and I feel vertigo for a moment. I shake off the dizziness and swim toward him.

I'm going to dunk that boy.

chapter twenty-two

Wolf

HOURS LATER, WE'RE both sufficiently pruny, and her nose, cheeks, and shoulders are pink.

"Alright, Red. Time to get out. You're getting fried, baby girl." I swim to the zero-entry end of the pool and walk out.

Red follows me to the pool house, where I show her where the beach towels are. I toss a towel around my shoulders and drape the other one around her, helping her dry off.

Goosebumps coat her soft skin from the air conditioning in here, and I kneel to rub her legs under the guise of drying her off. Honestly, I just want to fucking touch her soft skin again.

Her stomach chooses that moment to growl, which thankfully cuts the tension a little. I was getting dangerously close to sporting some serious wood. It's a real bitch getting a hard-on in swim trunks. And Red's skimpy swimsuit doesn't help matters much.

It was easier to ignore when we were in the pool and she was mostly underwater. And even though she says she doesn't care about us possibly being stepsiblings, I'm not sure that I buy it. The girl moved into a strange house with strange dudes just because her mom mentioned it.

I mean, fuck—we could've been *anyone*.

Murderous rage wells up inside me when I think about someone else touching her and tracing her soft skin, and my hands involuntarily clench around her thighs.

A quiet moan escapes her, and I flick my gaze to her face to read her. I've always been good at reading people—not as good as Sully, no one is as good at reading a room as that motherfucker—but good enough to tell that she's turned on. Her cheeks are flushed, her eyes are glassy, and her chest is rising quickly.

"Wolf." Her voice is low, and my cock twitches in response.

I lean forward, so my face is closer to her pussy and breathe the word, "Yes?"

"I need—" She groans and shifts from foot to foot, rubbing her thighs together and bringing her body closer to my face.

I nudge my nose along the crease of her thigh and pussy, and murmur, "What do you need, baby girl?"

"You—" Her word ends on a sigh as I slide my hands along her legs, my fingertips grazing the inside of her thighs from behind.

A knock on the door stops my movements. Only a handful of people are even on the property right now, but I doubt any of them would track me down at the pool house.

In one quick motion, I twist around and grab the Glock 19 strapped underneath the side table and stand up, placing Red behind me. Fierce protectiveness descends over me, slowing everything down until my goal is crystal clear: protect Alaina, eliminate the threat.

With my left hand, I reach back and gently nudge her behind me further. "Shh now, Red. Duck behind that chair, yeah?"

"What's going on, Wolf? You're freaking me out," she whispers just as another knock hits the door, harder this time.

"It's alright, baby girl, just get behind the chair, and if anything happens, you run to the bedroom down the hall and press the blue button on the intercom system." I glance over my shoulder at her and see her eyes are glassy, and her movements are a little jerky, but she's following my directions without breaking down, so I know she'll be okay.

"Okay, Wolf."

I wait a moment until she's tucked behind the black leather overstuffed chair. On silent feet, I step toward the front door to the pool house. I'm thankful that I had the foresight to close and lock it when we came in here for towels.

This could be a very different situation if we'd stayed in the pool for another twenty minutes.

I press my back into the wall next to the door and wait until the pounding starts again. I grip the door handle and count to three in my head, and then I wrench it open with one hand and bring up the gun to whoever's on the other side of the door.

"Dave," I grit out between my clenched teeth, my gun still aimed at Dave's forehead. "What the fuck are you doing? I could've killed you."

I drop my arm and engage the safety, holding it next to me as I stare at the head of our security team, who definitely should know better than to pound on a door unannounced.

"Apologies, Wolf. But I tried calling you and paging the entire system, but I didn't hear back from you."

I have to give Dave respect. He just stands there, respectful but not backing down. The man is made of steel—he didn't even flinch when I had that Glock to his forehead—and one of the most loyal. "Fuck, Dave. What's going on?"

"Rush will be here tonight. He called us since he couldn't get a hold of you. He wanted to give us a heads-up since our security measures were upped."

I tip my head back and exhale a breath, trying to will the adrenaline still coursing through my bloodstream to calm the fuck down. "Fuck, I haven't checked my phone all day. I've been in the pool."

"I know, Wolf, that's why I came to tell you personally. I knew you were with Miss McElroy—"

"Alaina." She tsks at Dave like he's a misbehaving kindergartener and not one of the deadliest men I know.

I look over at her. She's tentatively standing behind the armchair, so I tilt my head to the right, silently asking her to join me.

A smirk tips up one side of his mouth. "I knew you were with *Alaina*, so I came to tell you and check on things."

"Alright, Dave. Thanks for the heads-up. We'll be in the main house if you need anything else. Remind me to check the intercom system in here since I didn't hear anything. This isn't the time for shit to stop working correctly."

174

"Alright, Wolf, Alaina. Have a good evening." Dave turns on his heel and walks down the pathway that leads to the front of the house.

I watch him walk away as I debate on what to say to Red. On the one hand, she's going to be family soon, so she'll find out sooner or later. On the other hand, I don't know what the fuck is going on with Da these days, so it's possible he's pulling some weird Houdini shit, and Red'll be gone in a week.

It's tough to say what the old man is up to these days. He's cagey as fuck—come to think of it, I bet that's where Rush gets it from.

I rub my free hand over the scruff on my face. "Fuck it." If the old man can seemingly wing it, then so can I.

I double-check that the safety is on, and I place the gun back in the holder underneath the side table and turn to a wide-eyed Red.

"Hungry? I could go for some pizza. How about you?"

"I can always go for pizza." She stares at me as if she's unsure what's happening.

Baby girl, that makes two of us. I'm just making this shit up as I go.

I grab her tee from where it landed when we first got in here and slide it over her head.

"Perfect, unless you eat pineapple on your pizza. Then we're going to have to talk about the right and wrong way to enjoy pizza."

"Pfft. Pineapple is delicious"—she pauses and smirks at me, this mischievous little smile that has my dick getting hard—"but not on your pizza," she says as she slides her arms through her shirt. It settles down around her upper thighs, and I get my first good look at her shirt. It's a band tee.

"Aren't you just full of surprises?" I scan the faded screen print of London Calling on the front of her black tee. "Favorite Clash song?"

"Oh"—she tugs on the hem and shrugs her shoulders—"they're all good."

I nod and hold her hand, interlacing our fingers together. The corners of my lips tip up when I think about Sully seeing my girl—our new stepsister—in a Clash shirt. "Sully's gonna love you. He's a huge Clash fan."

"Hmm. What about you? What's your favorite Clash song?"

I lead us toward the house, grab our phones on the entryway table, and say, "Hateful, probably. But Train in Vain is up there too." She looks at me with raised brows. "What?" I quirk a brow. "You thought I wouldn't name one? By now you should know me well enough to know that I value truths."

"I guess I'm not the only one full of surprises then," she says as she squeezes my hand.

I lead her down the brick pathway to the main house. "C'mon, Red. Let's order a pizza and listen to The Clash while we wait for it."

She looks over at me as we walk down the brick pathway framed by colorful flowers and low-lying bushes. Her whisky eyes twinkle in amusement as she asks, "Will there be dancing?"

I flash her a wide grin. "Absolutely. I'll even let you pick the first song."

She playfully bumps her shoulder into me, and something warm tingles throughout my body. It's strange but not unpleasant. "You've got yourself a deal. I hope you like '80s music."

chapter twenty-three

Alaina

I TAKE A BITE out of my sausage and artichoke pizza; the cheese stretching from my mouth to my slice a foot in front of my face. Wolf watches me with a wide grin, eyes twinkling in amusement, and I can't help but laugh.

I haven't had this much fun with someone other than Maddie and Mary in years. Except for . . . *him*. My heart still clenches at the merest thought about him, so I do my best not to think about him often.

"Hey, where'd you go?"

"Hmm?" I finish chewing my bite, wipe my mouth with a napkin, and force a smile. "I'm right here. This pizza is delicious, by the way. I didn't know Boston had pizza like this."

Wolf hooks a finger around his beer bottle and brings it to his lips for a drink. The little smirk he sends my way increases the warmth that's been pooling low in my belly since I saw him standing outside the pool this morning.

If I'm being honest, I've felt the embers of attraction from the moment I saw him. There's something about the messy black hair and the tattoos and the fuck-it attitude that really does it for me.

And every time he smirks at me or teases me with that little sparkle in his espresso-brown eyes or flashes that delicious vee my way, it fans the flames. And so here I am, dressed in a damp bikini and old band tee, squeezing my thighs together and scolding my libido to chill out.

"I'm not surprised, it's a local favorite. How long did you live in Boston?"

I quirk a brow. "I never said I lived in Boston."

"Aye, but your ma did. That's how she met my da. They were at a local festival, or at least that's what he told me. Who knows, maybe they met at something else entirely." He waggles his eyebrows at me.

I throw my balled-up napkin at him and miss by a mile. "Gross."

"Oh, baby girl, we're going to have to work on your aim," he says with a chuckle. "I take it you didn't play a lot of sports in school."

"Nope." I pop the p with a smile. "But I was on the dance team, and I sang in the choir."

His gaze roams over my face, and I'm close enough to see the flecks of smoky gray in his eyes as they darken with desire. "I look forward to hearing you sing again. And watching you shake that sweet ass tonight. I've got the perfect song in mind."

My breath hitches at his tone, full of dark promises. Changing the subject, so I don't embarrass myself more, I blurt, "Maybe we can sing together sometime?"

He pauses, the beer bottle halfway to his mouth. "Nah. I don't sing."

"Everyone can sing, Wolf."

"I didn't say I can't sing. I said I don't sing, and I definitely don't sing with anyone." His voice is hard, leaving no room for argument.

Disappointment hitches in my chest, and I distract myself by tidying the table.

"But I do dance."

A bubble of excitement surges inside, and I try to contain my smile. Judging by his wide answering grin, I don't think I succeed. "Of course you do," I tease. He stands up and rounds the table, holding out his hand to me. I place my hand in his, and he pulls me up. Desire warms my limbs as we stand close enough that my tits brush his chest with every breath. I look at him from underneath my lashes, something warm rolling through my veins with every breath that brings us closer.

Shaking off the intensity, I break the connection and cross the kitchen to plug my phone into the speaker system. "I seem to remember you promising me the first song choice. Are you ready?"

He assesses me for a moment before a slow grin spreads across his face. "Aye. Hit me with it."

There's plenty of space between the breakfast nook and island to have a proper dance party, so I cue up my party songs from the 2010s playlist and hit play. I spin around so I can savor his reaction, and he doesn't disappoint. The sight of him with his head thrown back in laughter steals my breath for a moment.

I sway to the beat as I walk toward him, giggling the whole way. This is the second time today I feel this light and carefree. It hasn't escaped my notice that Wolf has been around both times. And I'm not even talking about what almost happened in the pool house. I can't stop wondering what would've happened if Dave knocked ten minutes later.

Or if he didn't knock at all.

What a cruel twist of fate that he's going to be my stepbrother.

Maybe, that little voice says, *or maybe he's going to be your boyfriend.*

Twisting my lips at the idea of calling Wolf mine, I eye him, eager to see his skills on our makeshift dance floor.

"I wasn't expecting this to be your first song choice." He grins and runs a hand through his hair.

"What's wrong with some Lil Jon? He breaks the ice nicely, don't you think?" I raise an eyebrow as I sing the lyrics and shake my ass.

"Aye, he does. But I get to pick next."

I shrug and twirl around, swinging my hips to the beat. Shimmying my shoulders, I laugh as I sing the ridiculous lyrics at him.

With each sway of my hips, a worry slides off my shoulders. And with each loudly sung lyric, a weight lifts from my soul. Until I feel unfiltered joy wrapping around me like my favorite jacket—comforting and warm.

With a carefree boldness I only feel around my cousins, I pull out all the fan favorites: the sprinkler, the grocery cart, and cracking pepper. And I'm not disappointed when he tips his head back in laughter and joins me for his own rendition of the Charleston.

With our gazes locked on one another and matching wide grins, I feel it. An electric current that shoots out and tethers us to one another, crackling in the air.

He's so goddamn charming that seeing him break out the mashed potato dance in nothing by black swim trunks and a smile stops my heart for a moment.

I shrug and keep dancing, bounding on the balls of my feet and really letting loose. I'm not even surprised that Wolf can dance. He moves effortlessly, swaying and staying on beat.

I'm not even surprised that he can dance, not really. He seems like the type of guy who's good at everything he tries.

We alternate song choices, and somewhere along the way, the songs get slower, and the bass drops. Our silly dances morph into something less innocent. A playful, teasing sort of dance that has Wolf leaning toward me when I lean away, heartbeat in my ears.

A sultry soundtrack to the desire in the air between us, soaking into my skin and heightening my senses.

He palms the back of my neck and pulls me in close. "C'mere, baby girl," he whispers against my lips. My tits press against his chest, and I bite my lip as I stare up at him through my lashes. I never realized how tall he is until this moment. I push onto my tiptoes just to see how close I can get, and it's not close enough.

With his hand gripping the back of my neck, he holds me still as we sway to the beat. My pulse roars in my ears—and in my clit, beating in tandem to the song.

With Maddie's voice in my head telling me to climb him like a tree, I slide my palms up his abs and chest, each bump and dip ramping up my desire. I wet my lips involuntarily and push against his hard chest until he takes a step backward. I keep pushing until the back of his knees hit a chair. I slide my hands up to his shoulders, the skin soft and hot and push him until he's sitting down. Using his shoulders as leverage, I straddle him, but I don't sink down. Not yet.

I give myself a minute to explore and run my hands up into his hair, pulling firmly. He groans and closes his eyes halfway. He likes a bite of pain with his pleasure—I can work with that.

In one swift movement, I sink onto his lap, his hard cock hitting all the right places. With my grip on his hair, I tug his face toward mine. I swipe my tongue across his lips, and all semblance of control snaps. He surges forward, hooking his arms around my back so his hands touch my shoulder blades. He kisses me with possession, dominating my mouth. I relinquish control and kiss him back, starving for the connection that feels a lot more than simple lust.

I roll my hips, moaning at the feel of his cock hitting my clit at just the right angle. I tear my mouth to the side, gasping for air, never stopping the movement of my hips. Wolf runs his nose along my neck, dropping hot, open-mouthed kisses.

"Wolf." I breathe his name, my breath hitching as he thrusts at the same time I sink down hard. "I-I'm close."

He groans, his breath skating across my flushed skin. "That's it, Red. Right there."

chapter twenty-four

RUSH

MUSIC BLARES FROM somewhere in the back of the house, and even though it's loud, I know my brother. He's got some bird with him.

That's the one good thing about this house—every little noise carries. I've been telling Da it's too big for the four of us for years, but he always insisted the extra space is necessary when we have the other members over—and for appearances. Fuck appearances, I'd rather feel the security of knowing my house is safe. And I don't get that from this museum we call home. That's part of the reason I suggested the lockdown. It seems we're on the verge of another motherfucking war.

I slowly walk down the hallway, muscles tense, and pull my favorite SIG Sauer from the back of my pants. Dave didn't mention approving entry to anyone, but he underestimates my brother's affinity for women. He's more than capable of sneaking someone in without raising any alarms. My trigger finger twitches when I think of who he could've brought home. Some random local or a plant sent here to send us all to meet our makers?

I don't trust anyone. Not with the way people are getting popped left and right, combined with the lack of intel on who the fucking enemy is.

The closer I get to the kitchen, the louder the music blares. It must be the built-in speakers that we rarely use. I only remember that we have them because I used some of the wiring for the upgraded security system I installed a few years ago.

Jesus Christ.

The music is loud enough to conceal a small fucking army storming through the house—what the fuck is he thinking? I could be anyone right now, and that motherfucker and his *guest* would be eliminated before they even heard a creak in the floorboard.

I should've just stayed at the shared flat in the city tonight and actually slept, but fuck me, I wanted to get home and check on my girl. I set up some basic security outside her place a while ago, and an agreement in place with a few friends in the city who keep an eye on her. Even though I haven't heard anything from them, the Mama Rosa's explosion has me fucking twitchy. I've been spending a lot of time at the pub, and now that there's an unknown player on the board, I don't know what I don't know.

And I fucking hate not knowing.

I stand in the entryway to the kitchen, still partially concealed by the shadows. I clench my jaw and tighten my grip around my gun at the sight of Wolf sitting on a chair at the breakfast nook facing me with a redhead straddling his lap. In only an oversized shirt.

I squint as I take in the situation—namely, the redhead. There's something vaguely familiar about the color of her hair.

If I wasn't so goddamn tired, I probably would've seen the situation clearer. But I hadn't slept more than a few hours in the last few days, and my patience was thin on the best of days.

Right now, it was nonexistent.

I take two steps inside the kitchen. "What the fuck, Wolf?" My voice menacing and loud, bouncing off the walls. The redhead jumps about a foot off of his lap, and I smirk. She's a jumpy little thing—*good*.

I walk over to the refrigerator where the control panel is and turn the music down. I never turn my back to Wolf, and it doesn't go unnoticed.

Eyes narrowing, he tightens his hands around her waist. Never taking his eyes off of me, he says softly, "Shh, Red. It's just my brother."

My gaze zero-in on the possessive way his hands flex around her waist, right below where her damp hair lays in waves down her back. I lean against the counter next to the fridge and eye my brother and his little toy. "What's this now?" I gesture to him and the redhead with my gun.

Wolf's brows crease as he stares at me for a moment. "You wanna stop acting like a dick and put the gun down?"

I bark out a sarcastic laugh. "Me?"—I scoff and push off the countertop—"I'm not the one endangering everyone by bringing some piece home while we're on the brink of war!" My voice rises as I talk, and by the end, I'm yelling at him. "She could be a goddamn Trojan horse, Wolf!"

Out of the corner of my eye, I see the redhead jump again and lean into my brother, and something inside of me pulls taut. I can feel the vein in my temple throbbing as I grip my gun again.

I recognize that I'm acting irrationally, but if I didn't always make sure we were safe, then who would?

I watch with narrowed eyes as Wolf taps the girl on her bare thigh, murmuring something in her ear too low for me to hear. She stands up and moves off of his lap, her hair hanging in her face. Wolf moves her behind him, and then I can't see her at all.

There's something achingly familiar about her—it must be the color. I've only seen that shade of red a few times in my life, and one of them is on my little bird.

Wolf takes a few steps toward me, his eyebrows drawn together and head tilted to the side. "Come on, brother. There's nothing duplicitous going on here. When's the last time you slept?"

I scrub a hand over my face and lean my head back to look at the ceiling. "I don't know. I caught a few hours in the last couple of days," I say on a sigh. I look back at my brother and say, "But you can't be bringing girls in here like usual, man, this is serious this time."

His jaw flexes. "I know it's serious," he grits out. "And I didn't bring anyone in,"—he tilts his head to the side—"this is Lana's girl."

At the mention of Lana, familiar warm brown eyes the color of my favorite whiskey peek over Wolf's shoulder. And my heart fucking stops.

"Declan?"

chapter twenty-five

Alaina

I FEEL DIZZY WHEN I lock eyes with Declan, my mystery man from O'Malley's Pub.

"Declan?" I ask again when no one answers me the first time. His eyes go wide, and his mouth falls slack for a split second before his face transforms into the familiar blank mask I'm used to seeing at the pub every week. Every week except last week, when he kissed me like I was the very oxygen he needed to live.

I take two quick steps back. "I-I don't understand. What's going on?" I look between Wolf and Declan, waiting for someone to explain what the fuck is happening. My back hits the counter, and I wince as the handles to the junk drawers dig into my spine.

What the fuck is happening right now? To my absolute horror, my eyes begin to fill with tears. A curse that I've had since I was young—anytime I get angry or scared,

I start to cry. It's a messed-up defense mechanism if you ask me.

The universe must take pity on me since neither one of them is looking at me. Instead, they're communicating with their eyebrows and clenched jaws. The silence is unnerving.

Wolf pivots, so both Declan and I are in view, but he doesn't say anything. I stare at him, willing him with my eyes to explain what's going on.

"Wolf?" I prompt. "You said your brothers' names were Rush and Sully. *Not* Declan. So, what. the fuck. is going on?"

Wolf slowly lowers his head to look between Declan and me. A cruel smile plays on his lips as he says, "Red, meet my brother Declan, but he goes by Rush." He takes a few steps to the chair that I was just straddling him in ten minutes ago and kicks it toward me. "Sit. It seems we have some things to catch up on, wouldn't you say, brother? Or should I call you Declan now?" He sneers, acid dripping from each word thrown at Declan.

I'm struggling to figure out the dynamic here, but one thing's for sure—I'm in over my head. I touch the sore spot on my back from where I jammed it against the drawer handle, and the pain is enough to break through the fog clouding my brain right now.

While Declan—*Rush*—and Wolf glare daggers at one another, I quietly open the second drawer and slip my hand inside.

"So, you just decided the best way to get information outta Lana's girl is with your tongue?" Rush snarls, his nostrils flaring. This is a side of Rush that I've never seen in all the weeks he's come to the pub.

Wolf laughs, this caustic noise that seems to egg Rush on further if his clenched fists are anything to go by.

I move the loose papers and takeout menus to the side and feel around for the gun that I found yesterday—or was that today? I feel like Alice after she goes down the rabbit hole and lands in Wonderland where time doesn't work the same, and everything is trippy and laced with double meaning.

"What's the matter, Rush? Are you jealous that I had Red's perfect pussy grinding against my cock while you were fucking around in the city?" Wolf taunts with a sneer.

The cool metal of the Sig Sauer touches my fingertips, and I slowly pull it forward. I wince when it bumps against something inside the drawer, but neither boy so much as spare me a glance.

I feel the violence shimmering in the air.

Rush cocks his head to the side. "Oh, you mean my sloppy seconds, *brother*?"

Wolf swings his glare to me. "What the fuck is he talking about, Red?"

Rush turns to face me, standing close to Wolf. "Yeah, Red, why don't you tell my brother here all about how you were all over me just a few days ago." Rush's smile is hard and taunting.

Hurt flashes across Wolf's face for a moment before what I'm now dubbing the Fitzpatrick glare takes its place.

Being on the receiving end of one Fitzpatrick glare is more than enough, two seems like overkill. I grit my teeth as I glance between them both, my hand firmly wrapped around the handle of the gun.

In one swift motion, I pull it out of the drawer and level it on them. My hands shake, and I don't have it in me to be embarrassed about that. My adrenaline is spiking again, and my fight-or-flight response is screaming at me to run. I stuff everything down deep where I can't reach it. Right now, all I need to do is get the fuck out of this Fitzgerald Fun House and get as far away as I can.

I wiggle my toes, remembering that I'm still barefoot and wearing a swimsuit and an oversized tee. A heavy coldness starts in the pit of my stomach and spreads outward, blanketing my panic and replacing it with numbness and cool calculation.

I take a step to the side along the wall, toward the hallway, never taking my eyes off of them. I'm smart enough to realize that they're the real predators in the room—I'm just a sheep in wolf's clothing.

"Here's what's going to happen. I'm going to walk out that front door, and you're going to let me." I take two more steps and watch their gazes track my every movement like true predators.

Standing next to each other like they are, I see it. Their thick arms crossed across wide, muscular chests, prominent brows furrowed over narrowed eyes, and similar strong jawlines. They're definitely related.

"I don't know what the fuck is going on, but I'm not going to play this little game. I don't even want to know how you got my mom to play along." I'm impressed with how steady my voice is.

Wolf uncrosses his arms and shakes them out, flexing his hands. He bounces on the balls of his feet as if he's getting ready to run after me. Fuck. He's going to call my bluff.

"Wolf," I plead in a low voice. "Please don't do this."

"Sorry, baby girl, I can't let you leave," he answers, regret in his eyes.

"Declan?" I flick my gaze to him, and he just shakes his head slowly, his gaze never leaving mine.

"Then you leave me no choice," I say as I take another step backward into the dark hallway.

"There's always a choice, little bird," Rush says as he looks over my shoulder and nods.

I whirl around to see what he's nodding at. "Wha—"

"Uh-uh-uh," a man says as he grabs the gun from my hand. "Looks like I got home in the nick of time, huh?" He chuckles, his voice dark and deep. "What would you do without me to always clean up after you guys? The safety's still on, anyway."

I'm frozen, and my chest feels tight at the sound of his voice.

He grabs me by the shoulder and spins me around, so I'm facing the kitchen again. "Come on, let's get this over with. I'm starving. It was a long-ass drive from up north."

My shock makes me surprisingly pliable, and I don't put up much of a fight as he frog-marches me back into the kitchen and over to the breakfast nook.

I spin around, my hair whipping him, heart lodged in my throat. And come face to face with one of the most gorgeous men I have ever laid eyes on. Messy dark-blond hair, long enough to reach his ears, scruff covering his sharp jawline, and eyes the color of the sea before a storm.

My ex-boyfriend.

A ringing noise fills my ears as the color leeches from his face, and his eyes go wide. "Holy fuck. Alaina?"

That's the last thing I hear before everything goes black.

chapter twenty-six

Wolf

I WATCH AS MY youngest brother, Sully, disarms the fiery little redhead in one quick motion. I hate the panic I see in her eyes, but I can't let her leave.

Not only because Da would have my head, but because *I'm* not sure what the fuck is going on. I glance at Rush out of the corner of my eye. His face is a void of emotion, but he's clenching and unclenching his fists. I've never seen him so fucking jittery.

It's freaking me the fuck out. I huff as I cross my arms and try to focus on what Sully's saying.

"When did he get here? I thought he was with the boys up north," I say quietly to Rush.

His intense gaze follows Sully and Red like a hawk, a vein popping out in his neck. "I don't know," he murmurs. "I don't know what the fuck is going on anymore, and I don't fucking like it."

Sully pushes Red toward the breakfast nook, and she spins around, hair flying to face him.

"Holy fuck, Alaina?" Sully croaks. A second later, her eyes widen before they flutter closed, and she faints.

I dart over to her, but Sully catches her before I get there. He clutches her with one arm behind her back and the other under her knees. He spins around to face us, holding her close to his chest.

"One of you motherfuckers better start talking. What the fuck is my ex-girlfriend doing in our house?" Sully roars.

I wouldn't be more shocked if Tom Hanks strolled through the patio door whistling Whitney Houston than I am staring at my brother completely lose his shit. Make that *brothers*.

Rush is holding on by a thread, and I'm not sure what's going to set him off: the fact that Red is Sully's ex or the fact that thirty minutes ago, I had my tongue down her throat or the fact that she's Lana's daughter. What I can't quite pinpoint is how he knows her—because there's no way he gets this high-strung over some bird he barely knows. No, I know my brother well enough to know that something else is at play here.

I take a step toward Sully and reach for Red. "Here, I'll take her to her room. Then I think we need to talk—all of us," I say sharply.

Sully hugs her closer to her chest as scoffs. "Please, she barely weighs anything. I'll carry her."

Red groans and puts a hand to her head. "Wh-what's going on?" Her fearful eyes search out Sully first, then me, and I have a hard time tamping down my jealousy.

I stare at him for a moment before I nod in agreement. "Follow me. You fainted, Red. We're taking you to your room to rest." I look back at Rush as I lead Sully out of the kitchen. "You too, Rush."

Rush stares at Red in Sully's arms with the intensity of a lion watching a gazelle waiting for the right moment to pounce.

They follow me down the hallway and up the stairs to the second floor. We turn left toward our bedrooms. "She's in the pink guest room." I stop in front of her bedroom door and take a deep breath. Tingles race down my spine as I reach for the handle. This feels like more than just putting Sully's ex-girlfriend, who's now my girl and possibly our new stepsister, in her bed after she fainted.

Well, that's a weird fucking thought.

But it's true. This feels like more than the simple act of opening a door. This feels like we're about to cross into uncharted territory, and I don't have the fucking blueprints.

I take a deep breath, twist the knob, and open her door.

This isn't the first time I've been in here, so I walk right to her bed and help Sully get her situated comfortably. I tilt her head to the side and make sure she doesn't have any bumps or bruising. I don't think she hit her head, but Sully's big ass blocked most of my view.

"She didn't hit her head," the man in question confirms like he was reading my goddamn mind.

She places her hand over mine on her face. "He's right. It was just a shock. I'm fine." Her big eyes are wide and pleading with me for something I'm not sure I can give her. I don't have any answers.

"Shit, man"—I grimace—"I forgot how easily you can read people."

He shrugs in response, staring at her for a moment before turning and walking out of the room.

194

Wolf

"Fuck," Rush murmurs as he walks further into room, peering at everything as he passes it. "I'd forgotten how absolutely *pink* this room is. Why didn't they give her the blue or gray guest rooms? Those are less . . . loud."

I shrug. "Dunno. Da probably figured she'd like the pink since she's a girl. Speaking of Da, I think we need to have a conversation with him, yeah?" I pin my brother with a stare.

Rush nods. "Yeah, but not here." His face softens when he looks at her on the bed, and that freaks me out more than anything. "Stay here and rest, yeah?"

I've never seen my brother look at anything the way he's looking at her—not even the one girl he brought around for a while.

She glances between Rush and me before she finally nods.

I follow Rush to his room across the hall, but I leave her door partially open. I want to be able to hear her if she needs anything. Once we're inside Rush's room, he goes right to his monitors and turns on all six of them and starts typing.

I grab a seat on his lounger in the corner and stare at Sully, who was already sitting on the couch across from me. Pulling out my phone, I dial Da and leave him a voicemail when he doesn't answer. "Da, it's me. We've got a bit of a situation here, but nothing that requires any baked goods. It's about our little birdie—call me when you get this." I end the call and lean my head back against the wall.

While Rush mutters to himself as his fingers fly over the keyboard, I figure there's no time like the present to start unraveling this clusterfuck.

"Why are you home, Sully? Last I heard, Da sent you up to Nolan to be our eyes and ears." I eye him carefully.

195

"I was. I spent three days there, and that was more than enough to gather that no one knows shit up there. And they definitely aren't planning a war. Then Nolan got called in for a family reunion across the pond, so when I got Rush's voicemail to come home early, I did."

"Fuuuck." I groan and tip my head forward to look at him. "Did Rush tell you *why* he wanted you to come home?" I drum my fingers on my legs as I wait for his answer.

"No," he snapped. "So imagine my surprise to come home and find Alaina in our kitchen."

"Mama Rosa's burned down tonight," Rush says as he turns to face us. "There were some casualties. I'm sorry, man. I know how much you loved that place—and those people."

Pressing a palm to his mouth, he lets it slide off, and his Adam's apple bobs a few times before he speaks again. "Do we know who?"

Rush shakes his head. "Not yet, but there was a tea party happening. I'm not sure if Matteo was there or not."

Sully hangs his head, his hands threading through his hair. "Goddamn it!" he roars as he stands up. He fishes his phone out of his pocket and calls someone. "You better not be dead, motherfucker," he mutters with the phone to his ear. "Voicemail," he grumbles. "Matteo, I just heard about Mama Rosa's; call me back as soon as you can." He ends the call and tosses his phone to the coffee table between us.

"We don't know who started the fire, but considering it was a frequent hangout of ours, and Matteo is climbing the ranks in the Russo family, it could've been for either one of us," Rush offers.

"Yeah, except that we're usually in the city on Fridays, not Mondays," Sully challenges.

"About that," I say with an edge to my voice. "Wanna tell us how you know Red?"

"Who the fuck is *Red*?" Sully sneers.

"No," Rush says simply.

"No? What do you mean *no*? That's not how this works, fucker. We don't keep secrets, and she"—I point toward her room across the hall—"feels like a pretty big fucking secret right about now."

Rush grips the bridge of his nose and sighs audibly. "Fine. Give me a minute to check something. I'm trying to see if I can see any footage of Mama Rosa's tonight." He spins his fancy-ass leather computer chair around and starts clicking, bringing different CCTV footage up on one screen.

I see the familiar entrance to O'Malley's Irish Pub on one screen, and curiosity gets the best of me. I walk over to stand behind him and wait for him to explain what we're looking at.

"Don't stand behind me," Rush snaps without even looking.

"Fine," I huff, rolling my eyes. I move to his right side. "What are we looking at? And why do you have security on O'Malley's?"

"These are CCTV cams I pulled to see if I can get any different angles. And this"—he points to the monitor with O'Malley's—"is for my own protection. I'm there every Friday night, it'd be stupid not to have eyes on it."

I nod. "That makes sense."

He snorts but doesn't reply. Five minutes later, he's pulled every CCTV cam in the area and nothing to show for it. I release a sigh and walk back to the couch, sitting down on one end.

Rush walks over to his mini bar in the corner of the room. He pulls out three highball glasses and pours us each three fingers of his favorite whiskey. He brings them over to the sitting area and places them on the coffee table before he sits down in the armchair next to me.

"Alright, brothers, I think we're going to need these for this conversation."

Sully's raised eyebrows match mine.

I reach for my glass and take a sip. The whiskey is smooth with a pleasant bite at the end.

"I'll start," I offer when no one says anything for a minute. "I met Red—*Alaina*—when I picked her up from the train station. And with the exception of the first night when Da and I had dinner with her and Lana—"

"How was her mom? Were they acting, I don't know, different?" Sully inquires.

"Different how?" I scratch the scruff on my jaw.

He shrugs. "Dunno. Cagey or overly nice or whatever the fuck people do when they're trying to con you?"

"Nah." I shake my head and take another sip. "If anything, her mom was acting like she didn't want Red around." I pause for a moment. "You ever hear of a parent who doesn't go to their kid's graduation because they were too busy shopping before?" I purse my lips and run a hand across the back of my neck.

Rush shakes his head slowly. "Hmm. That's . . . odd behavior. I'll look into Lana further now that we have Alaina to link to her." He stares into his nearly empty glass and mutters, "Still doesn't explain why I couldn't find anything on her before."

"So, it's only been us here. So, we've been hanging out." I feign nonchalance.

Rush glares at me as he sips his whiskey. "Sure as fuck didn't look like just *hanging out* when I saw you earlier."

"Jealousy isn't a good color on you, brother," I taunt with a sneer. "And so what if I like her?"

"Whoa. Slow down. Who said anything about liking her? You barely know her!" Sully interrupts, rage coating his voice.

"Yeah? And you do?" I challenge.

"Aye, I do." He glares at me, jaw clenched.

"And how's that?" His shitty attitude is pissing me off.

"I dated her."

I have to clench my fists to stop from smacking that smug grin off his face. Sully raises his brows at me in challenge, the asshole.

Rush stops swirling his drink and stares at our brother. "Yeah, about that. Why are we just hearing about this now?" he asks in a monotone voice. "When? And for how long?"

Sully finishes his drink in one swallow and slams his glass on the coffee table. "Two years ago. Remember the ambush in Brooklyn two summers ago?" He motions for a refill, and Rush obliges.

Rush and I both nod. I don't think any of us will forget that summer for a long, long time. Maybe not ever.

"We dated that summer."

"How did you meet?" I ask, taking a sip of my drink.

Sully exhales and tips his head back to look at the ceiling. "We met when I got community service at the library in the city."

"No shit? Red's got a record?" I whistle under my breath. "Gotta say, I did not see that coming."

"She doesn't have a record, dumbass. She was there for school credit." Sully stares at me with a sneer.

"Okay, so why haven't we heard about her until now?" Rush clenches his hand around his glass as he stares at our brother.

Sully stares at Rush, eyes hard. "I wanted to keep something for myself." He shrugs. "But in the end, it didn't matter."

"What happened?" Rush grits out.

Sully shrugs in response. "The Brotherhood."

We're all quiet for a moment, and I'm trying to figure out what the fuck Sully's riddle means.

"Well, speaking of the ambush. Do either of you recall how it all started?" Rush asks as he fiddles with the loose thread on the chair. His uncharacteristically nervous behavior sets me on edge. What the fuck is he up to now?

"How could we forget? I broke my wrist." Sully deadpans.

"No, I mean, do you remember why the junior council started fighting—or should I say over *who*?"

I nod and run my fingers through my hair, pushing it back. "Aye, some little bird all four of them wanted to claim."

Rush nods and his eyes light up with anticipation at whatever knowledge bomb he's about to drop on us. I flick my gaze to Sully to gauge his reaction. Furrowed brows and coiled muscles. Great.

"Exactly. And do you remember what the three of us decided?" I hear the note of glee in Rush's voice, and the hair on the back of my neck stands up.

"The pact," Sully murmurs.

"Aye, our pact." Rush finishes his drink and rotates his glass in his palm. "So what'll it be, brothers?"

No one speaks for a moment. Rush can barely sit still, and then it hits me. I cock my head to the side. "Are you talking about enacting the pact . . . with Alaina?"

He nods, his face serious. "That's exactly what I'm proposing."

chapter twenty-seven

Sully

"NO. NO, *FUCK no*. You don't know what you're asking of me. Not only did this bitch—"

"*Don't* call her a bitch," Wolf growls.

I glare at him and grit my teeth. "Not only did she just up and fucking disappear one day, but now she's—what—magically living in our house? Why am I the only one who thinks this is a problem?"

Wolf glances at Rush, and I've never been more thankful for my ability to read people. I see through the bullshit mask Rush has on to his giddiness at the prospect of sharing Alaina.

I rub the back of my neck and stare at the floor, thinking about what I can say to get them to understand. "Remember how I went back to the city a few days after the explosion?"

Wolf snorts. "Yeah, I remember. It was fucking stupid too. You had a bunch of broken bones, and you looked like shit. We all did."

I nod, still looking at the floor. "Yeah, I went to the NYPL because I couldn't get a hold of Lainey. I was supposed to meet her the night of the ambush, but for obvious reasons, I didn't show up. My phone got fucked at the warehouse, and Buzz couldn't get anything off of it, so I had no way of getting in touch with her. The last thing I remember for sure texting her was that I couldn't meet that night." I scrub my hand over my face and exhale, my shoulders weighing down with the phantom terror I felt for those few days. "And since we knew there was a rat, I was coming apart at the seams thinking about something happening to her. So I went to the city to find my girl."

"What happened?" Wolf asks after a moment of silence.

A cruel laugh slips past my lips as I think about what happened that day.

I walk up the steps of the New York Public Library on a wing and a prayer. It's a true testament to New Yorkers that no one even bats an eye at me covered in cuts and bruises. I've got a broken wrist, a dislocated shoulder, broken nose, and a dozen visible cuts and bruises.

It feels like an entire goddamn marching band is playing inside my head, and all I wanna do is see my girl. My phone is fucked, and I don't have her number memorized yet. I know we're done with our NYPL project, but I'm hoping to sweet-talk the program director, Ira, into giving me her number or address or some shit. I just gotta see my girl. Feel her in my arms. Anything to calm down the rising panic in my chest that some-one got her.

"She was a goddamn ghost, that's what happened. The program director didn't have her personal info—a fact he only admitted after I properly threatened him. And none of her classmates were at the library anymore. And in all the time we were together, I never asked her where she lived." I laugh without humor.

"Fuck," Wolf breathes out, pity coating his word.

I look at both of my brothers and deliver them the truth—my truth. "I went back to those steps every single day for a month, hoping and fucking praying that she would show up." I pause and stare out the window, the backyard lights emitting a soft orange glow into the night.

She never did.

I still think about her, and what my life would look like now had I answered her calls that day. Or text her back. Or did anything different, really. For a long time, every redhead I saw was her. I'd do a double-take, wishing it was her.

It never was.

"So, yeah, I know her."

I storm out of Rush's room, rage making my limbs heavy. They don't know what they're asking of me. How can I just ignore the fact that the reason my heart is no longer beating is now sleeping ten feet away from me.

I lost track of how much pussy I drowned myself in after I realized she wasn't coming back. But it never mattered. It never erased her from my mind. She fucking imprinted on my goddamn soul, and I've done everything I can to erase her mark on me for the past two years. And now these motherfuckers are asking me to—what, dive back in headfirst?

I'm not at all surprised to see the girl in question standing in the hallway outside Rush's room. She's mastered the art of looking innocent while covering up the callous snake she is on the inside.

I crowd her against the wall, careful not to touch her. I'll never make that mistake again. She stares at me with wide eyes shimmering with tears.

Unbidden, a memory of the first time I saw her runs through my mind as I stare at her.

I walk up the never-ending stairs to the New York Public Library, Johnny at my side. Plucking the front of my shirt away from my sweaty chest, I open the heavy wooden doors and step inside what will be my penance three days a week for the foreseeable future.

I stop inside the threshold to take in the architecture and luxury of the space. The judge did me a favor when he assigned my community service at the library.

I run my hand through my hair as I look around the room and make a few snap judgments—a pack of Stepford girls in matching school uniforms, a handful of stoners, and her. Hair the color of wildfire and an air of indifference calls to me like a moth to a flame. But it's her eyes that give her away.

I take one step toward her, and Johnny comes up behind me, clapping me on the shoulder. "Wait up."

I glance at him until he removes his hand. Da sent him to the city for the summer—to keep an eye on me. I'd be insulted if I actually thought Da thought I needed a babysitter. Instead, it's all a ruse to work a few different associates in the city— strengthening the bond and all that shit.

I sigh as I think about all the shit I have to do when this community service is over today.

"I'll wait for you today, kid, but otherwise, you'll be fine here." Johnny's careful not to let his voice carry.

I can feel the eyes of the Stepford clan on me, but there's only one person who deserves my attention, and she's sitting by herself, meticulously arranging her notebooks.

"Don't worry about me, Johnny. I'll be just fine," I murmur, never taking my eyes off the redhead.

I walk toward my girl, and Johnny follows a step behind me. "You'll be done in just four weeks, James. You did the right thing. I'll be around until you're done today," he says as he claps me on the shoulder a few more times.

"Yeah, okay." I turn to watch him walk toward an overstuffed lounger in the front of the library.

I shift to face my girl, and I feel the smirk tip up the corners of my mouth. She blinks several times, and the prettiest pink flushes the tops of her cheeks. "This seat taken?"

Those three words sealed my fate more than anything else in this life—not my brothers or the Brotherhood, or even when my parents bailed. And fuck me if I don't hate her a little bit for it.

I lean in further, our faces millimeters apart. Tingles sweep my body, and I press my hands harder into the plaster. The bite of pain anchors me here, so close but so far from the love of my life that left my sorry ass behind like nothing. My long-buried rage soars to the forefront of my mind, threatening to erupt.

It takes conscious thought not to let myself get sucked into the swirling brown depths of her eyes. It's always the amber flecks that get me—it's such a goddamn unusual color and one I'm always drawn to.

But what pierces me through the hole in my chest that used to beat for her—and only ever her—is the yearning in her eyes.

Her lips part, and she exhales my name on a breath. "James."

And that's enough to shatter what control I had left.

I crush my lips to hers, pushing every thought and feeling I've ever had for her into this kiss. All the love and lust and devastation and grief only fuel the fire that rages for this one girl. My punk rock princess.

When her hands tentatively fist my tee and pull me closer, I feel like I lose my grip on my sanity for a moment.

Sliding my hands down the wall, I palm her perfect, lush ass and lift her into my arms. Lainey slides her hands into my hair and pulls my mouth to hers. Our tongues tangle, and she moans like she's in ecstasy. I crush my body to hers, and suddenly, it's like no time has passed.

That feeling—that goddamn feeling—startles me out of my lusty haze. I wrench my mouth away from hers, but I don't put her down. I don't think I can yet. I rest my forehead on hers and close my eyes, trying to calm my racing heart.

"Fuck you, Lainey. Fuck you for leaving, and fuck you for coming back." The tortured words are ripped from me involuntarily.

I open my eyes to see a single tear fall down her cheek and heartbreak in her eyes. "James," she whispers.

I slant my mouth over hers in a brutal kiss that's over as quick as it starts and drop her on her feet.

I take a small step back and scan her face. Satisfied that she's not going to fall over or faint, I nod to myself and take another step back. I keep going until I'm at the top of the staircase.

She hasn't moved from her spot against the wall, just silently watches me as I walk away from her, tears steadily rolling down her flushed cheeks.

I give her one last lingering look before I turn on my heel and jog down the stairs.

I hear the first sob when I hit the bottom stair, but I can't make myself go back to her.

Not yet.

Maybe not ever.

chapter twenty-eight

Alaina

I'M NOT SURE how long I stand outside Rush's room, my heart aching and pulse thundering in my ears. Eventually, I slide down the wall and pull my legs to my chest, laying my head on them.

Memories of my summer with James flash before my eyes, and I close my eyes against them, willing them to leave me.

But that's the problem. That's always been the problem. James is unforgettable.

"I made a playlist for you." James puts an AirPod in my left ear before putting the other one in his right ear. He scrolls on his phone for a minute, glancing at me once before I hear the first few notes of Yeah Yeah Yeah's "Maps."

My breath hitches, our gazes lock and hold as we both listen to Karen O serenade us with her promise that no one loves you like she loves you. I lick my suddenly dry lips. This feels like a premonition and a promise. When the song ends, the next one starts, and I sink to the floor, stretching my legs out across from me. James moves to sit next to me, and we listen to this guy pour his heart out. He sings about the freckles in our eyes being mirror images, and when we kiss, they perfectly align.

By the third song, I feel warm and tingly all over. I intertwine our fingers, content to listen to this curated playlist he made for me for the rest of my life. By the fourth song, my heart feels full, and I lay my head on his shoulder. This playlist is a peek into James's soul, and I'm not passing up an opportunity to dive deeper.

I startle out of my memory when I feel a hand on my shoulder.

"Hey." Wolf's voice is close.

I lift my head from my knees and tilt it back against the wall. I can't look at him yet, but out of the corner of my eye, I see he's bent down in front of me, balancing on the balls of his feet.

I release a big sigh. "Hey. So . . . your brother is my ex-boyfriend," I say as I look at him with a humorless smile.

He stares at me for a moment, his gaze scanning my face. "Aye."

I stretch my legs out in front of me, wincing as the pins-and-needles feeling climbs up my legs. "There's one thing I don't understand though."

"Just one?" He teases me with a wink.

"Why do you call them by different names?"

Wolf stands up and extends his hand toward me. "C'mon, Red. We need alcohol for this conversation."

I stare at his hand, not moving a muscle.

"C'mon, baby girl. You're safe with me, and I know you have questions. Let's get some of those sorted out, yeah?"

I nod a couple of times. "Yeah, okay." I place my hand in his, and he pulls me up with more force than I was expecting, and I bump into his chest. His still very naked chest. It's only then that I realize that I'm still wearing an oversized tee over my bikini. "I, ah, should change real quick."

"Alright"—he nods his head to the door next to Rush's—"I'll be in there. You've got five minutes before I come get you."

"Okay," I murmur.

Once I'm safely inside my room, I lean against the door, softly bumping my head against it a couple of times. Of all the people in the world, what are the odds that I have a history with not one, but two of my possible new stepbrothers?

No, really, what are the odds? One in a million—or eight million, I guess. I laugh at the absurdity that is my life.

I should've stayed in the city this summer. *But then you wouldn't have met Wolf*, a voice counters.

Pushing off the door, I cross the room to my bed, where I stashed my lounging clothes from earlier.

As I change, I think about how Maddie and Mary are going to lose their minds when I tell them about this, and I laugh. Like full-on belly laugh that quickly morphs into hysterical laughter for a solid two minutes.

By the time I compose myself, I'm feeling a little better. I swipe under my eyes to catch any lingering tears and pop into the bathroom to splash cold water on my face.

I barely hear a knock before the door opens, and Wolf strides in.

"Knock much?" I quirk a brow at him, my hands on my hips. "I could've been naked."

He playfully sighs. "We've been through this before, Red, remember? Besides, I heard that weird laughter mental breakdown for two minutes and thirteen seconds, so I figured you were probably decent."

I flush, embarrassment warming my cheeks. "You heard that?"

"These walls are thin, Red. Best to remember that, yeah?"

I think about the couple of times that I pulled out my vibrator and worked myself over, and I feel a blanket of warmth roll through my body. Strangely, it's not embarrassment, more like *everything is super weird and I'm not sure where we stand, but I'm definitely still interested.* Whatever that feeling is called.

"Wait. How do you know how long I had my"—I wave my hand around—"whatever?"

He shoves his hands in the pockets of his gray sweatpants, drawing my attention to the seriously impressive bulge he's sporting. In the words of my cousin, *god, I love gray sweatpants season.* Even though it was definitely in the upper eighties today, the mansion stays cool.

Wolf shrugs. "I timed it."

His arrogance lights a fire inside, and for a moment, I forget that he's brothers with my ex-boyfriend and whatever the hell Rush is.

"What the hell would you do that for?"

He grins, this feral sort of thing. "Wanted to make sure you weren't having a seizure or going into some sort of crazy episode. If it went to three minutes, I was gonna check on you."

I don't say anything for a moment. "There are so many things I could say to that, but honestly, that's the bottom of the weird list for the day. So it's just going to have to wait."

He shrugs again and turns to walk out of my room. "C'mon, Red. Let's get you that drink."

"And questions," I add, following after him. "Don't forget the questions."

"I wouldn't dream of it." Wolf reaches behind his back to grab my hand. He laces our fingers together and tugs me until we're walking side by side all the way down to the kitchen.

Wolf walks to another faux-paneled cabinet and opens it like a door. "What's your poison?"

"Um, whatever you think. I'm not picky."

He pulls out a bottle, glasses, and shot glasses, setting them all on the table in the breakfast nook. "It's a vodka night," he says as he walks over to the fridge. He pulls a bottle of Sprite from the soda drawer and joins me at the table.

"How so? Why not tequila or whisky?"

"Vodka is for spilling secrets. Tequila is for dropping inhibitions. And whiskey is for closing deals."

"Huh. I've never heard of that before. Did you make that up?"

He pours us each a shot before making us a mixed drink. "My brothers and I did, yeah."

"Hm." I'm not sure how this all fits together—or how these guys all fit together, but I've got my fingers crossed that Wolf will help me figure some of it out.

Holding up his shot glass, Wolf clinks his against mine. "A toast: to the truth."

"And to vodka," I add, staring right at him.

"And to vodka," he murmurs. Then, at the same time, we both toss back our shots. I wince at the burn, but Wolf takes it like a guy who's well-acquainted with vodka shots.

Two shots later, my limbs are tingling, and I have just enough of a buzz that I'm ready to start the Spanish Inquisition.

"So, what's with the nicknames? Is it some sort of road name or something?" I mentally pat myself on the back for how put together that sounded. I mean, I just finished a binge-watch of *Sons of Anarchy* last month, and I could totally see the three of them in an MC.

He nods. "Something like that. We've had them for so long that it sounds strange to hear my given name."

"What's your real name?"

"Conor."

"Middle name?"

A smile tips the corners of his mouth. "Nicolas."

"Conor Nicolas Fitzpatrick," I breathe the words out, testing them on my tongue. And I'm not even surprised that I like the way they feel and sound.

"That's me," he murmurs.

Then a thought hits me out of nowhere, breaking up my little lust party. "Wait a minute. Why do they call you Wolf?"

He sips his drink and licks his lips. "Ah, Red, I don't think you're ready for that answer yet."

"What?" My mouth falls open. "You said you'd answer my questions," I accuse.

"I said I knew you had questions. I never said I'd answer all of them." He stares at me, indecision marring his handsome face. "If you're still here in six months, I'll tell you, yeah?"

I nod, thinking about all the possible reasons he can't tell me why or how he got his nickname.

"So, how did you meet my brother?"

"Which one?"

His jaw clenches, and he tips back another shot.

I look over the rim of my glass at him, taking in the tattoos, the menacing vibe he can get to in less than ten seconds, and the guns I found hidden all over the house. "The Brotherhood?"

Wolf stills, eyes narrow in suspicion. "What do you know about the Brotherhood?"

I shrug and try to wipe my face clean of the glee I'm feeling on the inside. After so many surprises in one day, it feels good to connect at least a couple dots. "I remembered something James—ah, Sully—said once."

"Sully told you about the Brotherhood?" Wolf rubs his chin, staring at me without really seeing me.

"Not really. Just mentioned it one day, but I remember thinking it was a gang or something."

"A gang, huh? What made you think that?"

His face is unreadable, so I can't tell if I'm on the right path or he's just humoring me. I don't really have much to lose, and if Wolf wanted to, he could always ask Sully himself.

I stare out the French patio doors at the dark night illuminated by the moon, and more memories of Sully—god, that's going to take some getting used to—and our time together comes back to me.

I shrug. "Frequent busted knuckles, an interaction at a restaurant, his two burner phones, and guns."

He raises his eyebrows. "That all?"

I tip my chin up. "That, and combined with all of this"—I wave a hand in his general direction—"that you guys have, yeah."

He nods to himself and takes another sip of his drink. "He showed you his guns?" His voice is quiet, curious.

"After I, uh, saw them the first time by accident, he didn't hide them from me." I clear my throat as the memory of how I saw one of his guns comes to mind.

Wolf smirks. "And what exactly were you two doing that caused you to see it *on accident*?"

I pin him with a challenging glare. "Do you really wanna know what we were doing that had Sully's shirt off?"

He grits his jaw before slamming another shot and slamming it down on the table. "We're not a gang."

His complete subject change isn't unnoticed, but I decide that I'm feeling generous right now. And I'm just waiting for him to bring up that kiss with Sully in the hallway. I'm not sure that I wouldn't change the subject if he asked me about it. The truth is, I don't know what I feel—I know I should feel guilty that I essentially made out with Wolf's brother when we're . . . doing whatever it is we're doing.

But I don't. For some unexplainable reason, it didn't feel like cheating. It just felt . . . right. I sigh, thinking about what went down in the hallway not too long ago.

It didn't feel like the closure we never got—it felt like we were waging war on one another, fueled equally by passion and heartache. And I'm not confident there will be a winner, not in the way I fear Sully wants. At some point, I know I'll have to have a conversation with him about what really happened that night.

But for now, I shift my attention to Wolf, which isn't hard. Plus, I really want as much information as I can get.

"Not a gang"—I tick a finger—"or an MC"—I tick another finger—"or Italian." I slowly curl my fingers inward to make a fist. "But you're definitely something, Conor Nicolas Fitzgerald."

I watch as a shiver works its way down his body when I say his full name.

"Aye, we're something, alright, baby girl." His voice is low, gritty from alcohol and overuse.

My heart stutters, and butterflies start to flutter in my belly. "Are we still talking about the Brotherhood, or are we talking about . . ."

"Tell me how you know Rush," he demands.

"Dodging another question so soon, Wolf?" I taunt. I sigh. "I didn't really meet Rush until the other night."

I busy myself by pouring another shot, hoping that he doesn't notice my omission. I mean, technically, yes, I didn't meet Rush until that night I cornered him at O'Malley's. But I'd been dying to meet him for an entire year before that.

Something inside urges me to keep that quiet, that it's something private between Rush and me. I hope that's not a mistake.

"Don't you have any questions for me?" I ask, steering him away from how I met Rush. I tip the shot back as he asks me his next question, and I nearly choke.

"Aye, I've questions. Where's your Da?"

I sputter and cough, the vodka burning the entire way down. "I-I'm sorry, went down the wrong pipe." I pat my chest a couple of times. "Did you just ask about my dad?" He nods but doesn't offer anything else. "I already told you. I haven't seen him since I was little."

An hour later, when we've run out of questions we're willing to ask or answer, and we've had more than enough liquor, Wolf stands up and holds out his hand to me. "Time for bed, Red."

Hope flutters in my chest. "I like the way that sounds," I say, grabbing his hand. I let him pull me to my feet, swaying a little.

Without a word, Wolf bends down and hooks an arm under my knees and another around my back, lifting me in his arms. I reflexively loop my arms around his neck, coming face to face with the tattoo on his neck.

The intricate lines mesmerize me, and I trace them with the tip of my finger.

Leaning my head against his shoulder, I whisper, "Thank you. I could've walked though."

"I know, but I like way you feel in my arms."

He brings me all the way into my room and places me on my bed. Indecision clouds his handsome face as he stares at me for a moment.

He turns to leave, and I lean onto my knees and reach out to grab his hand. "Wait." Wolf freezes but doesn't turn around. "Stay." My voice is low, and the thread of vulnerability is loud in the quiet of the room.

chapter twenty-nine

Wolf

MY PULSE IS loud in my ears as I stare at the grooves in the door, mentally calculating why this would be a bad idea.

"Please," she whispers, and the rawness of her voice is what seals her fate.

I sigh and scrub my hand down my face, the letters inked onto my fingers catching my attention. Live. I look at my other hand. Free.

What would I do if she wasn't Sully's ex and didn't have a connection to Rush? What would I do if I just follow *our* code—our pact to live free?

Squaring my shoulders, I stride toward her door. I hear her exhale in defeat, but I'm not leaving. I close and lock her door and set the code on the panel to arm it. I'm feeling paranoid as fuck, and I don't like it.

I turn around, and I see the relief and hope straighten her shoulders, and a grin slowly spread across that beautiful face.

I'm not the least bit surprised that she captured the attention of my brothers. She's fun and smart and so goddamn beautiful my chest hurts.

I stand next to her bed and reach behind me to pull my shirt off with one hand. She groans, this quiet, low noise in the back of her throat, and I have to tell my dick to chill the fuck out.

Starting something while she's this messed up would be fucked-up. And since I plan on keeping her long after this shit with Da and Lana expires, I don't want to scare her off.

"Get under the covers, Red." She obeys without hesitation, and I file that bit of information away. I climb into her bed and lay down next to her, the scent of sugared peaches overwhelms me. "Stop staring at me and go to sleep."

She sighs, this little noise of frustration. "I'm trying. But—it's just—I can't relax with you in my bed looking like"—she waves her hand over my chest—"this."

I can't help the grin that spreads across my face. I tilt my head to look at her. "Like what?"

She stares at me, those whiskey-brown eyes of hers wide and open. "You know how hot you are, Wolf, so don't even act like you don't know what you being half naked in my bed would do to me."

I have a feeling that she wouldn't have shared quite so much if she wasn't tipsy. When I don't answer her, she tosses and turns, wiggles around until I've had enough. I reach over and expect to grab a handful of that perfect ass covered by those tiny shorts she was wearing earlier. Instead, I'm met with warm, soft skin.

"Fuck me," I groan under my breath, hauling her close to me. She snuggles closer, draping her limbs over me.

Someone decided to test me today.

I glare at the ceiling and mentally give whoever got bored and decided to fuck with me today the finger. I won't break that easy.

I'm strung tight, but I close my eyes and will my body to relax.

BEEPING WAKES ME up in the middle of a deep sleep. It's quiet enough that it infiltrated my dream—suddenly, the lion I was looking at opened its mouth, and instead of a roar, it beeped. I open my eyes, taking a moment to realize where I am. When I hear the blaring alarm, that means not only did someone break through the perimeter, but they've broken into the house now.

Somehow in our sleep, we drifted even closer, and Red's half laying on my chest. I shake her shoulders to wake her up, but at the first touch of my hand, her head whips up to stare at me.

"What the hell is that?" Her eyes are wide and blood-shot. Fuck, I hope she's not still buzzed.

"Put some pants on, Red. We gotta move." I slide her off of me, gently pushing her lower back to get her out of bed. I jump out of bed and reach underneath the bedside table for the extra guns. I pull out two SIG Sauers—of course, they're Rush's favorite.

In three strides, I'm at the panel beside the door, typing in the code to unlock the bedroom door. If Rush and Sully followed protocol, they'd be in the secure room by now. I intercom the gray room.

"Talk to me, Rush."

"Breach, west side, the window in the study," Rush says just as another alarm wails.

"Breach, west side, library," Sully adds.

"Someone needs to get Alaina," Rush orders. I hear typing through the intercom, so I'm sure he's got the security system pulled up.

"I already got her," I tell them as I glance over my shoulder to see Red dressed in leggings, a sweatshirt, and sneakers.

"That was quick," Rush comments. "Three perimeter cameras are down. West side."

Ignoring him, I glance at the panel, overriding the Pink Room's restricted access and see if I can tap into the library's intercom camera. "When's backup arriving?"

"Five to ten," Sully says.

"Fuck. That's too long. They'll be on top of us by then. We can't stay in this room." I can't see how many people are in the house—it's too dark. "Rush, remind me later to help you install night vision capability in the intercom," I mutter as I check the gun.

"What do you mean? Where are you?"

"We'll meet you in Gray," I say to the intercom and turn toward Red. "C'mere, baby girl"—I reach my hand toward her—"it's alright."

Red takes a few steps toward me, clasping her hand in mine. Eyes wide and hair disheveled, she's the most beautiful thing I've ever seen. Protectiveness swells up inside me, a tidal wave of fury at whoever dared to break into my home and put my girl at risk.

I don't question the unfamiliar feeling; instead, I harness it into a finely pointed blade of chaos.

I lock that shit down and focus on the girl in front of me. I can't protect her if I'm swept up in my rage. There will be time for that later.

"We're going to Rush and Sully." I scan her face for an impending freakout. I don't exactly have time to coddle her, but I can't have her melting down out there either. "Ever shoot a gun before, Red?"

She blinks at me with wide eyes, and I take that as my answer.

She stares at the gun, raises her eyebrows, and shakes her head before turning those doe eyes on me. I tuck the extra gun into the back of my pants and hold on to the other one.

"It's alright. We'll add that to our list of things to do tomorrow. Stay with me, yeah?"

"Okay, Wolf," she murmurs.

I grab her hand and tug her so she's plastered to my side. I don't know which direction they're coming from, and I won't risk her life on a guess.

I take a moment to center myself.

Gunfire breaks out close enough that I'd guess they're on the stairs. We have maybe thirty seconds before they're in front of her door. The gray room is thirty steps away, but it's fortified in a way none of the other rooms are.

It's a risk we have to take.

I inhale and wipe away Conor, I exhale and become Wolf. Calm, calculated, merciless.

"You're going to go in front of me. Run to the gray room. It's the last door on the right. I'll protect your six, yeah?"

Red grasps my hand with both of hers. "You're coming with me, right?" Panic laces every word.

"Aye." I swipe my thumb over her hand a few times and lean toward her, placing a hard kiss on her forehead. "Let's go."

I open her bedroom door, wait for a moment to make sure we're not walking into an ambush, and step out quietly. Whoever the fuck is here lacks training and discipline. They're loud as fuck as they ascend the stairs.

With my hold on her hand, I guide her into the hallway, pushing her behind me as I face against the staircase. "Go," I whisper.

She doesn't hesitate, taking off at a quiet run for the last door. I walk backward, never taking my eyes off the staircase, finger on the trigger. I hear the quiet snick of the door opening, and I spare a glance to see Rush pulling her in the room. I quicken my steps, and as soon as I'm in front of the door, the intruders hit the landing.

Without hesitation, I fire three quick shots—two to the first guy's chest, one to the second guy's chest. The door opens wide behind me, and I spin to duck inside, kicking it closed just as bullets hit the door.

Red yelps with each bullet, stepping back until her back is plastered against the wall.

Her reaction seeps some of my adrenaline high away. I take in the way her chest heaves and her wide, panicked eyes flick around the room. I curse whoever decided to hand me this perfect creature only to show me that she doesn't belong in my world. Fuck them. Rage courses through my veins as the unfairness of it all settles on my shoulders.

Her eyes settle on me, and I fucking hate the relief I see in them. "Wolf?"

"It's armored, Red. We're fine. Aren't we, Rush?" I turn away from her.

Rush is hunched over four security monitors, typing something on the keyboard. "Aye. Backup's here in three, two, one."

Right on cue, I hear another set of gunshots and yelling. I watch it all play out on the security feeds. One guy sneaks off to the other side of the second floor, toward my da's room, and I see my chance to exercise my demon while exacting a little vengeance.

"I'll be back," I say as I stride toward the door. "One got away from Dave's men."

No one stops me as I leave the security of the gray room and jump headfirst into the chaos.

chapter thirty

Alaina

"WOLF?" I DON'T look at him when I say his name. I know he's right there, even if I couldn't see him, I'd know. I can feel him.

It's this heady mix of awareness, safety, and lust all swirling together, giving me the ability to sense his presence.

"Hmm?"

I see him shift his attention from his phone to stare at me. I scoop more bubbles from the side of the jacuzzi tub and gently smooth them along the top of the water near my chest. Best not to flash too much—I'm not sure I could handle that tonight.

Though Maddie always says that the best sex is when your emotions are high. Somehow, I doubt she was talking about nearly getting killed. It's been hours since I left what I'm calling the command center. It's a perfect name considering all the monitors and bullet-proof exterior. Rush gave me the all-clear to leave, so I beelined for maybe my favorite part of the house—my bathroom. If ever there was a time to soak in the clawfoot bathtub, this was it.

"What did those guys want?"

He sighs, and from the corner of my eye, I watch him type something on his phone before placing it on the counter behind him. "Truth for a truth, Red?"

I look over my shoulder at him. He's leaning against the bathroom cabinets by the double sinks, his head tipped back against the drawer where I stashed my makeup. His muscles are coiled and alert, but his eyes look tired.

There's something different about him—he's quieter, less playful. His cocky smirk is gone, replaced with a blank intensity. How can someone look void of emotion but still radiate such rage and agitation?

I flick my gaze all over him again, triple-checking for injuries. His knuckles on one hand look a little red, but not nearly as bad it could've been. The thought of Wolf getting shot sends nausea churning in my belly.

"I'm fine, Alaina, see?" Wolf holds his hands out to the side, inviting me to look my fill. Though I'm not sure I'll ever have enough of looking at Wolf Fitzgerald.

I meet his gaze and nod. "What did they want, Wolf?"

"I don't know." His voice is quiet in this calm bubble we've created in my bathroom.

I can almost pretend that nothing happened tonight, except for the fact that my hands won't stop shaking, and my stepbrother slash boyfriend is sitting in the bathroom watching me take a bath in a very not sexy way.

"Does that sort of thing happen a lot?" I swirl my hands underneath the water, watching the ripples they create as I wait for his answer.

"Yes and no. Do we get into altercations with people who want to harm us? Yes, but not as often as you'd probably think. Do these . . . altercations happen at our house? No." Wolf sighs and looks at the ceiling. "We're in uncharted territory, Red."

I nod like I understand, but I don't. I don't understand what the hell is going on. Or why guys with guns broke into this heavily fortified house. Or why Wolf, Rush, and Sully acted like the cast of *Scarface* with their armored room at the end of the hall and guns stashed all over the house and Rush's crazy security computer setup.

And I definitely don't understand why I'm still here.

I sigh and sink into the tub further. "I'm going to get out soon and lay down. I'm sure there are other things that need your attention right now."

He stares at me for a moment, tapping his finger against his bottom lip, eyebrows drawn. "You sure? I don't mind staying."

I nod and look up at him from underneath my lashes. "Yep. I'm fine. I'll see you later."

He exhales, his shoulders hitching, and says, "Stay in your room, yeah? I'll come back in a little bit."

"Okay, Wolf." My voice is small as he leaves my bathroom and then my room. The door slams closed behind him, and I'm proud of the fact that I don't flinch.

The gunshots have stopped, but it's not quiet. There're tons of noise happening all over the house, but inside the bubble of my room, it feels like I'm the only person around.

Wolf

TWO HOURS LATER, after Red's safely secured in her room with a guard posted outside her balcony and on the second floor, I'm in Rush's room with my brothers.

Situated on the couches around the coffee table, we dial Da.

"Rush." The background noise fills the room. I glance at my phone—six o'clock—which means it's midday for him.

The need to take out my frustrations on the guy sitting in the carriage house surges through me once more. I take a breath and remind myself to exhale the violence still simmering around me.

"You're on speaker, Da. Sully and Wolf are here."

"Hold on." We hear the noise quiet down, then a slam, and then silence. "Talk to me."

"Break-in at Summer Knoll tonight."

Da exhales, the sigh audible. "How bad?"

Rush sighs. "Two of ours. Six of theirs. By our best estimation, three or four got away."

"Goddamn it," Da roars. Three seconds later, we hear the crash of glass breaking.

I catch Sully's gaze and flash him a smirk. Looks like I'll be winning that bet. He said Da would upend a table, but I wagered he'd throw the nearest object.

Rush continues without missing a beat, "They found our blind spot in the perimeter, cut the cameras, came in on the west side of the house—multiple points, and immediately went to the second floor."

Da's heavily breathing fills the silence.

"Then they went for your room. Any idea why they'd do that?" I ask him, bracing for the deflection he's been shoving at us for weeks.

"My room?"

"Aye, your room. I caught the fucker myself," I confirm, rage boiling low when I think about the asshole going through Da's closet and dressers.

"Did he squeal?" I can hear the smile in his voice. I bet the bastard is imagining all the ways he'd get the guy to talk if he were here. There's a reason he got named the Butcher.

"Aye, he did. I left him with Dave for now. I'll be paying him a visit tomorrow." I smirk, imagining how my visit with him will go. That's what growing up in the Brotherhood does—strips your emotion so when you end up in a gunfight, you can talk about the casualties and torture as easily as the weather.

"Good. Call me for anything big."

"Is there something we need to know, Da? We can't do our jobs with only half the information," Rush reasons, brow furrowed. I know how much it's killing him that he doesn't have all the facts.

"Ah, fuck." Da sighs. "I need a few more days to finish a couple things here, but it's clear to me that I need to be there. There are things we need to discuss."

Sully raises his eyebrows. "What the hell does that mean?"

"Not on the phone, boyo. We'll talk when I get home," Da snaps. "How's our bird—she alright?"

I don't like the way his voice gets quiet when he talks about her. Something about it rubs me the wrong way.

"Aye, she's alright," I confirm.

"Good, good. I'll see you boys when I get back." Without waiting for a reply, Da hangs up.

The three of us are left staring at the black phone screen before raising our gazes to look at one another. Sully's the first one to break the silence. "What the fuck was that?"

Rush leans back into the chair, drumming his fingers on his leg. "I have no idea. But I think we'll finally get some answers as soon as he gets back. So we just have to wait until then."

I nod in agreement. "So, we wait."

chapter thirty-one

Alaina

I BOUNCE INTO WOLF'S room, brimming with glee. I know I should be way more freaked out that a bunch of dudes just broke into the mansion two days ago, but for some reason, I still feel safe here. With them.

And I'm strangely good at compartmentalizing everything.

Besides, it's my birthday tomorrow. And I refuse to wallow on my birthday eve, not when I have someone like Wolf to spend time with. And maybe even Rush.

I haven't seen much of my mystery man since that middle-of-the-night gunfight. My nickname for him is so much more fitting than I originally thought. Maybe Wolf can pass along an invite? I rake my teeth across my bottom lip at the thought of spending time with both of them—*between* both of them.

Fleetwood Mac's *Rumours* plays on the record player, and Wolf's lounging in his bed, shirtless, of course, laptop open on his lap.

He pauses to stare at me, eyebrows raised. "Huh. I expected more fear and less . . . joy."

I meander over to the record player and scan his vinyl collection on the shelf next to it. "You keep saying that, Wolf, but I told you that night that I was fine." I flash a smirk over my shoulder at him.

Closing his laptop and putting it on his nightstand, he says, "We'll see. I'll just be here, waiting for your big freakout. Because it's coming."

"If you say so." I shrug and stride to his bed, a smile playing around my mouth. Hesitating only briefly, I climb into his lap, straddling him and looping my arms around his neck. Since the moment I saw him, I've felt a connection, and it's been growing ever since. And somewhere between the truth bombs and the break-in the other night, something shifted between us.

I'm totally crushing on Wolf.

I'm still coming to terms with the fact that he might be my stepbrother one day. I know other people won't understand—and if I'm honest with myself, I'm not sure that my mom will understand, but that's a bridge we'll cross when we get there. And that's assuming she notices—and that she comes back here.

The heat of his palms against my waist is like a brand—warm and possessive. He touches me as if we've been doing it for years, not days, and with an authority that entices me.

Those deep, dark eyes of his captivate me, especially when I can see the flecks of gray swirling. He chuckles. "What're you up to?"

"Who, me?" I fake confusion, my eyebrows high in exaggeration. Leaning in so we're cheek to cheek, I smile against his light scruff. "Come to the city with me."

His hands flex on my waist, and "No can do, baby girl. We're on lockdown, remember?"

Pulling back to look at him, I work to keep my shoulders loose and the disappointment off my face. But I'm not totally done yet—I play my trump card. "But it's my birthday tomorrow, and I want to celebrate it in the city with my boyfriend. My cousins are in town and everything."

Wolf

HER LIPS BRUSH mine with every word, distracting me from the fact that she just called me her boyfriend.

It's like the universe is listening, because the record player actually scratches, and Fleetwood Mac stops playing.

Red climbs off my lap and hurries to the other side of the room to lift the needle. "Shoot. I hope that didn't actually scratch the record." She flips the switch off and leans down to inspect the vinyl for damage, completely oblivious to my heart attack over here.

My entire body seizes, muscles taut and breath stalled in my throat. I've never needed the boyfriend label to get pussy—most of the time, I barely get to buy a bird a drink before she's dragging me to the nearest flat surface. I happily oblige, and then we go our separate ways.

Sure, some birds have tried to tie me down over the years, but I've never even been tempted before. Red could tempt the most devout man. I'm loyal to The Brotherhood, and this life doesn't lend well to caged little birds. Besides, I don't have the capacity to keep one.

Especially not one like Red.

Whatever good inside me was systematically eradicated year after year as the Brotherhood's rifle.

A month with me and everything good in her would be crushed by the rage and chaos that live within me. Sometimes it's easier to think of it as a living, breathing thing, but the truth is it's not. It's just me. The wild, bloodthirsty side of me that only surfaces when the Brotherhood needs it.

They created this side of me, nurtured it, and one of these days, I won't be able to stuff it back in the box during daylight hours anymore.

Maybe not in a week or even a month, but eventually, she'll wise up and leave my ass behind. Fuck, if my parents can drop me without a second thought, what the fuck chance do I have at keeping a girl like Red?

Better to uproot that shit outta my life now. I don't need to wake up one morning and realize I caught fucking feelings, and then she fucking leaves the next day or some shit. Because that's exactly how karma works. And these hands are permanently stained red, so I can't imagine I have any good karma left.

I stare at Red's profile as she fiddles with the record player, and I know what I have to do.

To save her.

From me.

And to save yourself, a voice whispers in my mind. I shake the thought away, no need to complicate things when my mind is made up.

I've never been one for lies, but I'm willing to make an exception. For her.

She spins to look at me, the dark blue skirt flaring around her legs. I drink her in as she is—faded Stevie Nicks band tee knotted in the front, all-white Vans, that silky-soft wavy hair floating around her shoulders—she's fucking radiant.

And I realize that I've missed everything she just said. "Hmm?"

She rolls her eyes. "I asked if you would invite Rush for me too. And be ready to leave in an hour, okay? I ordered a car service to take us to the city, and we can spend the night in my dorm." She waggles her eyebrows at me, eyes dancing with excitement. "No one will care. Then we can come back here in a few days."

If she looks hard enough, she'll see the visions of what could have happened the other night flashing through my mind. What will definitely happen again—maybe not tomorrow and maybe not this house, but that will not be our last gunfight. Not in this life. I've made my peace with that—fuck, sometimes I crave that. But there's a reason I don't do girlfriends, and this is one of them.

So it's better that we end this now before she gets any more invested.

Jesus fucking Christ, I sound like a goddamn high school girl. I grind my jaw, and I can feel the vein in my temple throbbing.

Fuck it.

I take a breath and lock the disappointment and regret down—way down, where I can't feel it. Blanking my face, I look at her and prepare to let her down easy.

"I'm not your boyfriend."

Okay, that's not exactly letting her down easy.

She stares at me, mouth ajar, a light flush staining her cheeks. "Of course. I didn't mean anything by it. I just thought—"

Her once-bright smile dims, and if I wasn't in the middle of a nervous fucking breakdown, I'd jump at the chance to spend a few nights tangled up in Red.

And that thought is enough to send me spiraling. I don't do relationships. Fuck, I barely do repeats. And here I am fucking *jumping* at the idea of snuggling some birdie I haven't even fucked yet?

I don't think so.

I need to shut that shit down. And quick.

I take a breath and school my face, preparing to obliterate any chance of us.

"Thought, what? That because we fucked around a couple of times that we were exclusive. Or did you think it meant something more than what it was: a convenient hookup?" I scoff. "Come on, Red. I thought you were smarter than this."

She shakes her head a little, her eyes welling with tears. My hands tingle with the need to wipe away her sadness.

"Don't cry, little bird. It's not entirely his fault. I asked Wolf to get close to you." Red and I whip our heads to the doorway at the same time to see Rush standing there, leaning against the doorjamb, oozing nonchalance. But he can't fool me, I see the jealously in every tense muscle, and that only flares my own.

"Thanks a lot, asshole," I snarl the words through clenched teeth, flexing my fists to stop myself from laying his interfering ass out.

"What?" Rush shrugs. "It's the truth."

"No, it's not really."

Red sniffs, pinning her accusing gaze on me.

Rush quirks a brow. "Didn't I tell you to seduce her for information the day Mama Rosa's blew up?"

"What?!" Red shrieks, her gaze swinging to Sully. "Mama Rosa's *blew up*?" I didn't even see the sneaky fucker behind Rush, leaning against the wall in the hallway.

Sully clenches his jaw and looks away. Goddamn it, now I'm going to have to talk to him about this too.

"Yes. It was a few days after you got here," Rush tells her, his gaze bouncing around her face.

She nods and flicks her gaze to me. "And when was this phone call with Rush? Before or after the *Sopranos* marathon?"

I force myself to hold her gaze when I utter, "Before."

Shoulders hunched, she looks down and the floor. "I see."

I heave a sigh, my stomach knotting as I stare at her slumped shoulders. She looks like someone kicked her goddamn puppy.

"Come on, Red, you knew the score."

She tips her head up to look at me, and her expression guts me. Heartbreak, disappointment, and resignation mar her beautiful face, washing out her freckles. "Yeah, I guess I should've known, huh?" A self-deprecating smile tips up the corners of her lips. "Alright, well as fun as this has been, I'm out."

She takes a step toward the hallway when Sully's arm snaps out in front of her, stopping her. "It's not safe to go to the city alone."

She sidesteps him. "Maybe for you, but I'm no one, remember?" she challenges, a bitter smirk on her face. "And not that it's any of your business, but I'm meeting people there. So I won't be alone."

Burning coats my stomach, and I feel like I'm going to erupt any second. "A guy?"

She whips around fast enough that her long hair slaps Sully in the face. She advances on me, her finger pointing aggressively. "No. No, you don't get to reject me and then act jealous at the thought of someone else paying attention to me." She jabs her finger into my chest. "That is *not* how it works, Wolf."

I take a step toward her, pushing her finger into my chest. I skim my hand down her arm, cup her elbows, and gently pull her, so our bodies are flush. "You make me fucking crazy," I growl the words in her face.

"Yeah? Well, you're the most mood-swinging moth-er*fucker* I've ever met!"

Her chest is heaving, I can't help the smile that spreads when she swears. She must be really mad to drop a *motherfucker* on me.

"And stop doing that infuriating, sexy smolder thing at me because I am *so* over it."

I lean my head toward her, just barely skimming her nose. "Sexy, huh?"

"That's all you got out of all of that?" Her voice lowers into an exasperated murmur.

Fueled by the burning desire to lay claim to her, I crush my mouth against hers. And for a few seconds she melts in my arms, kissing me back like the last twenty minutes didn't happen.

Then it's over. She rips her mouth off of mine and steps back. I don't even try to keep her.

She puts a shaking hand to her swollen lips. "You can't"—she clears her throat—"you can't keep kissing me like that. It's not—it's not fair, Wolf." Her voice is soft and pleading. "We don't want the same thing. You know I want that magical kind of love." Her smile is small and wistful. "And you . . . you don't. And that's fine."

Her gaze begs me to disagree with her, to declare some sort of promise to her. But I can't do that.

Fuck, I wouldn't know how to start even if I wanted to.

In another life, we'd explore this growing attraction between us, but not in this one. Not at the expense of her soul.

My gaze is unyielding as I stare at her. When I don't say anything, she nods once, turns on her heel, and walks out.

All three of us watch her walk down the hallway, and it's only after we hear the front door slam that Rush breaks the silence.

"Right then. You're"—he points a finger at me—"a fucking idiot."

I clench my jaw. "You got something to say, Rush?"

His gaze narrows. "Yeah, I do. You're just going to let your girl walk away like—"

"She's not my girl." I shrug, feigning nonchalance, but judging by the exasperated look on Rush's face, I'm not convincing anyone.

Rush raises a brow. "That so? Then you don't mind if I move her into my bedroom—into my *bed*?" He flashes this condescending smirk at me, and I clench my fists to keep them from flying into his face.

"You'd like that, wouldn't you, asshole? Except then what would you do about your little bird stashed away in the city, huh?" My tone is a cruel taunt.

He smirks. "I don't know what you're talking about."

"Sure ya don't, asshole." I sneer at him.

"Look"—Rush sighs and pinches the bridge of his nose—"I'm not losing her because you can't get your head out of your ass."

I shake my head and grit my teeth. "Nah, you don't understand, man. It's not the same for you."

Rush's mouth flattens. "Oh? I wasn't raised in the Brotherhood? I didn't get my hands bloody in middle school? I didn't lose a fucking parent? Huh? Is that how it's different for you?" His voice gets colder with every word, and by the end, derision drips from each syllable.

Shame coats my body, and it's uncomfortable as fuck. Tipping my chin to my chest, I exhale, guilt weighing me down. "Fuck. I'm sorry, man."

Rush stares at me and nods once. "Fix it, Wolf."

"Fix it?" I scoff. "What the fuck am I supposed to do? She's not from this world, man. And I've never had a relationship in my goddamn life!"

"What the fuck did you think I meant when I said it's time for the pact?" Rush yells, a vein throbbing in his temple. "That means we're in a *relationship* with one girl, dumbass." He pinches the bridge of his nose and stares at the ceiling. "And we'd bring her into our world."

"Well how the hell am I supposed to know? I've never been in a four-way relationship before!" I yell back at him, the back of my neck getting hot.

"Three-way," Sully interjects.

"What?" I snap at him.

"A three-way relationship. I don't want to have anything to do with this shitshow you're trying to corral, Rush. Count me out." He stares at Rush and then me for a moment before he storms away.

Rush looks at the space Sully was for a moment before he looks to me. "We'll have to work on that."

"As if we're somehow going to make Red *not* Sully's ex who crushed his black heart?" I scoff. "Good luck with that. Not even you are that good, man."

"Oh, ye of little faith." He flashes me that cocky condescending smile he knows I hate. "I'm out. Call me when you get your head outta your ass." He turns to walk away.

"Where the hell are you going? We're on lockdown!"

He waves a hand behind his head as he walks away to do god knows what. Probably plot someone's demise and take all their assets.

I scrub my hands down my face and blow out a breath. "Fuck."

chapter thirty-two

Alaina

ONCE THE CAR I ordered drops me off back at my empty dorm in the city, I make my way into my dorm suite. Stale air greets me, and I immediately open up some windows in my room and the shared living space.

It's already getting humid outside, but I'll take the humidity over stagnant air and the smell of old fried food any day.

After I unpack my bags, I sit on the end of my bed and text my mom to let her know that I'm here. Not that I think she'll text me back or really care, but it feels like the right thing to do.

I'm sure I'll have to go back to that house at some point, if for nothing else than to get the rest of my stuff. I still have a lot of my things here, but I left my laptop there.

My mind spins as I recall the last week—snagging on the last conversation I had with Wolf. Embarrassment rolls through me, leaving a flush in its wake. I can't believe I called him my boyfriend. I wince and shake my head. So stupid, Lainey.

I'm not even sure what made me say it, except that I wasn't really thinking, and it kind of felt like we were something. But maybe that was the adrenaline talking. Maybe the break-in affected me more than I realized?

I exhale and flop back on my bed. Warmth wraps around my heart, washing away the embarrassment as I stare at the glow-in-the-dark plastic stars on my ceiling.

Mary and Maddie got them for me for my birthday years ago, and we had to sweet-talk the janitor to let us borrow his ladder to put them up. They always make me feel special—and loved—on my birthday. Every day, really.

I glance at the clock—they should be getting here in a couple of hours.

I roll over onto my side, tuck my hands under my head, and stare out the window into the city that never sleeps. My eyes feel heavy, and before long, my eyelids start drooping.

I shake myself awake a couple of times before I finally give in and close my eyes. I'll just rest my eyes for a few minutes, I think.

"HAPPY BIRTHDAY TO you. Happy birthday to you! Happy birthday, dear Lainey, happy birthday to you!"

Blinking my eyes open, I find Mary's and Maddie's smiling faces right in front of me. It takes me a few moments to figure out what's happening.

"Come on, sleepyhead! We have a full day planned for you." Mary's awfully chipper for someone who probably has some serious jet lag right now.

Yawning, I struggle to sit up in bed. I'm surprised to see that I'm in just my tee. I must've woken up sometime in the middle of the night and taken my skirt, socks, and bra off.

"What time is it?" I ask, covering my mouth as another yawn escapes me.

"Six o'clock!" Maddie answers, bouncing on her toes.

"You know I'm excited to see you, but can we do this later—in like three more hours?" I groan and try to snuggle back underneath my covers.

"Ah, ah, ah. Time to get up!" Mary peels the blanket off of me and shakes her head.

I try to hide the grin on my face as I peek up at their smiling faces. "Can't I sleep in just a little bit?"

"Nope, we've got plans for our birthday girl," Mary says with a wide grin.

Maddie nods. "Exactly. Starting with breakfast from your favorite brunch spot."

"How'd you get brunch reservations there on such short notice?"

Maddie hooks a thumb over her shoulder toward Mary. "Someone didn't sleep on the plane."

Mary shrugs. "I'll take a disco nap today. I'll be fine."

"Disco nap." A slow smile spreads across my face. "Does that mean we're going out tonight?"

"Babe. It's your birthday. Of course, we're going out tonight! You only turn nineteen once!" Maddie bounces on the balls of her feet. "Now, out of bed, we've got a stack of birthday pancakes to eat!"

I laugh and pull back my comforter. "I'm so glad you guys are here." Reaching one arm toward each of them, I curl them in for a group hug. "Thank you."

A COUPLE HOURS LATER, we arrive back at our dorm suite, my stomach and heart full. We walk into the living room and all flop down on the couches.

"Disco nap?" Maddie asks, her eyes already half closed.

"Mm-hmm." Mary reaches behind her to grab the cream-colored throw blanket and drapes it across her. "Wake us up in an hour, Lainey."

I can't contain the smile that spreads across my face as I stare at my two best friends napping like toddlers after brunch. I exhale, and a wave of exhaustion sweeps over me. But I don't think a nap can fix this. My soul is tired.

I know I shouldn't be this disappointed about some guy I haven't known for long, but I can't help it. The whole thing with Wolf, Rush, and Sully is . . . just so weird. Like, what are the odds that these three men—all of whom I've had a real connection with—not only know each other but are related?

My face flushes when I think about the fact that I've kissed all three of them. And try as I might, I can't stop my mind from imagining what it would be like to kiss them all—maybe even at the same time. My breath hitches as I daydream about Rush's mouth on mine, Wolf's hands on my body, and Sully—

My heart aches, ripping me from my fantasy. I can't get over the look on his face when he saw me. Heartache, devastation, and a tiny kernel of hope. But all of that was erased in an instant and replaced with rage, contempt, and maybe worst of all—indifference.

I know we've both changed in the years since we last saw one another, but for that one single second, I felt that old connection snap into place. It was only then that I realized I've had the same feeling with both Rush and Wolf.

I told the girls the abridged version over brunch, but I didn't see the point in giving them the play by play. Because then I would have to admit that I'm quite possibly crushing on three guys.

My three stepbrothers.

And . . . and I'm still processing that fact.

I'm sure Mary and Maddie wouldn't judge me, but I'm not sure I can say the same thing about everyone else. Anxiety bubbles up inside my chest when I think about my mom's reaction to that sort of declaration.

If Mom doesn't end up with Cormac, it's possible I'll never even see them again. So, maybe telling her won't even be an issue.

I let my mind wander and think about what I would do if Wolf suddenly showed up here, prepared to woo me back. I stifle my giggles as I imagine Wolf on his knees with his inked fingers wrapped around a bouquet of flowers, begging me for a second chance. But that scene doesn't feel like Wolf to me. He's more likely to show up with specialty pizza and vinyl records.

Maddie once explained the art of The Woo as a rite of passage and swears that every girl should experience it at least once.

You can tell a lot about a man by the way he woos you.

I've never really been in a situation where I've been wooed before, but a secret part of me wishes that I'll get to experience that with Wolf.

Sure, I'm a strong, independent woman.

But I'm also a romantic at heart. What girl isn't?

Before I know it, an hour has gone by. I haven't moved an inch from my sprawled out position on the couch, and even though I didn't sleep, I feel refreshed, lighter.

I cue up a song from my 80s playlist on my phone and crank up the volume. Both girls startle awake, and I attempt to smother my giggles when they yelp.

"Come on, sleepyheads," I tease with a laugh.

"Not cool, Lainey, not cool," Maddie grumbles.

"Ah, but what's a bit of payback between cousins?"

Mary tosses the blanket back and pushes her hair off her face. "Alright, I'm up. Please turn that down though."

I smirk and stop the music. "Hey, you said wake you up in an hour. You didn't specify how."

"It's fine. We've got birthday cupcakes to pick up, so we should get ready. I picked out our outfits for tonight!" Maddie sits up and grins. "We brought you back a dress!"

"What? You guys didn't have to do that!"

"Psh, we know that. But we saw it and thought of you." Mary shares a look with Maddie.

"Well, thank you. That's very thoughtful of you." I quirk an eyebrow at them. "What's this about cupcakes now?"

chapter thirty-three

RUSH

FROM UNDERNEATH THE brim of my Red Sox hat, I watch the object of my obsession with laser focus. I wonder if she can feel my gaze as it caresses her. I imagine wrapping her dark-red hair around my fist and claiming her lips. I imagine the noises she'd make and the way her body would lean into mine.

The green dress she's wearing hugs every single inch of her curves, and I'm sure my eyes are not the only ones drawn to such perfection tonight.

I bring the glass to my lips and take a sip of the single-malt whiskey, letting the burn settle in my throat before I swallow down its sweetness. The beat from whatever song is playing thumps as the lights automatically dim. It must be nine o'clock already.

I followed our little bird to the city last night. Just because Wolf and Sully can't see beyond right now to the big picture doesn't mean I have the same issue.

Alaina is absolutely perfect—and perfect for us.

There's no way I'd let her leave the mansion, especially since she was there during the perimeter breach, without protection. Dave offered one of his best men to shadow her in the city, but as much as I trust Dave's judgment, I wouldn't trust anyone with her safety but my brothers and me.

All it takes is one guy with a grudge against Da or fuck, even me, and her light's snuffed out forever. If that means being her tail for a few days in the city before I can persuade her to come back to Boston with me, then that's what I'll do.

I watch her and her cousins make their way to the bar for another round, laughing and smiling with one another.

I know the moment she finally sees me. It never takes too long for my little bird to find me, and tonight is no exception. She stares at me for a moment longer, her gaze searching my face before she turns and follows her cousins back to their table, drinks in hand.

I let my gaze follow the lines and curves of her body as she leans over the table to place the drinks down. I lift two fingers to the nearby waitress to signal another round, my gaze never straying from her.

The music cuts out, and Jack lifts his hands to cup around his mouth. His voice booms across the pub. "Listen up, it's our songbird's birthday today."

The crowd erupts in cheers and whistles, and the corner of my lips tip up in a smirk. I spot the blush heating her cheeks from here, her fair skin making it easy to tell when she's embarrassed. My fingers itch to explore just how far that blush spreads.

"And she's kind enough to grace us with her voice tonight, so let's give it up for our songbird," Jack yells into the pub.

The same waitress drops off my fresh whiskey and takes the empty glass without a word, and I murmur my thanks. I bring the glass to my lips and take a sip, watching Alaina walk hand in hand with her cousins to the stage at the other end of the pub. All three girls climb on the stage, and they look like an explosion of color. Brightly-colored dresses and vibrant red hair. Her cousins are beautiful, no doubt, but they don't hold a candle to my girl. Her very presence commands the attention of every person in this pub.

Movement out of the corner of my eye grabs my attention, and I see Benny slink in from outside. He steps over to my booth and leans against the wall.

"That's a good way to get yourself shot, Benny."

His eyebrow quirks in challenge. "Inside O'Malley's? C'mon, Rush, no one would dare mess with you here. 'Sides, I'd never let them in."

I place my gun back on my lap under the table and give the stage my full attention again. "You wouldn't even know you had let them in, Benny. We're on the brink of war, and people get reckless when they think they have something to prove."

The girls get situated on the stage, and the other bartender, Levi, hops up there to join them, guitar in hand. He settles at the back of the stage, and the opening notes of "With A Little Help From My Friends" ring out in the pub.

I sit up a little; this is a new song for her.

Benny whistles under his breath. "She sure is something, isn't she?"

I spare him a glance to assess which redhead he's salivating over, but Alaina's voice demands my focus. She's singing about getting by with a little help, and the other two girls back her up. By the time she's singing about needing somebody to love and shaking a tambourine, I'm ready to storm the stage and snatch her off of it.

"Mine." The words are growled out, but Benny knows they're for him.

"Of course, boss, I didn't mean the songbird. I've got my eye on the one in blue." Benny's words are measured.

The guitar fades out, and only the girls' harmonized voices remain in the pub before they fade out. The crowd cheers and whistles, and the girls all murmur their thanks.

"Thanks for celebrating our girl's birthday with us tonight! We've got some new ones for you. We hope you enjoy them," Maddie says into the mic.

Alaina grabs her mic stand and leans back to say something to the guitarist. He nods and sets his guitar on his lap.

"Hey, guys, thanks for indulging us tonight," Alaina says into the mic with a smile. Then she opens her mouth, and I swear to God, if I wasn't already sitting down, I'd be flat on my ass.

I marvel at the goosebumps that race down my arms when Alaina sings the chorus to "Creep."

My phone vibrates in my pocket. I pull it out to see a text from Wolf.

I ignore it and place my phone back in my pocket, fixing my gaze back on my songbird. He can wait. But this performance can't—there's something happening in O'Malley's tonight. Something truly special, and it's emanating from the little bird on stage.

Goosebumps race down my spine as I watch this magnificent creature leave everything on this stage in the middle of New York City.

She's successfully captured every single person's attention. The final note hangs in the air, and for a moment, no one moves, then the entire pub erupts in cheers, jumping to their feet.

"Thank you so much," she says with a smile and a small laugh.

Jack brings her a shot of something, probably tequila, and hands it up to her, saying something I can't quite hear over the cheering. She accepts the shot and tosses it back before giving Jack the shot glass back.

"Woo," she says with a slight grimace. "Okay, guys, that's all we have for you right now. But stick around, and we might be back on this amazing stage soon!"

She twirls around, reaching out to hug the bartender-turned-guitarist on stage. And every possessive urge I've ever had roars through my body, demanding I take what's mine. Fuck the consequences.

It's a shitty time to claim a woman. I wasn't sugar-coating it earlier, we really are on the brink of war. But the thought of another man touching what's mine while I *wait for the right time* is enough to send me into a rage.

I will have her.

And god help anyone who stands in my way.

chapter thirty-four

Wolf

MY FOOT BOUNCES with each second that ticks by and I'm not with my girl. I stare out the windshield as we leave the streets of Boston behind. I overheard Red talking to her cousins earlier, and I'm pretty sure they agreed to meet at O'Malley's at nine. Glancing at the clock on the dash, that gives me a little over an hour, and I'm still 120 miles away. I hit the gas and focus on the road.

I shake my head in disbelief that it was Rush, of all people, that talked some sense into me earlier.

Don't get me wrong, I'm so fucking grateful he did, but I haven't quite figured out why. Why is he the voice of reason? And why her?

I know that he's the one who enacted the pact, but now that it's not this abstract idea made fresh off adrenaline, I'm not sure how to navigate it.

How will it work? Do we rotate rooms, or do we all room together? I love my brothers, and I'm willing to try this whole sharing thing, but I like my own space too.

Just thinking about having Red in my space—permanently—has me gripping the steering wheel a little tighter.

"I really fucked up." My statement hangs in the air, unable to disguise the guilt that rings true in my words.

"You did," Sully confirms.

"I'm going to fix it," I promise.

He shrugs. "Doesn't matter to me either way."

"You say that now, but you forget that I've known you your entire life. You can't fool me that easily, little brother," I tell him, not unkindly.

"You're no brother of mine," he snarls. "My brother wouldn't be fucking my girl, and he definitely wouldn't be thinking about fucking keeping her!" he roars.

I glance at him out of the corner of my eye. He's staring straight ahead, chest heaving, and hands clenched.

"You said my girl," I say quietly. "You said my girl, not my ex-girlfriend."

"Fuck off, I did not." He crosses his arms and turns to stare at me. "Don't try to psychoanalyze me. Besides, we both know that I'm better at it."

I nod. "That's true. But then why are you coming along?"

"Someone needs to watch your six."

"Rush is there," I counter.

"Rush is preoccupied. And we're on the brink of war. So, I'm here for you, not her."

"Appreciate it."

He grunts and turns up the volume, effectively ending our conversation, which suits me just fine.

SEVENTY MINUTES LATER, we're walking down the block toward O'Malley's. I'm twitchy, and I know it's not entirely nerves for the grand gesture I have planned.

"You feel that?" I mutter, looking over my shoulder again. I feel like a goddamned bobblehead with the way my head is constantly swiveling, looking for anything out of the ordinary. But I don't spend enough time in this fucking city to even know what would be unusual.

"Yeah, I feel eyes on me. And I don't fucking like it."

We approach O'Malley's, the forest-green awning gently swaying in the breeze. It's so hot and humid tonight that the slight breeze feels more sauna and less cooling. I pluck the bottom of my black tee away from my stomach, trying to get some airflow to cool down.

We stop in front of the pub by a few guys hanging out in front of the open door. I hear the chatter from inside, but I don't hear any singing yet. Good, hopefully, I didn't miss her.

"'Sup, guys, Benny," I greet them, a smile on my face. That's my role, after all. I'm the good-time guy, the one who's always down to party. Fuck, I think I can hear the bitterness in that thought. That's next-level fucked-up.

I catch myself before irritation rises—I'm here for Red, no one else.

Sully just nods in greeting, a scowl on his face. Great, he's not selling shit tonight. I elbow him and motion toward the guys with my head. He rolls his eyes and says, "Benny."

I recognize a few of them from Brotherhood meetings, and the others are associates—including Benny. He's the bouncer for O'Malley's, and rumor has it he's trying to get in with the Brotherhood.

"Yo, Benny, what's with the candles set up every-where?" I eye the white pillar candles on every table and scattered along the bar top.

"Just a precaution. Jack started it last night. We want to be sure to have something in case we get a blackout."

"No shit?" Sully peers into the pub.

Benny nods. "Yeah, they're talking about rolling brownouts soon, but you never know."

"I suppose eight million people running their AC twenty-four seven for the last week is enough to cause a blackout." Fuck, I hope not. That'd be a shitty way to spend your birthday.

"You seen Rush yet?" I ask Patrick, the other bouncer.

"Yes, sir. He's inside at his booth." He meets my eyes without challenge.

My eyebrows hit my hairline, and I look at Sully. What the fuck is that supposed to mean?

"Alright, man. Thanks." I clap him on the shoulder as we walk past him and into the dimly-lit pub. I stop inside the threshold and let my eyes adjust to the low light.

I spot Rush sitting in the shadows in a booth kiddie-corner from the stage. I jerk my head to the corner. "There he is. I gotta talk to Jack about something."

Sully nods and heads toward Rush's table without a word.

It's crowded tonight, so it takes me a minute to find Jack. He's at the far end of the bar talking to two women—both redheads, but neither one is my Red. I wait and see how long it takes him to notice me standing here, staring at him.

Two minutes and thirty-eight seconds.

He walks out from behind the bar, flipping a bar towel over his shoulder, a wide smile on his face. "Boyo!" He grabs my outstretched hand and pulls me in for one of those half hug things. "It's been too long. I only get to see Rush's ugly mug every week," he says with a chuckle, stepping back.

"You losing your touch, old man?" I smirk. "Over two-and-a-half minutes before you spotted me."

"Ach, you try focusing when you have the attention of two pretty little birds." He flashes me a smirk.

"Speaking of pretty little birds. I'm looking for a red-head. About this high"—I hold my hand level with my chest—"eyes like whiskey."

A knowing glint sparkles in his eye. "Aye, I might know of such a girl."

"You know where she is?"

"I might, I might." He crosses his arms smugly.

I'm hanging on by a thread, clamping down my irritation. "Something to say, old man?"

"Watch your tone, boyo," he snaps, body rigid.

I grit my teeth, but I don't apologize. Jack has a complicated relationship with the Brotherhood. He's not a member, but he's not *not* a member. He knows too much to be just an acquaintance, but not enough as a member. Even if he was Brotherhood, I would outrank him as VP of the junior council.

But I like Jack, and I don't want to disrespect him, so I tip my head ever so slightly toward him.

He exhales and relaxes a little. "What do you want with the songbird?"

I quirk a brow and give him my best blank look. "Right. I need you to turn on the stage lights in five minutes. Is it cool if I borrow Patrick's guitar?"

He tilts his head to look me over. "What for? You sing-ing tonight?"

I grin. "Sure am, Jack. Sure am."

"Well, holyyy shit." He whistles through his teeth, his bushy orange brows wiggling. "Never thought I'd see the day the Lone Wolf takes the stage."

"Fuck off, man," I say with a chuckle. "I always told you it'd take something big to get me back onstage."

"Ahh," he says, a twinkle in his eye. "I see you found your something big then, huh? You sure you won't have to go toe to toe with your brother for this songbird? He's here damn near every week to watch her."

"Really." I tuck that piece of information in my mind before I shove it aside. I don't have time to think about it now.

Jack nods, scanning my face, probably looking for a clue that I'm going to freak out on him.

He scrunches his face, lips pursed, and he leans in. "We can't have another infestation, no matter how spe-cial you think the bird is, boyo." His voice is low, but the overhead music is loud as fuck, and no one gives two shits about us talking.

"Don't worry so much, Jack. I'll catch up with you later. I've got a grand gesture to get to."

His laugh hits my back as I turn around to make my way toward the stage. "Good luck, boyo, sounds like you'll need it."

"I make my own luck," I yell over my shoulder.

I nod at a few familiar faces sitting at the tables, but I don't stop to talk to anyone. I'm working on a limited amount of time here, and the element of surprise is key.

I find Patrick's guitar in its case in the back corner of the stage. It's his extra one that he keeps here just for this purpose—but usually, it's him that's playing in

Penelope Black

the pub. He told me all about it at the last Brotherhood prospect meeting.

I sit on the stool, on the dark stage, and quickly tune the guitar. I take a moment to take a breath, and then I strum the opening notes of "Shallow."

I flick my gaze to the bar, and Jack kills the overhead music and slowly turns on the lights. The dramatic switch is enough to garner the attention of everyone in the pub.

But I only have eyes for one person—Red.

I know it'll seem like an unlikely song choice to everyone in this place—everyone but one person. And that's the only person I'm looking at as I sing.

chapter thirty-five

Alaina

AS SOON AS Jack cuts the overhead music, I turn around. I don't hear anything over the chatter, but then I hear it. The beginning notes to "Shallow" from A Star is Born, and I just know it's Wolf.

When he flips the stage lights on, my heart skips a beat.

"Holyyy shitballs, that man is sex on a stick," Maddie stage-whispers.

Mary snorts, but I can't take my eyes off of him long enough to look at either one of them.

Dressed in a Clash tee, dark jeans, and all-black Vans with tattoos peeking out from underneath his collar and filling his arms, he's a vision. He's like every fantasy come to life—I mean, Jesus, he already was, but with a guitar on his lap and his eyes on me, it's almost unfair how attractive he is.

I discreetly pinch my arm to make sure this isn't a dream—it wouldn't be the first time I've had a sexy dream about Wolf. He sings the opening lyric, and I know this is it: this is the moment I've read about in all my favorite books.

This is The Wooing.

I'm being fucking wooed.

I stop myself from literally swooning while he sings to me, never breaking eye contact. Holy shit, his voice is amazing. Bold, low, and smooth, it wraps around me, sinking into my very soul.

Without even thinking about it, I slide off my stool and weave my way through the tables and chairs and people to make my way to the stage.

When he pauses to hold out his hand to me, I don't hesitate. He stands up and pulls me onstage, moving to the side of the mic stand to make room for us to share.

I swear to God, I've never been so close to swooning in my entire life. I lean into the mic and lock eyes with Wolf, and I prepare to sing my goddamn heart out.

Goosebumps erupt all over my body as I stare into his eyes and sing the chorus. I pour every emotion I've ever felt—and all the ones I long to feel—and I crack my soul open for him to see.

When he joins me to sing the final chorus, a tear slips down my cheek. We sing the last note and never take our gaze off one another as the entire pub erupts in cheering and clapping.

I can feel the wide grin on my face, but there's no wiping it off. In one quick movement, Wolf sets down the guitar on the forgotten stool and steps into me. He palms my ass in his inked hands, picking me up, and I wrap my arms and legs around him. He takes two steps and jumps off the stage.

I slide my hand into his hair, and we meet in the middle for an earth-shattering kiss.

We ignore the wolf whistles as he walks me backward until my back's against a wall to the side of the stage. He presses me to him and kisses me back with all the passion—and angst—that song invoked. I feel reckless and free . . . and seen.

I pull back from him and stare at his beautiful eyes, blackened with desire. "Conor, that was absolutely beautiful," I breathe out. "That's the best birthday present I've ever received, and I can't believe you drove all the way here just to sing. For me."

"Fuck, are you crying?" His gaze darts around my face.

"No," I say with a watery laugh. "I'm just so happy you're here." I sniff.

"There's nowhere I'd rather be, Red. Nowhere." His intense stare pierces my soul.

"Does that mean . . ." My lips brush softly against his with each word.

"You're my girl, Alaina."

"Are you sure? What about all the things you said earlier?" I bite the inside of my cheek, thinking about all the times he told me he doesn't do relationships.

"I'm an asshole, baby girl. And that's probably not going to change much. But I'll try. For you, I'll try. And"—he sighs and stares into my eyes for a moment—"I freaked out a little, okay?"

The vulnerability in his gaze takes me by surprise. "But why?"

"I don't do relationships, Red—"

I scoff and roll my eyes.

"Just listen. I've never done them, and I can promise you that I'll fuck up again. But the thought of never seeing you again, never feeling those pretty pink lips against me, fucked me up more than the idea of having a serious girl. And I am very serious about you, Red."

The cocky smirk he flashes at me actually has me leaning toward him. It's like goddamn catnip—irresistible and makes me lose my goddamn mind every time it's near.

"Kiss me already," I whisper against his lips.

He doesn't hesitate, pressing his body against mine and pushing me against the wall. He slants his mouth over mine, my lips already feeling swollen. What is it about O'Malley's that has me against the walls?

"Yo! Lovebirds getting frisky in the back!" Maddie yells from across the pub.

Wolf pulls back and runs his nose down my neck in just the right place to send shivers down my spine. "Your cousin's a cockblock."

I giggle. "I'm surprised she lasted this long without butting in sooner."

I look around Wolf and see Maddie standing up with her hands cupped around her mouth.

"Hellloooo, remove your mouth from my cousin, bro."

"She's definitely tipsy. No way she yells like that sober," I say with a laugh as I wiggle in Wolf's grip. He slowly sets me down, never taking his hands off of me. "I better check on her. Plus, I promised Jack the girls and I would sing tonight."

"But it's your birthday," he says into my neck. His warm breath leaves tingles in its wake, and warmth pools low in my belly. Damn tease knows that's my weak spot.

"Exactly. And shouldn't the birthday girl get everything she wants on her birthday?" I tease him, quirking my brow.

His hands flex around my ribcage as he tips his head back to stare at me. "And what is it you want, Red?"

I push onto my tiptoes and say against his mouth, "Everything."

I feel rather than see the shiver that rolls through his entire body. He groans into our kiss.

I pull back before we get carried away again.

"Alright, Red. You'll get everything," he promises.

And even though I'm scared that this is one giant mistake that's going to come back and bite me in the ass, I believe him. I stare into his dark eyes, mesmerized by the promises shining from them.

A smile tips up the corners of my mouth, and I stare at this beautiful man I get to call mine.

A shiver of anticipation rolls through me, and I bite my lip as I think about what else I'm going to ask for tonight. He did say everything.

"You're going to get us in trouble with your hellcat cousin if you don't stop looking at me like that, Red," he groans out, eyeing my lips.

"Like what?" I tilt my head to the side, a small smile tipping my lips.

One inked finger traces my swollen bottom lip, and my breath hitches. His gaze is transfixed on the path his finger makes, and I'm transfixed on his expression—reverent.

"You're going to be the best kind of trouble."

"I know." I slowly nod, and the tip of his finger slips in between my lips. I just barely flick my tongue against it, and his groan reminds me of a wolf claiming his spoils. It only turns me on more.

"Alright, alright, that's enough for now," Maddie says from right next to me.

I jump at the sound of her voice, and his finger slips off my lips. "Okay, Maddie. Let's sing," I say, still staring at Wolf.

"Yesss!" I see her fist pump out of the corner of my eye.

Wolf steps back, unpinning me from the wall. "Alright, birthday girl. I'll be in that booth over there"—he points to Rush's usual shadowed booth in the back—"with Rush and Sully."

"Sully came?" Surprise colors my voice.

He nods, looking at me for a moment. He must find whatever he was looking for, because a moment later, he's grinning like crazy. "Oh, I am going to enjoy this."

I'm not sure if he's talking about me singing or something else, but I don't have time to ask him. Maddie pulls on my hand and walks toward the stage. "You can make googly-eyes at your man later. It's time to sing!"

Maddie buzzin is always a fun time, and I laugh, following behind her to the stage. We climb the couple of steps and join Mary on stage to start to set up the mics and mic stands how we like them.

When we're all set up, Mary is to the left of me, and Maddie is to the right. At their nods, I nod to Jack behind the bar. He cuts the overhead music and flips the stage lights on.

I lean into my mic and open my mouth to greet everyone, but Jack whistles for everyone's attention. I swear his whistles are heard in the next borough they're so freaking loud.

Jack stands up on a barstool and yells, "It's a songbird's birthday today, and we are going to celebrate!"

Everyone in the bar cheers, and I glance to the table in the back to see all three of them staring back at me. A dirty smirk tips my lips up, and I toss a wink in for good measure.

chapter thirty-six

Alaina

JACK HOLDS UP a shot glass in the air. "A toast! To one of the three best songbirds O'Malley's has ever seen!" He pauses, waiting for Levi to bring us each a clear shot. It looks like it'll be tequila night, after all. We hold our shots in the air, and I look around the room to see that everyone in the pub is holding their drink in the air to me.

My cheeks warm at the thought of so many people celebrating me. Even if Jack's practically making them.

"To the birthday girl!" Jack toasts and tosses back his shot.

"To the birthday girl," everyone repeats before cheering their glasses with whoever is closest to them and taking a drink.

"To me," I say and clink my shot glass against Maddie's and Mary's.

"Happy birthday, Lainey."

We toss back our shots, and I wince at the burn. "You know how much I love it when you use your twin mojo like that." I smirk. "You guys ready to sing?"

"Hell yes! Let's rock 'n roll, baby!" Maddie crows.

Mary smirks at her sister. "Let's start with 'Valerie.'"

Mary turns to the crowd and starts belting out the lyrics while Maddie and I harmonize and back her up on the chorus. We grab tambourines and hit them against our palms with the beat, shaking our hips and grinning wildly at one another.

Mary kills it on the bridge, and I find myself sending up another gratitude prayer for these two women to whoever's listening up there. I don't know what I'd do without these two—and I don't ever want to know.

This might be one of the best birthdays I've ever had. I should've known though, every birthday spent with these two is always amazing, but this one feels extra special. Tingles roll through me like a wave when my gaze connects with Rush's—then Wolf's—and finally, Sully's.

Three different men who've captivated me.

I sing the final note, and my gaze involuntarily darts to the back booth where Wolf, Rush, and Sully sit. A couple of guys stand around the booth, and one sits down right next to Rush.

Reluctantly, I tear my gaze from him and scan the cheering crowd with a smile.

"Thank you so much, everyone!" I say into the mic as I hook it back in the stand.

"Let's hear it for our songbirds tonight!" Jack's booming voice reverberates around the pub.

I scan the pub, looking for the orange-bearded man in question, when I see commotion at the back booth out of the corner of my eye. Rush stands up and gets in some guy's face. Wolf and Sully stand up and flank Rush, and my heart pounds at the prospect of a fight breaking out.

Not that Jack isn't used to the occasional disagreement or fight—that's why he has bouncers—but the thought of them fighting has nausea churning in my stomach.

"And happy fucking birthday, Lainey!" Maddie yells into the mic.

The crowd obliges her drunk birthday declaration and whoops and claps once again.

"Thank you!"

I step off the stage, intent on heading to the back booth, when Jack steps in front of me.

"Great job tonight, girls. Happy birthday, kid." Jack places a shot glass in my hand and a peck on the top of my head.

"Thanks, Jack." I toss back my shot and swipe Maddie's too. "She's already going to be hurting tomorrow, no need to pile it on." I spy Wolf walking toward the hallway to the bathroom, and I see my chance sneak another toe-curling kiss. I toss Maddie's shot back and hand the empty glasses to Jack. "If you'll excuse me, I have to use the restroom."

"Ah, sure thing, kid. Come to the bar before you go. I have a little something for you." Jack turns on his heel and heads back to man the bar.

I turn toward Maddie and Mary. "Bathroom break, either of you need to go?"

"Nope," Maddie says, popping her p.

"I'm good, Lainey," Mary says, scanning the room. "We'll be at the bar."

"Okay. I'll come find you there. Stay with Maddie, this place really filled up in the last hour."

"Of course," Mary scoffs. "Later, babe."

I make a mental note to talk to Mary tomorrow. She's been on edge all day, and I'm not sure if something happened on vacation or it's jet lag.

I turn the corner to the hallway that leads to the restrooms, and deja vu hits me like a freight train. This is exactly where I kissed Rush.

A secret little smile curls up the corners of my lips as I recall how possessively he held me that day.

I jog a few steps to catch up to Wolf. When I'm within reaching distance, I lean forward to grab the back of his black tee and give it a little tug to get his attention. "Wolf, hey."

He stops, but he doesn't turn around. It's dark back here, and the lightbulb above us starts flickering, distracting me. "Oh, crap, I hope we don't lose power. I forget to check if we're getting a rolling brownout tonight. Do you know?" I stare at the flickering lightbulb as if it can give me the answers I'm looking for.

My stomach churns. Why the hell isn't he turning around? "Hey, what's going on?"

I reach for his hand, and he lets me. I use my hand on his as leverage to spin him around to face me. And what I see stops me cold.

A nervous giggle crawls up my throat. "I'm sorry. I thought you were someone else." I tug my hand off of him, but his reflexes are fast, and he holds onto my wrist with an iron grip. "Ow. Hey, you're hurting me."

He steps forward, underneath the flickering lightbulb, and his features look demonic. Black hair similarly styled to Wolf's and sharp angles outline his face. Red contacts stare back at me as he smiles at me, all teeth.

I try to step back, but he tightens his grip on me. "Uh, uh, uh. Patience."

Panic claws at me as I fight to stay calm and get the hell away from this guy. "Look, I'm sorry I grabbed your shirt, but I have friends waiting on me, and they'll be worried by now."

He stares at me for a moment. "Three, two, one," he whispers.

And the lights go out.

"Time to go." He starts to drag me down the hallway.

Panic floods my body, and I start thrashing to get away from him. I'm kicking my own butt for not taking Wolf up on the offer to train in self-defense the other day.

He pulls me down the hallway toward the bathrooms, and I properly lose my mind. I start screaming and kicking and grabbing for anything I can get purchase on. But there isn't a single painting hung on the walls or a lone stool to grab.

"Shh, now. There's no need for that noise," he scolds. "Besides, they won't be able to hear you over the show."

Before the last word leaves his mouth, I hear popping noises, followed by breaking glass and shouting.

He drags me past the bathrooms, and we're five feet away from the emergency exit that leads to the back alley. But I do remember one thing I learned in school a few years ago: you decrease your chance of survival once they take you to a secondary location. I fight against him with everything I have inside, but it's not enough.

He stops right in front of the door and turns to look at me. "This is going to hurt."

I see him raise a handgun, and I think that this is it—my life is over. A highlight reel flashes before my eyes, but a split second later, he brings his gun down on my head.

And then I don't think about anything at all.

chapter thirty-seven

Wolf

RED STARES AT me as she sings the last note in the song before staring at Rush and then Sully. I'm about to say something snarky as fuck to Sully when Matteo sits down next to Rush.

My muscles tense, ready to jump into action if necessary. We're on good terms with the Italians, and I know for a fact that Sully and Matteo have done business together in the past. But these are uncertain times, and to trust someone could mean your death.

"Bold, Rossi, coming into my bar, sitting at my table as if you have a right." Rush's gaze cuts to Matteo and narrows.

"I'm not here for politics, Fitzgerald." He flicks his glance to Sully and me for a moment before focusing on Rush again. "I heard you three were in town tonight, and since you're normally a hard man to get in front of, I had to take my chances."

"Thank you so much, everyone!" Red says into the mic, and I keep her in my line of sight while keeping an eye on Matteo.

"I'm listening," Rush says, pointedly eyeing Matteo's guys standing in front of the booth.

"I know you heard about Mama Rosa's."

"Let's hear it for our songbirds tonight!" Jack yells, distracting me.

"Aye, we did. And we're sorry to hear that. Glad you made it out, man," Sully says.

Matteo dips his head in acknowledgment. "Thank you. Rest in Peace, Aunt Carm, God bless her soul." He leans forward and lowers his voice. "Little Italy just went up in flames two hours ago, and word on the street is you're next."

"Us?" Rush asks with raised brows. "What makes you say that?"

Matteo leans back. "Just a rumor I heard from someone who heard it from someone else. It could be bullshit." He shrugs. "But I like O'Malley's, and I like Jack—"

"When the fuck have you been here?" I interrupt.

Matteo looks at me and shrugs. "A time or two in the past. Anyway, I just wanted to give you a friendly heads-up. That's all." Matteo slides out of the booth and stands up.

Before he can get two steps, Rush is in his face, snarling, "You better not be fucking with me. And if I find out you're setting us up, I'll bury you."

"And happy fucking birthday, Lainey!" Red's drunk cousin, Maddie, yells into the mic. I can see the pretty pink flush on her cheeks from here. I'm itching to wrap this up so I can go grab my girl. I've got plans for us tonight.

Matteo stares at Rush. "Nah, I wouldn't do that to you."

Sully and I slide out of the booth and stand on either side of Rush. "That's what they all say, Rossi," I say.

"Yeah?"—he smirks—"they're not me." Matteo signals to his guys and walks out of the pub and into the warm night.

"Thank you!" Red yells and waves at the cheering crowd.

Our little interaction is mostly unnoticed by everyone except for Jack, who steps in front of Red as she hops off the stage.

I watch Jack hand her and her cousins another shot, and she downs hers pretty quick. He pats Red on the shoulder and steers her toward the bar, and the compulsive need to be near her dims only slightly. Jack'll protect her if he has too.

"What the hell was that?" Sully murmurs, crossing his arms across his chest with a scowl.

"Fuck if I know, I need a smoke. You comin'?"

"Nah, I need a drink." Sully heads toward the bar, and I wait for Rush's answer.

Rush stares out the open front door for a moment before nodding. "Let's go."

We step outside, and one of the bouncers, Patrick, dips his head to us. "Heya, guys. How ya' doin?"

He's a nice enough guy. I've seen him around at some Brotherhood shit. Rush ignores him and stands right outside the door, angling his body so he can see inside the pub while he takes a drag.

I tip my chin at Patrick. "We're good, man." I light the cigarette dangling from my mouth and inhale. "How are things here?"

"Can't complain." Patrick closes the front door.

"Leave it. My girl's in there," Rush snaps, sticking his hand out to block the door from closing completely.

"Sorry, man, Jack's rules. If people smoke out here, then I gotta close the door, so it doesn't get in the bar." Patrick rubs the back of his neck, perspiration beading on his forehead.

Rush exhales, blowing smoke into the humid night air, and all three of us watch as it wafts directly into the pub.

"Yeah, okay. Sorry, man, it's just . . . I need this job, ya know?" Patrick looks at the sidewalk as he talks.

I eye the way Rush tenses up, his posture deceptively loose, but his fingers flutter against his leg, and I just know he's seconds away from reminding Patrick who he is.

I used to hate this part of the life—the intimidation, pulling rank, even the violence—but now I understand why it's necessary. And I trust that Sully and Rush won't ever let me step over that line again—the one that separates us from monsters.

We are, after all, created in our Da's image—three butchers in our own rights. We learned from the best.

I could step in, but then we wouldn't know if he can hack it in the Brotherhood. That's why they started the prospecting phase—it's a test.

Rush stubs his cigarette out on the brick wall and drops it in the ashtray. "I understand. But the difference, prospect, is that if you disobey an order from Jack, you'll only lose your job. If you disobey an order from me, you'll lose your head."

Patrick visibly swallows and flicks his gaze between us. "You're right. Apologies, to both of you."

I shrug in response and stub my cigarette in the ashtray. I look inside the pub and see Red going toward the back by the bathrooms. "C'mon, Rush. Let's go check on Red."

Rush stares at Patrick for another minute before he turns on his heel and walks inside the pub. I clap Patrick on the shoulder as I pass him and head to the bar where I spot two redheads.

I'm two steps away from them when the lights go out.

There's a moment of silence before everyone talks at once. I whip out my phone and use the flashlight app to illuminate the space around me. I spin to the bar, expecting to see Red, but come face to face with her cousins instead.

"Where is she?"

"What do you mean? She just followed you to the bathrooms. I saw her," her cousin Mary says.

"Jesus. Are you drunk? I'm right here." I point to myself with my index finger.

Mary crosses her arms and snaps, "Do I sound drunk?"

"Relax, sister, it's probably just a scheduled brownout," Maddie slurs.

Mary hooks a thumb at her sister. "She's the drunk one."

"Yeah, I really don't give a fuck. I just need to find Red. You two stay here until I get back." I turn around, cursing the fact that I have not one but three redheads to look after tonight. Red would kill me if anything happened to these two—especially if one of 'em is drunk. And I'm not fucking anything up so soon after I got her back.

I'm going against the crowd, fighting my way to the back of the bar when everyone is mass exiting out of the font. But I can't leave Red back there alone in a blackout. There's one light back there on a good day.

When I'm halfway to the back of the pub, I hear a rapid succession of crackling pops. I freeze for a second, straining to hear for the telltale whistle that it's fireworks and not fucking gunshots.

When I don't hear any whistle, only more loud, quick pops, my heart catapults into my throat.

Alaina.

I take off in a run to the back of the pub, the flashlight on my phone bouncing off the walls. "Red!" My voice sounds panicked, and I can't stop the flood of fear that courses through my veins.

I skid around the corner in the hallway and burst into the ladies' restroom. "Red! Are you in here?" My voice reverberates off the walls as I slam the stall doors open, finding nothing.

I sprint out of the bathroom and push the door to the men's room open with more force than necessary.

Heart pounding, I pull up my phone and dial Rush.

"Where are you?" Rush answers, but I'm only half paying attention. I spend two seconds looking around before I turn on my heel and run back into the hallway. "Wolf? Where the fuck are you?"

"Do you have eyes on Red?"

Rush pauses. "No. And neither does Sully, he's right next to me."

I run my hands through my hair as I spin around.

Where the fuck is she?

The flashlight illuminates the emergency exit door, and I jog over to it. The hair on the back of my neck stands up as I push the emergency exit open and step into the alley.

The gunshots are quieter out here, and the smell of rotting garbage is overwhelming, but what catches my attention is the flash of dark-red hair illuminated by the sign at the end of the alley.

I take off like a goddamn cornerback. "Alley. Now!" I bark into the phone and stuff it in my pocket as I pump my legs faster.

I watch as someone throws my entire world in the side of a blacked-out utility van from 500 feet away. She isn't screaming or fighting back, and my gut clenches at the possibilities of what that could mean.

I jump over a spilled garbage can, sliding on the dirty concrete. Every step feels like somcone's jabbing a needle into my heart, fear lodging itself in my throat.

But I won't give up.

I'll never give up on her.

Someone stands inside the open side door, staring at me from beneath a ski mask. I hope the motherfucker can read the slow and torturous death I'm promising in my gaze.

Because that wolf—that primal, vengeful, violent part of me that's been buried for years has been unleashed. Heaven help anyone who gets in my path now.

The guy slams the side door closed as I pull my gun from the back of my pants and fire a few rounds, aiming for the tires and driver's side door.

The van peels out from the mouth of the alley, squealing the back tires, and I push myself even harder, running like Red's goddamn life depends on it.

I should've protected her better.

I have too many enemies in this life.

I reach the end of the alley and run right into the middle of the road, scanning each direction for the van.

The streets are empty.

I rest my hands on top of my head, never letting go of my gun, and release a guttural roar.

Rush and Sully run up next to me, guns out, brows furrowed.

"What happened?" Rush asks.

"They took her." My breaths are heavy as my mind spins. "They took our girl."

I scan the area, trying to get a better look at the situation from the middle of the street. A crowd of people from inside O'Malley's huddle in front of the dark pub, some crying and injured. But the restaurants on either side are brightly-lit. In fact, every other building around O'Malley's is shining bright in the dark summer night.

This was a set-up.

chapter thirty-eight

RUSH

"TELL ME EVERYTHING, start from the beginning." My words are careful and measured.

I've never seen Wolf this full of rage before, not even when his biological father reached out to him for the first time from prison, asking for money.

As Wolf details everything from the last fifteen minutes, I pull up my phone and call one of the best hackers in the country—aside from me. He answers the call, and per professional courtesy, I say, "I'm calling in a favor."

"Send me the request," he replies.

I hang up and pull open my encrypted file sharing app I built just for this purpose. I tell him what I need and the coordinates and request priority service, offering two favors for the rush.

After that, I filter search the dark web for any information that might help.

"Son of a bitch," I snarl. "There's a fucking hit out on Alaina." I glance from my phone to Wolf's rage and Sully's forced indifference.

"What the fuck does that mean?" Wolf yells, muscles tense.

"It means . . . that someone offered to pay a million dollars for the capture of one Alaina McElroy." Icy rage boils in my veins at the audacity of someone putting a hit on my girl.

"At least it's not dead or alive, right? That's gotta be something," Sully mutters.

"Sully, call the boys and have them reach out to every contact they know," I delegate. We need to have the junior Brotherhood members on the streets.

"On it." Sully whips out his phone and starts dialing.

"Wolf, reach out to the Blue Knights and Matteo."

He pauses for a moment, staring at the empty street where the van was. "We have to find her." He stares at me, eyes tight and fists clenched.

If Sully's the calm before the storm, and I'm the eye of the hurricane, then Wolf is the active volcano, rage ready and willing to cause mass destruction.

Good.

If we have any hope of finding Alaina, we need him to have his head in the game. I eye Sully, noting the tremble in his hands as he calls our soldiers to duty. He might be fooling himself, but he's not fooling me.

"We will, brother, we will."

"I'll go to war for her, Rush. Are you ready for that?"

Someone dared to challenge me by taking my girl from my bar. And make no mistake—Alaina is mine.

"Aye, we're already at war."

"The streets will run red with my vengeance," he promises, voice pitched low.

I stand next to him and stare at the empty street. "I'll burn the whole fucking city down to get her back."

To be continued . . .

A Note To Readers

Thank you so, so much for picking up Wolf!
And I hope you're not too angry with me for that
ending. I know I left you dangling on that cliff, but
rest assured that the next book, Rush, will be out in a
few short months!
I can't thank you enough to taking a chance on
Alaina, Wolf, Rush, and Sully—and me!
And I cannot wait for you to read what
happens next!
Pre-order Rush, book two in The Brotherhood
series at books2read.com/Brotherhood2

Acknowledgments

Thank you to my readers—ahh! I'm still pinching myself over the fact that I *have* readers! I'm eternally grateful for you taking a chance on me.

Thank you to my loving and supportive husband, who continues to cheer me on at every turn—and make me dinner every night. Loveyou!

To my tiny humans: thank you for being the best kids a mama could ask for. I love you both more than all the stars in the sky.

To my wonderful family who's encouraged me for months—thank you, thank you, thank you.

Thank you to my wonderful beta readers Claire, Savy, and Tracey. I'm so grateful for your insight and support!

Thank you to each and every author who has been so kind and supportive while I asked one million questions over the last six months. There are far too many of you to thank, and for that alone, I'm forever grateful. They've embodied one of my favorite quotes: in a world where you can be anything, be kind.

I would be honored if you had the time to leave a brief review of this book. Reviews are the lifeblood of a book, and I would so appreciative.

Thank you all so much.

xoxo
—*pen*

Enjoy Wolf? Make sure you stay in the loop!
Join my Facebook group, Penelope's Black Hearts.
Follow me on Instagram @authorpenelopeblack

Printed in Great Britain
by Amazon